AFTER THE STORM CAME THE PIRATES....

I'd been lying awake for half a strike when the door flew open and Dennis's footsteps pounded against the stairs. "Thomas, we need you," he shouted. "Something's wrong."

Alice was up in a flash, long legs flying across the shelter and onto the steps. I sprinted after her. Outside, I took a deep breath and followed their gazes across the sound to our colony on Hatteras Island.

"I can't see anything through the cloud," I said, rubbing my eyes.

Alice shook her head. "That's not a cloud. It's smoke." She took a hesitant step forward. "Our island is on fire."

OTHER BOOKS YOU MAY ENJOY

ELEMENTAL

BY ANTONY JOHN

speak

An Imprint of Penguin Group (USA)

SPEAK
Published by the Penguin Group
Penguin Group (USA)
375 Hudson Street
New York, New York 10014, U.S.A.

USA / Canada / UK / Ireland / Australia / New Zealand / India / South Africa / China
Penguin Books Ltd, Registered Offices: 80 Strand, London WC2R 0RL, England

For more information about the Penguin Group visit www.penguin.com

First published in the United States of America by Dial Books, 2012
Published by Speak, an imprint of Penguin Group (USA), 2013

THE LIBRARY OF CONGRESS HAS CATALOGED THE DIAL EDITION AS FOLLOWS:
John, Antony.
Elemental / by Antony John.
p. cm.
Summary: In a dystopian colony of the United States where everyone is born with powers of
the elements, water, wind, earth, and fire, sixteen-year-old Thomas, the first and only child
born without an element, seems powerless, but is he?
ISBN 978-0-8037-3682-5 (hardcover)
[1. Fantasy. 2. United States—Fiction.] I. Title.
PZ7.J6216Ele 2012
[Fic]—dc23
2011049539

Speak ISBN 978-0-14-242516-9

Printed in the United States of America
1 3 5 7 9 10 8 6 4 2

The publisher does not have any control over and does not assume
any responsibility for author or third-party websites or their content.

To Molly—intrepid explorer of new worlds

Atlantic
Ocean

The Colony

Shallowbay
Bay

Pond Island
Bridge

Bridge   Store

To the   Clinic   Lookout
mainland   The shelter
              Grove   Watertower

The Sound

HATTERAS
ISLAND

Broad Creek

ROANOKE
ISLAND

To Bodie
Lighthouse

N

0   2 miles

CHAPTER 1

T hunder rattled the aging wooden cabins, but no one stopped to listen. There wasn't time for that. The coming storm was written in every distant flash of lightning, and in the sick, heavy clouds hanging over the ocean. The pelicans flying by in tight formation groaned in warning. Even the air tasted strange and unnatural.

So how had Kyte, Guardian of the Wind, missed it completely?

Usually Kyte predicted storms a day in advance. He'd tell us how strong the wind would be. With a Guardian of the Water, he'd warn how high the ocean would rise. And though I found it hard to imagine the clear blue sky roiling with clouds, and the usually calm ocean turned inside out, I knew better than to doubt him. It was his element, after all.

"Swell rising," yelled Kyte. He crouched beside a stick planted firmly in the sand. It marked the highest point he expected the ocean to reach. As everyone turned to look, the water washed right over it and dragged it out to sea.

1

He closed his eyes. Tension carved lines in his face. He was engaging his element, but it had never looked so difficult before.

"Wind speed increasing," shouted another Guardian.

"I know. It's *my* element," exclaimed Kyte, as though he owned the wind itself, not just the ability to read it.

Meanwhile, my father stood side by side with my older brother, Ananias, at the colony's rainwater harvester. They looked alike: same thick, dark hair and serious expression. They conjured sparks from their fingertips, tiny flames that grew and combined into a white-hot glow. Ananias directed the heat onto a bent nail while our father straightened it and drove it back into the oak paneling. However bad the storm might be, we couldn't afford to lose our only water source.

All the Guardians were busy now, their elements in full effect. As the first and only child born without an element, I watched them enviously. I couldn't summon fire, unearth food, predict storms, or catch fish barehanded. But I could toss sandbags against the stilts supporting our cabin, and so I did—one after another, as my arms burned and sweat poured down my forehead.

"Shouldn't you be loading the evacuation canoes, Thomas?" Kyte's voice was low and threatening.

"Alice is taking the last bags now," I said, pointing to the girl sprinting across the beach—sure-footed and powerful— two bulky canvas bags slung across her shoulders.

He followed my eyes, and shouted: "Do you like having to do everything yourself, Alice?"

As she turned her head, the wind tousled her dark hair. She peered at Kyte from the corner of her eye, but she didn't answer.

"I'm talking to you, Alice!"

She dropped the bags. "Does it matter what I like?" Her eyes drifted to me, and she cocked an eyebrow. "Anyway, you've spent years trying to keep Thom and me apart. Why do you want him to help me now?"

Kyte's face reddened. "How dare you speak to a Guardian like that? You're not an Apprentice yet, remember."

"And I hope I never will be." She smiled. "Are we done now?"

The other Guardians stopped what they were doing, and watched with interest. Kyte obviously knew it too. He'd have to take action—punish Alice yet again—just to save face. It was all so predictable.

Couldn't we have just one afternoon without Alice battling the Guardians head-on, when she could be spared their pointless attempts to tame her? The storm would be upon us soon. There wasn't time for this.

"Why do you think you missed this storm, Guardian Kyte?" I asked. The words came out quickly, a thinly veiled attempt to distract him. "Since your element is wind."

Kyte's mouth twisted into a mocking smile. "Why? Did you foresee it before me, Thomas? Did you just forget to mention it to us?"

I sensed the Guardians' stares shifting to me. "I wasn't meaning to criticize. It's just strange. Almost like your element didn't . . ."

3

"What? Like my element didn't *what*?" Kyte lifted a sandbag as though it weighed nothing and launched it several yards. "I'd think that you of all people would have more respect for the elements."

Without a sound, my younger brother, Griffin, joined me. Being deaf, he'd learned to read the Guardians' body language better than anyone. Having him beside me should have been a warning to say nothing. But I'd only spoken up to save Alice.

"I'm just trying to understand."

"And you think now is the time for that?" Kyte raised his hands toward the darkening sky. "Some of us have work to do, and not enough time to do it. Can you at least respect *that*?"

My pulse raced. Anger coursed through me. "You wouldn't be in such a hurry if you'd predicted the storm like you're supposed to."

"Until you have something to offer this colony," he spat, "I suggest you keep your thoughts to yourself."

"Exactly," echoed my father. I hadn't heard him approach. He placed a reassuring hand on my shoulder, but his voice was loud and fierce. He fixed his eyes on Kyte. "After all, those with elements should always be allowed to speak."

"True. And if Thomas discovers an element, I'll be sure to listen."

"And how do you suggest he finds one?"

Kyte shrugged, but the mocking smile was back. "It's difficult, for sure. Especially so late in childhood."

My father's grip tightened. Pain swept through me. "As things stand, he's nothing."

4

"As you say," returned Kyte smoothly. *"Nothing."*

I felt anger flash through my father's claw-like fingers—sharp enough to make me wince—and then he pulled away. I waited for him to come to my defense again, to match Kyte word for word. He'd supported me for sixteen years. I expected nothing less now. But when I looked at him, it was as if he was done fighting. Or worse, as if he agreed with Kyte.

Nothing. The word hung in the air like a fork of lightning seen long after it has vanished. Of course it was difficult for Father to have a son with no element—it was even harder for me—but he'd always told me to be patient. Had he been lying all those years? Was *this* how he really felt?

There were only fourteen people in our colony, but every single one of them stood still and silent, eyes fixed uneasily on the ground.

My hands balled into fists by my sides. My heart beat wildly. *I can throw insults too*, I thought. I could've asked Kyte why his weather predictions were increasingly unreliable. I could've asked my father why his element was so much weaker than his oldest son's.

But I didn't say anything. Because in the end, they still had an element, and I didn't. Something was better than nothing.

I kept my head up and began to walk—quick, uneven strides that couldn't carry me away fast enough. My father called to me, but I didn't turn back. As soon as I crossed the dunes, I broke into a run. Sand slipped beneath me. I couldn't seem to get a grip on anything—the earth, my pulse, my life.

I didn't stop running until I reached the narrow woods that

ran like a spine down the center of Hatteras Island. I placed my left hand against a pine tree and punched the trunk with my right. Mosquitoes landed on me, and I didn't flick them away. I closed my eyes and welcomed a different kind of pain.

"Are you all right?"

I spun around. Alice stood before me, bags still hanging from her shoulders. She must have run too, but she didn't even seem out of breath.

"I'm fine."

"Liar." Her blue eyes blazed. She was a year younger than me, but that was easy to forget when she was angry. "Ignore them, Thom. Ignore them all."

"Easy for you to say."

"Why? Because I have an element, and you don't?" She snorted. "I can barely conjure a spark, let alone make a fire. It's a pathetic excuse for an element, and you know it."

"At least it's something."

She dropped the bags and folded her long tan arms. Sinewy muscles showed through the dull coat of white sand. "When are you going to start fighting back?"

"I just did, remember?"

"I don't mean for me, or Griffin. I mean for *you*."

"Who should I be fighting? Kyte?"

"Anyone. Everyone. Go ahead and hurt them. Do it so they'll never look at you the same way again."

"Is that how you got so popular?"

Alice just smiled. "See? So much anger inside you. You need to let it out."

6

There was a rustle behind us. A girl stood beneath the canopy of a young tree. She fingered the ends of her long blond hair anxiously.

Alice huffed. "What a surprise. I didn't expect Kyte to send you so soon, Rose. I figured he had more important things to do than worry about Thom and me."

"My father didn't send me."

"Course not." Alice retrieved her bags and walked away. She didn't look back.

Once Alice was out of sight, Rose knelt down on a bed of pine needles. She tugged the ends of her white tunic toward her knees, but the material rode up again. Her skin was smooth and pale, unblemished by scars. "My father shouldn't say those things to you," she murmured, voice almost lost on the wind.

I sat down with my back against the trunk. "Have you told him that?"

She looked away. Suddenly I felt guilty instead of angry.

"Alice doesn't think an element is important," I said. "But she's wrong. If I had yours—if I could read water the way you do—everything would be different."

Unlike Alice, Rose didn't disagree. I was grateful for that. "You'll find your element," she said, summoning a smile. "I'm sure of it."

"Why do you keep saying that? You swam like a fish before you could walk. Elements reveal themselves early. Not when you're sixteen."

Her smile never faltered. "Look at your brother. Griffin's

right leg doesn't work properly. He has ears, but he can't hear. Maybe you have an element, and it just doesn't work."

I wanted to believe her, but I'd already passed the age of Apprenticeship. There would be no silver lining to the cloud that had followed me my entire life.

A gust of wind bent the trees and scattered the needles. The first drops of rain came with it.

"I believe in you, Thomas," she said. "Always have. I want you to know that."

For a moment, she held my gaze, and I knew that she was telling the truth. I might be nothing to the colony, but I mattered to Rose. Her fingers drifted to the wooden bangle on her left wrist. She twisted it around and around. It was what she always did when she was nervous.

She had carved the bangle herself. Just as she'd sewn the band of white cloth that held her hair back from her face, and the pretty linen tunic that fit her so differently than the ones stitched together by the Guardians.

My pulse quickened again, but this time there was no hint of anger. Instead I felt something even more powerful. Something I'd been feeling more and more over the past two years. Something that left me as empty as having no element.

"We should go," I said quickly, before my face gave me away.

I pulled myself up and offered my hand to Rose. She didn't take it, though. Then again, no one but my father touched me, or held me. It was as if having no element was contagious. And who could risk losing their greatest power?

Rose stood now. She was much shorter than me, but looking at her was like watching myself: same unsure expression, same way of shuffling her feet like she wasn't sure what to do with them. Was she thinking the same thing as me too? Deep down, did she want to touch me as much as I wanted to touch her?

"You're right," she said, breaking the connection. "We should go."

No. An element wasn't the only thing I'd never have.

CHAPTER 2

Three canoes sat on the creek, filled with bags of supplies and fresh water in canisters—enough for an overnight stay in the hurricane shelter. Usually I'd have been dreading a trip to the smelly, sweaty shelter on Roanoke Island, two miles to the west. Not this time, though. For once I could only think of getting away—from the Guardians' stares, and my father's lies, and the colony that felt smaller every day.

With a lingering gaze at me, Rose climbed into the front of the canoe on the left. Her brother, Dennis, the youngest member of the colony at nine years old, joined her. He pressed his hands against his head as if it hurt. Rose rubbed his back gently.

Alice already sat at the helm of the middle canoe. She rolled up the sleeves of her dirty, misshapen blue tunic, and grasped the paddle tightly, eager to get moving. As her older sister, Eleanor, shared yet another embrace with their father, Alice rolled her eyes. Or perhaps that gesture was intended for her grandmother, Guardian Lora, who sat in the middle of the sisters' canoe and complained to nobody in particular that the rain was increasing. The other Guardians claimed that Lora was coming along to look after us, but we all knew it was because she was too old and frail to ride out the storm in the colony.

I followed Lora's eyes to the clouds. We'd never set off so late before. I wondered if we'd make it across before lightning hit. If I'd had the element of wind, I'd have known the answer. If I'd had the element of water, I'd have been attuned to the swell, the tempo of the incoming tide.

I had nothing.

I took my usual place at the rear of our oak canoe. It tilted from side to side, but I barely noticed. We spent so much of our lives on water that the constant movements felt as familiar as the gentle give of sand on the beach. Griffin sat in the middle and faced me so that he could communicate with his hands during the crossing.

Meanwhile, in the bow seat up front, Ananias conferred with our father. He spoke with the confidence of a boy who'd been treated as an adult for years—though he was only eighteen. When they were done, Father waded toward Griffin and me. He paused beside Griffin, but when he leaned forward, it was me he hugged. He gripped my hair between his fingers and held me tight.

"I'm sorry," he whispered fiercely. "You have no idea how sorry I am. None of this is your fault. I need you to remember that. Always."

I felt tense in his arms. I wanted to scream that it didn't

matter whose fault it was. Was it any consolation for Griffin to know that his limp wasn't his fault? Or his deafness? Or those sinister visions that kept everyone at arm's length? No. Griffin and I were more than brothers. We were the colony's outcasts, the constant reminders that not everything is created perfect. Knowing it wasn't my fault didn't change that at all.

"I'm sorry," he said again, breaths ragged in my ear. He was squeezing me so hard I could barely breathe. Something rushed through me then, like a message direct from his heart, begging for forgiveness. Against my will, it calmed me. I hugged him back.

"It's all right," I said, even though we both knew it wasn't. "I'm all right."

As soon as he let go, I knew I'd done the right thing. He looked so grateful.

Finally, he turned to Griffin. Father never held him the way he held Ananias and me, but this time was different. Still smiling, he took a deep breath and rested his hands on Griffin's bony shoulders.

Griffin's eyes grew wide in astonishment, and his face opened like a sun breaking through clouds. For a precious moment, everything seemed right.

But then the smile disappeared. His expression shifted. He looked frightened—horrified, even.

That's when the noise began.

At first it was a low sound, like waves breaking in the distance, but it had a knife-like edge that made Ananias spin around instantly. We dropped our paddles and crawled toward

Griffin. He'd already grasped Father's hands and locked on. Father tried to pull away, muscles bulging beneath his dirty cloth shirt, but it was futile.

Almost everyone in the colony had seen Griffin like this before, overcome by a blind panic that gave him superhuman strength. For years I'd tried to block out the memory of those moments—or what followed—but as Griffin's voice twisted into a keening wail, I couldn't think of anything else.

I lunged at Griffin and sent him tumbling onto the hard bottom of the canoe. Father stumbled back and collapsed into the waist-deep water. With the wind knocked out of him, Griffin struggled to breathe, let alone make a sound, but I could tell he'd snapped out of the trance now. There wouldn't be any more moaning, just a faint whimpering as he curled up in a ball.

I didn't need to look around to know that we were being watched. I could literally feel the silence. Everyone in the colony remembered hearing that sound, and what had followed.

"We don't need to go," Dennis cried, his voice high-pitched and desperate. "It's a storm, nothing more."

Kyte shook his head. "We'll not take that chance, son."

"Then come with us. It's not a really bad storm, I promise. That's why you didn't foresee it—"

"Enough!" Kyte was clearly embarrassed at having his weather prediction challenged by his own son. "It's time you left. Paddle evenly. Conserve your water."

Paddle evenly. Conserve your water. This is what the Guardians said every time we set off for another stay in the hurricane shelter. Following these words, we'd dig our paddles into the murky green water and watch them create eddies as the canoes slid forward. We'd laugh at our own strength and Alice's determined attempts to get to Roanoke Island first, like this was a race, not an evacuation. And we'd secretly revel in the knowledge that the only person of authority would be Guardian Lora, who was too weak to walk unaided, let alone control seven of us.

Now there was no laughing. No reveling. No one moved.

"He said go!" My father's voice lashed at us, fueled by fear and anger.

As I scanned everyone's faces, they looked away. They pitied my brothers and me, I was certain. The first time Griffin behaved this way had been nine years before, while he'd been sitting on the beach with Rose's grandparents. One moment, they'd held him fast; the next, his little hands had gotten such a grip on them they couldn't pull away. When they'd launched a sailboat that afternoon, it had taken three Guardians to hold Griffin back, even though he was only four years old. We hadn't even recovered from the shock when the meaning became clear: Rose's grandparents' boat capsized in a sudden squall. Their bodies were never recovered.

Three years later, Griffin had latched on to a boy named John as we played on a rope swing. We'd pulled Griffin away then too, and John had climbed the tree, laughing. But he hadn't gripped the rope properly, and fell. He'd been so still that we were sure he was just pretending to be injured. Then we saw the stream of blood.

After the grieving period, the Guardians had made me explain to Griffin that he wasn't to blame. I'd done as they asked, though I wasn't sure whether they were trying to convince him or themselves. It was the last day anyone had willingly touched my brother. No one wanted to be his next victim.

I knew that Griffin hadn't caused the deaths, of course; it was more like he somehow knew a bad thing was going to happen to someone before it actually did. He wasn't the first person in my family to have the ability either. I'd grown up hearing rumors about my mother's "talent" for foreseeing future catastrophes—even heard people wonder aloud if she was somehow the cause of them.

I'd always told myself that it was wrong for the Guardians to say such things when she wasn't around to defend herself. Then one night, as Griffin slept peacefully in a cot beside us, my father told Ananias and me that our mother had indeed been a seer, just like her mother before her. But all she had been able to foresee was death, and since no one had wanted to spend their final moments in fear of a fate they couldn't avoid, they were wary of her.

Like mother, like son.

Now I stared at my father, saturated and shaking. I wanted to ask him if he was as frightened as I was, but I couldn't. We had an audience, and he was determined to appear strong.

Instead I knelt beside Griffin, still curled up in the bottom of the canoe. Making sure I had his attention, I placed a finger against my chest and pulled my mouth into a frown. Finally, I pointed to him: *I. Sorry. You.*

He watched each gesture with a glazed expression, and when I finished he didn't sign back. I needed to see him touch his heart, to show that he forgave me. After all, we weren't just brothers—we were confidants, fellow outcasts. Strangers in our own colony. But I knew he wouldn't—or couldn't—do it. The last time he'd had a seizure, he hadn't communicated for a full day afterward. No words or laughter, just emptiness.

I glanced at Ananias, and wished I hadn't. Gone was the Apprentice, the boy with the confidence of a Guardian. Now he looked as panicked as I felt. Neither of us was ready to go, but the Guardians wouldn't allow us to stay. Silence weighed heavily, and somehow I knew that only we could break it.

I picked up the paddle and nodded to Ananias that it was time to go. He followed me in a daze. Neither of us said goodbye to our father—it was as though the word had changed meaning, become too final. Instead, we drove our paddles into the water and propelled ourselves away. For a dozen strokes I closed my eyes and focused on the splashing sound, and the monotony helped me to forget.

But then I glanced down at Griffin, and realized he was staring at the receding figure of our father. He didn't even blink. It was like he wanted to take in as much of the man as possible before he disappeared forever.

CHAPTER 3

alfway across the sound—the waterway separating our colony on Hatteras Island from Roanoke Island—the rain became torrential. Heavy drops collected in pools around Griffin's legs, but he didn't seem to notice. He was as silent now as he had been loud before.

We fought our way through choppy water around tiny Pond Island and followed the hulking bridge to the eastern shore of Roanoke Island. The bridge was old and decrepit— remnant of a long-ago civilization—and a small section was missing from the middle, making it difficult to cross. The Guardians had left strong wooden planks on either side of the gap, which could be lowered in case of emergency; but walking on a long, narrow board eighty feet above the water was something only Alice wanted to try. Besides, the canoes were faster, and could carry more provisions.

We paddled hard along one of the channels that cut into Roanoke Island. At the end, we tethered the canoes to a pon-

17

toon. Alice and Eleanor unloaded their supplies as Lora muttered curses.

"Let me rest," the old woman groaned. She was standing knee-deep in the water, fragile arms clinging to the pontoon. "I believe you would have me die out here, Alice."

Alice caught my eye. As gusts of wind whipped at her tunic, I'd swear she smiled a little. "I hadn't thought of that, Lora," she said. "Not until now, anyway."

Eleanor cast her sister a warning glance, but it was pointless. Despite their physical similarities—they were both tall and willowy—their temperaments were as strikingly different as their hair: long, curling brown locks for Eleanor, and unkempt raven-black hair for Alice. Where Eleanor glided with gentle grace, Alice carried the energy of an all-consuming storm. Where Eleanor seemed to look through people to the weather beyond, Alice stared at them with a blazing intensity that dared them to look away. Everyone adored Eleanor. Alice counted me as her only friend. Then again, she frustrated the Guardians even more than I did. How could I not have liked her?

Lora picked up on Alice's defiant tone, and cocked her head. "What was that? What did you say, child?" She emphasized the word *child*, as if she weren't completely at Alice's mercy.

Alice just smiled. She would be turning sixteen in a few months. Her element was unusually weak, but she'd still be honored with the title Apprentice of the Fire. There would be a celebration. A feast. She certainly wouldn't suffer through a halfhearted meal passed in cold silence, as I had done. She wouldn't have to press her hands against her ears to block out her father's tirade. She wouldn't be granted an additional year to discover her element—simply putting off the moment when the Guardians would acknowledge she had no element at all.

"Thomas. . . . Thomas!" Ananias stood over me. Rain ran down his face. "Can you help Griffin?"

It wasn't really a question, but I nodded anyway. "Are you all right?" I asked.

Ananias secured our canoe to the pontoon with deliberate slowness. He knew what I really meant. "Griffin could be wrong."

"He's never been wrong before."

"But Father knows there's danger now. He'll be on his guard. So will everyone else." He spoke earnestly, like he really wanted to believe what he was saying. But behind the stubble and the serious brows, he looked concerned.

I turned to Griffin. He hadn't moved at all. One side of his body was submerged in rainwater. *We go*, I signed.

Griffin blinked, but he didn't reply.

We go, I repeated. I waved my arm in a wide arc above my head to signify the weather. *Storm*.

He sat up, shivering.

I pulled off his saturated cloth shirt and gave him the spare from my canvas bag. I knew he'd be drenched again before we reached the shelter, but I just wanted him to stop shaking for a moment. He pulled on the shirt without looking at me.

Ananias took my bag so I could stay with Griffin. But Griffin either didn't need my help, or didn't want it. Without even a glance in my direction he crawled out of the canoe and onto the pontoon. Then he followed the others along the cracked road, fighting wind and rain, his weak right leg sliding through dirty puddles.

Finally only Alice and Lora remained. "Come on," grumbled Lora as I approached. She didn't look up. "Alice has me propped up against this pontoon like a ship's figurehead."

"Or a lightning rod," offered Alice cheerily.

When I drew close, Lora's expression shifted. "Oh, it's you," she said, startled. "Where's Ananias?"

"Carrying our bags."

She opened her mouth as if to speak, but sighed instead. "Well, you can carry my bag, then."

"Don't you need support?"

"Alice's help will be enough." She fixed me with her withering gaze. "I'm not an invalid yet."

I stared right back. For once, it was Lora who looked away first.

We trudged along the half-mile stretch of road that led to the hurricane shelter. To either side, marsh gave way to scrub grass, and then the ground was littered with rubble, the remains of a bigger settlement. No one knew precisely when the area had been abandoned, or why, but it was impossible not to marvel at what the colonists had accomplished: buildings of smooth stone, and bridges that soared for a mile or more across the waterways. And a hurricane shelter that was still miraculously intact after who knew how many years?

Near the shelter the crumbling road intersected with another, equally battered one. The buildings still stood here, in various states of disrepair. I'd named the place Skeleton Town after them; they reminded me of the rotting fish that sometimes washed ashore on the beach. The name had stuck ever since.

I wondered how Lora felt, returning here now. Her husband had died in one of the buildings—fell through a rotten floorboard and slid deep into a hidden shaft. The walls had collapsed on top of him. The Guardians had attempted to pull him out with ropes, but it was no use. He was completely trapped. Lora had passed him food and water and talked to him until, finally, he'd stopped answering.

Every one of us had been hurt here at some point: mostly from the broken glass littered around the buildings. The safest place was the center of the road. No one deviated far from it.

I glanced at the buildings to either side. Where had the strange materials come from? What had destroyed the place? Why did the colonists leave? Skeleton Town was one gigantic mystery, and every time we returned I found it more fascinating.

Suddenly, there was a flash of movement in the building to my left—a person, I thought, although that was impossible. I stared through the remains of a window. Broken furniture littered the floor. Shelves dangled from the walls at awkward angles. But there was no movement. It must have been the wind and rain playing tricks on me.

When we reached the intersection, Alice whistled. "Just look at these buildings," she said. "I reckon there were hundreds of people living here once. Why do you think they left, Guardian Lora?"

"I don't know. It was uninhabited when we discovered it many years ago." It was Lora's usual reply.

"But you must've thought about it."

"Well, it was probably the Plague. Like on the mainland."

"But there was no sign of the Plague when you settled here, right?"

"No. I suppose not."

"Hmm." Alice paused. "Mother says Skeleton Town may have been destroyed in the storm that grounded your ship on Hatteras Island."

"Possibly."

"I don't think so. There's no way everyone on board would've survived a storm that was powerful enough to destroy a town." She clicked her tongue. "Which reminds me: Why didn't Kyte predict *that* storm?"

"For the same reason he missed today's. Nobody's perfect, Alice. You of all people should be aware of that."

Lora no doubt sensed that Alice's questions were far from over—she clamped her mouth shut and stared straight ahead. None of the Guardians liked to discuss the hazardous voyage that had brought them to Hatteras Island years before we were born. All we knew for certain was that they had taken to the ocean in a desperate attempt to escape the Plague.

They weren't alone, either. Every now and then we'd glimpse clan ships on the horizon. The crews never disembarked, but sometimes they anchored offshore and the

Guardians would row out to trade with them. When they departed, the fifty or so people on board—young and old— would stand against the rail and wave to us. Those were the only times we could be sure we weren't alone in the world.

We shuffled on in a slow-moving line as clouds raced by and rain pummeled us.

"Why don't the clan folk ever stay?" I asked. "They could tell us about the ocean, and what's beyond it, right?"

"No. They'll not risk bringing Plague aboard their ship," replied Lora, clearly more at ease with my questions than Alice's.

"But there are no rats on Hatteras."

"They don't know that for certain. And we don't know there aren't rats on their ship. Have you forgotten what happened after John died?"

No, I hadn't forgotten. His parents had been distraught, unable to cope. So had his older sister, Elizabeth; she'd loved her brother, and when he was gone, she'd felt alone and neglected. Everyone had known it, but no one had intervened. We'd simply given the family room to grieve.

Elizabeth hadn't grieved. She'd escaped.

She'd taken a sailboat and headed for the mainland. Her parents had chased after her in a canoe, but didn't reach her until the next day. By the time they'd brought her home, she was showing early signs of Plague: chills, fever, seizures, and swelling around her groin. So they'd carried her to an abandoned cabin several hundred yards from the rest of the colony.

I remembered my father imploring them to cover their

mouths and bodies, but they hadn't listened. By the following day, they had the Plague too.

I never saw them after that. My father said they had asked him to divvy up their belongings. Then they'd taken a package of food and water, and paddled over to Roanoke Island, the three of them together. Ten days later, Father had crossed the bridge. We'd stood on the shore and watched him go, saw smoke from the fire he'd started to burn their decomposing remains. He'd rowed their canoe back, alone, and hadn't spoken for a week.

I hadn't forgotten that at all.

"If the people on the clan ships won't come ashore," pressed Alice, "how do they survive? How do they have anything to trade?"

"There are other colonies besides ours."

"What other colonies?" I asked. For a moment I shared Alice's frustration at Lora's dead-end answers. To me, she seemed entirely full of secrets—important ones. "Where are they? Why haven't we met people from them?"

"Everyone has a place in the world," replied Lora, "and this is ours."

"Now, yes," agreed Alice as we arrived at the shelter. "But what about before the shipwreck? Why won't you tell us where you came from?"

Lora stopped in her tracks, and despite her frailty, it was Alice who almost toppled over. Lora kept hold of her granddaughter, and clasped my arm too. I felt the pressure of her touch, heat that grew from her grip like a dull ache.

Lora stared at her hand, then at me. The muscles in her cheeks seemed to spasm. "You have so much to be thankful for. Don't you realize that?"

My pulse raced, but for once I refused to answer.

She pushed my arm away, but looked even more flustered now than before. "And you," she spat, turning her attention to Alice, "you ask too many questions."

Alice met her gaze and didn't blink. "And get too few honest answers."

CHAPTER 4

The hurricane shelter looked the same as it had the previous year—same heavy door, same thick walls. So did the grassy square beside it; and the water tower behind, which leaned precariously, defying gravity.

We pushed inside, and followed the staircase down. The shelter was a squat building, built mostly underground. Compared to low-lying Hatteras Island, where the waves almost kissed the cabin stilts at high tide, it felt extremely safe. Even the storm raging outside the narrow band of windows near the ceiling sounded distant. We were insulated from danger here.

I wished my father had come with us. In the heat of the moment I'd been confused, but now I realized that we could have made room for him in one of the canoes. Or would Griffin have already foreseen that? Perhaps there was no way to escape fate.

In the half-darkness we gathered in a circle and ate scraps of cured fish along with freshly harvested yucca flowers and sea rocket stems. I washed it down with small sips from my water canister. Despite the humidity I was thirsty, but I rationed my water. Unless the storm was devastating, the Guardians would arrive the next morning and tell us it was safe to return to the colony, and then I'd gulp down every last drop.

Griffin's portion sat untouched beside him. I tried to get him to eat, but he didn't seem to notice me. With his back pressed against the wall of the shelter, eyes blank and face drawn, he looked catatonic.

He wasn't the only one not eating. "Are you all right, Dennis?" I asked.

The young boy shook his head.

"It's the storm," explained Rose. She ran her hand up and down his back. "He *feels* it."

"Well, it is a bad one," said Lora.

I listened to rain drumming against the shelter. All I could think about was my father, and whether he'd be alive by morning.

Lora watched me. "Everything will be fine. You must have faith in the Guardians."

"Even when they're wrong?" muttered Dennis.

All eyes turned to him. I'd heard Alice cross the Guardians, but never Dennis. He was usually so wary of speaking out of turn.

"It's a storm, not a hurricane," he continued. "It's bad, but we could've stayed on Hatteras. We *should've* stayed."

"Now, now, Dennis," said Eleanor, no doubt trying to spare him Lora's wrath. "There's more to our element than predicting weather, remember. We need to consider the effects of the

27

storm. How the wind might change the height of the ocean. How rain can erode the beach. How—"

"I've done all of that already."

"Nonsense," snapped Lora. "Your father has shown you basic skills, that's all. You'll learn to harness your full element once you're an Apprentice, not a moment sooner."

Dennis shook his head. "Too late. Eleanor's already taught me everything."

"How could she? Eleanor doesn't even know everything—"

"She does! And so do I." Dennis's small dark eyes were wild. "I know the wind is thirty-three knots. We've already had an inch of rain, but we'll only get two. The ocean will swell by eighteen inches, but it won't rise above the cabin stilts. I know all of it. I've felt it all already."

Now that his outburst was over, the focus shifted to Eleanor. As an Apprentice of the Wind, she needed to tell Dennis he was mistaken. She needed to restore order. But she turned away instead. Even in the half-light, she looked flushed.

I wondered if Lora would punish both of them. An Apprentice training a young one was unthinkable; surely his element was too raw. He should have been taught by his father, Kyte, just as Eleanor had been taught by her mother.

"You should enjoy being young, Dennis," Lora said with eerie calm. "You have people who care for you. Food to eat. All we ask is that you listen and learn. There's time enough for you to become an Apprentice, to take on that responsibility." She summoned an unconvincing smile. "Or are you afraid there'll be no storms left by the time you turn sixteen?"

Dennis folded his arms and jutted out his lower lip. "What's the use of having an element if I'm not allowed to use it? Right now I'm no different than Thomas."

Rose grasped his arm and shook it. "That's a horrible thing to say. Tell him you're sorry."

"Why? It's true. He doesn't have an element."

"Maybe there are more elements than we know," said Ananias quickly. "After all, Griffin has the skill of foresight."

Lora turned the full force of her glare onto Ananias. "That's no *skill*. Predicting others' misfortune is a curse."

"You think we don't know that?" I snapped. "Look at him. He can't eat or sleep because of what he saw."

"If he saw anything at all. Being right twice doesn't make him a seer. Have you asked him what he saw today?"

"No. I'm not going to make him relive it, no matter what it was. And I won't let anyone else, either."

Dennis shivered. "Griffin frightens me. He hasn't moved since we got here. What's wrong with him?"

"Nothing's wrong with him," I said.

"How would you know? Our father says you're strange. Says we should be careful around you. Anyway, why don't you have an element?"

"Enough!" shouted Ananias.

Maybe I should have been offended, but I wasn't. I'd asked the same question a hundred times, and never once had a satisfactory answer. I turned to Lora, wondering how she'd reply.

The old woman licked her dry lips. Her breaths were

unusually quick. "I think you should go sit by yourself, young Dennis. You've said quite enough for one night."

With a defiant glare, Dennis shuffled over to the far wall. I wasn't angry with him, though.

"You can hardly expect him to learn if you won't answer his questions," I said.

"His question was impertinent. As is your tone."

"My tone? My father may be dead, but you're worried about my *tone*?"

Lora's expression didn't change. "I think maybe you should leave us too."

"Nothing would make me happier."

As Eleanor told a story to clear the air, I joined Dennis and Griffin in exile against the far wall. When I touched Griffin's shoulder he flinched, but still didn't open his eyes. His dark, curly hair was lank from sweat and his face was gaunt. We probably looked alike.

I opened my bag and pulled out one of the battered books my father had found in the remains of Skeleton Town. Pages were missing, but Griffin didn't usually care—it was a chance to lose himself in a different world. This time, he wouldn't take it.

I could think of only one other thing to try: a piece of driftwood and a burnt twig. Griffin was an extraordinary artist, the best in the colony. I placed the driftwood in his lap, the twig in his fingers, and waited.

Something seemed to stir in him, and Griffin brushed the twig across the wood, leaving shadowy black lines. Although

30

I wasn't sure what he was drawing, I could see him relaxing, his breathing slow. As Eleanor murmured her story, Griffin's picture began to take shape: Guardian Lora asleep, an expression of peacefulness softening her sharp features. It was one of his finest—far more than Lora deserved. I wished he'd saved his talent for someone else.

When she was done telling her story, Eleanor came over and knelt beside Dennis. She glanced over her shoulder like she was making sure no one was listening. But then her eyes locked on me momentarily. I got the feeling she wanted me to hear.

"Are you sure about eighteen inches of swell?" she asked Dennis.

He nodded.

"Hmm. I thought twenty, but you're probably right. You usually are. Your element is so much further along than mine was at your age. But try not to be in too much of a hurry, all right?"

She stroked his spiky hair and lowered her voice to a whisper. "Remember the first time you sensed a storm coming? You were only three, but you knew what was happening. I could tell just by looking at your face you had the element, same as me. And it's only gotten stronger." She swallowed. "But I know what you're going through, remember? I know how it feels—the *echo*. All that fear and uncertainty."

"How come no one else's element has an echo?"

"They do. No one talks about it, but if you watch their faces, you'll see—everybody suffers somehow."

"Sometimes I can't sleep. It's like something's pressing against my head."

"I'm so sorry." Eleanor took his hand and held it. "My father wouldn't let me focus on my element until I was your age. I thought if I started things earlier, you'd hone your element quicker—maybe get control of the echo quicker too. But it's worse now, isn't it?"

He nodded again.

"Oh, Dennis. This is all my fault." She sighed. "How long have you been feeling this storm?"

"Since last night. It's so much worse over here, though."

"I know. That's why I hate coming to Roanoke Island. But it makes sense, I guess. We only come here when there's a storm, and that's when the echo is worst." She stared at her fingers, splayed out across the hard stone floor. "Listen, you have to believe me—eventually the echo gets better. It did for me . . . like a weight being lifted, little by little. You'll feel it too. And when you do, you won't care about a title. Or even whether people listen to you. You'll just love being able to relax again."

She held him then, and let him cry into her hair, while we all pretended not to notice.

CHAPTER 5

Soon it was too dark to do anything. Ananias took one of the slow-burning candles the Guardians had discovered when they first explored Skeleton Town and lit it with a single spark from his fingertip. We placed blankets on the floor and settled down to sleep.

As the murmur of deep breathing filled the room, I wondered if I was the only one still awake. Then I heard Lora moaning beside me, the noise punctuated by occasional sharp breaths. I was still furious at her, so I blocked it out as long as I could. But there was something very uncomfortable about that sound.

"Are you all right?" I whispered.

Lora opened her mouth to speak, but nothing came out. Her tongue clicked, as though stuck to the roof of her mouth.

"Do you need water?"

She nodded, but when I picked up her canister, it was already empty. I didn't want to give her mine—I'd been rationing myself—but she sounded worse with every passing moment. Muttering a curse, I placed my canister against her lips and watched the water dribble into her mouth and out again.

"Building," she croaked. "Clinic."

I heard the words clearly, but didn't understand. I leaned closer. "What did you say?"

She took a deep, shuddering breath. "Take main road. Left side. Second building. White stone. Broken glass door." She paused to swallow. "Shelves on right. Second shelf down. White container. Aspirin."

"What?"

"White container," she wheezed. "Aspirin."

Her voice was quiet, and it took me a moment to realize she was sending me into one of the buildings in Skeleton Town. At least, it seemed that way. But she couldn't be, of course. It was forbidden. Lethal.

"Where do you want me to go?" I asked again.

"Main road. . . . Left side. . . . Second building." Step by step, she repeated her directions.

I hesitated. "What is aspirin, Guardian Lo—"

"Go!"

I sat upright, pulse racing. In the dim candlelight I could see that everyone was already asleep. I was tempted to wake Ananias, to check with him that Lora wasn't delusional. But she hadn't sounded delusional, just desperate.

Going into Skeleton Town during a storm seemed crazy. Or maybe that was the point. Lora probably hoped I'd refuse—

further evidence that I wasn't fit to be an Apprentice even if I had an element.

Well then, I'd prove her wrong. I wanted to see the shock on her face when I returned. I needed her to be in my debt, answer *my* questions.

I stepped around the sleeping bodies and padded up the stairs. As I opened the door, rain drove at me from every angle. With a deep breath, I stepped in the direction of the abandoned buildings across the road. I could barely make out my shoes as they swept through torrents of water.

I crossed the road and pressed my hands against the first building I found. I shuffled along to the corner and turned left. The building here was built from rough stone, and although I couldn't see it well, I was sure it wasn't white, so I leaned into the wind and pressed on. When I glanced behind me, it was as though the shelter had disappeared completely.

The next building appeared to be white. I could see its ghostly outline. I rushed toward it and followed the stone with my hands until I reached the door—broken glass, just as Guardian Lora had predicted. I turned the handle and pushed, but the door wouldn't open. I tried to force it, but it held fast. In desperation, I crouched down and attempted to climb through the hole in the glass. Halfway through, my foot snagged the edge and I tumbled onto the floor.

I didn't need to see my arms to know that I'd landed on glass. Even when I stood, the shards remained attached to me. It felt like a hundred tiny bee stings. I picked out each piece while my eyes grew accustomed to the darkness.

The building seemed to groan under its own calamitous weight. Wind whipped through holes in the windows. I took a step forward but tripped over an object that lay across the floor. My shoulder caught the edge of a table as I fell. It spun me around.

My head hit the ground first, my right cheek pressed against the floor. Water trickled into my open mouth. I spat it out and turned to face the ceiling.

Being on the floor reminded me that Lora's husband had died in one of these buildings. Which made me think of my father back on Hatteras. At that very moment he'd be fighting the storm too, with sandbags and hastily nailed wooden shutters, desperate to preserve what little the colony possessed.

Unless he was already dead.

I pictured Griffin earlier that afternoon—the way he'd latched on to our father with every part of his fragile body in a last-ditch effort to ensure he wouldn't leave us. Why had I pulled him away?

I groped around for an object I could use to pull myself up, and my hand landed on something smooth and hard. Immediately there was humming—a low, unnatural sound that resonated through every part of me. As soon as I let go, the humming stopped. I tried to see what the object was, but it was too dark.

I stood gingerly. Taking tiny footsteps, I made my way to the wall on my right. I placed my hands flat against it and shuffled along until I felt the shelves. They were exactly where Guardian Lora had said they would be—four of them, one above the other. I found the second shelf down and felt a rush of adrenaline as I anticipated finding the container.

The shelf was empty.

I checked it again. Checked that I had the correct shelf. Checked that there weren't other shelves beside me. But no, this was the one. And there was nothing on it.

That's when it hit me: How had Lora known the shelves were here? Did she already know the shelf was empty? Had she sent me to the same building where her husband had died?

I'd crossed Lora earlier, demanded answers she was unwilling to provide. Was this her revenge?

Gritting my teeth, I followed the wall toward the door. My head hurt where it had hit the ground, and every rapid heartbeat sent waves of pain to that spot. I knew I needed to calm down, but I was way too angry.

Just when I spied the door a couple yards away, my right hand ran across cables dangling from the ceiling. Something bright flashed against my hand, startling me. A spark beside my feet ignited paper strewn across the floor. I extinguished it by kicking water over it. Plunged into darkness again, I could still see a bright spot in the center of my vision.

I found the door and avoided catching the glass edge as I eased my way through. When I was outside, I stomped away from the building and didn't look back. I tried to stay focused, but couldn't. I was furious. Whether or not I was an Apprentice, I was surely more useful to the colony alive than dead.

I could see a little better outside, but I still hugged the

building. I couldn't afford to get lost. My head felt hot, but the rest of me was shivering. A long night in Skeleton Town was the last thing I wanted.

After several steps the wall felt rougher, and I knew I was next to a different building. When that building ended, I kept moving straight ahead across the road toward the shelter. Five steps. Ten steps. Fifteen.

Something didn't feel right. The shelter wasn't where I expected it to be.

Suddenly there was a sound nearby: something moving, or scraping. Had someone come to find me?

"Who's there?" I shouted.

No response, so I rushed in the direction of the sound. When I reached the spot, I stretched out my arms and felt only wind and rain.

I heard the sound again, nearer this time. Again I hurried toward it, and my shoulder collided with the smooth wall of the shelter. I knew it would hurt in the morning, but I didn't care. All my energy was focused on following the wall. When I finally reached the door, I threw myself inside.

I clung to the rail and descended the stairs, footsteps unsteady, shoes slippery. The candle still glowed, but no one stirred. I wound my way toward Lora. She lay on her side, exactly where I'd left her.

"Two," she murmured, eyes shut tight. "Two tablets."

"There was nothing there. *Nothing.*"

It seemed as though her entire body recoiled. "Should've

sent Ananias," she said, more breath than words. "Or Eleanor. Or Alice. Anyone but you."

"There was nothing there."

I wanted her to open her eyes. To apologize for what she'd done. But as the moments passed, I began to notice things: her expression, taut and unchanging; her legs, pulled tight against her chest. She looked helpless. She was suffering.

"Blanket," she mouthed.

My mind drifted back to the building. Had there been other shelves after all? Had I stopped looking too soon?

"Blan . . ." This time she couldn't even complete the word.

With so many bodies crammed together, the night felt even hotter and stickier than the day, but I spread my blanket across her anyway. Her arms glistened with perspiration.

I lay down as her rasping breath steadied. She said the word *tessa* over and over until her voice faded away entirely and I knew that she had finally fallen asleep.

As I rolled away from Lora, I noticed that Alice had edged closer to me. I could even see the whites of her eyes, so I guessed that she'd been listening.

"You're drenched." She stifled a yawn. "Where have you been?"

"Into Skeleton Town."

"What for? And why did she keep saying 'tessa'?"

"How did you hear—" I began to say. But then Alice's eyes grew wide. She was looking upward as though watching someone standing over me.

I rolled over and collided with Griffin. He knelt beside Guardian Lora and placed his hands under her head. She didn't say a word, even when he lifted her head into his lap and stroked her hair tenderly.

Then I realized why.

Lora had always been one of the cruelest Guardians — never satisfied, always doubting. But at that moment, all I could think was that her challenge to me had been real. And because I had failed her, our colony had lost another member.

With only thirteen people left, it was hard not to wonder if we were all as fragile as her. And if so, who would be next?

CHAPTER 6

A nanias was the first to wake, shortly before sunrise. When he saw Griffin, Alice, and me, he nudged Eleanor. The five of us encircled the body of Guardian Lora.

Eleanor turned away from her dead grandmother, and Ananias wrapped her in a tight hug. She buried her face in his hair.

Alice rubbed her tired eyes. "We should release Lora to the water." With the storm over, her voice sounded loud and intrusive.

Eleanor stepped back and dried her eyes with her tunic. "We should wait for the Guardians to arrive first."

"There isn't time. She died just after you fell asleep. I overheard the Guardians say that bodies must be released to the water within a half day of passing."

"You *overheard* this?"

Alice shrugged. She had an uncanny knack of overhearing all sorts of things—more than the rest of us put together.

41

Some of the Guardians even accused her of spying, though she always denied it.

"Well, then," said Eleanor, "we should carry Guardian Lora to the water and offer a blessing for safe passage."

Alice stood and waited for the others to help her.

"Someone needs to stay here, Alice." Eleanor tilted her head toward Rose and Dennis, who were still fast asleep. "They'll wake up soon, and need reassuring."

"So stay here and reassure them."

"No. Releasing Guardian Lora's body is something Apprentices should do."

"Well, there are only two of you, so you're going to need help. Anyway, you think I can't toss a dead body into the water?"

Eleanor gasped. "This is our grandmother, remember."

"Believe me, I remember—how much she hated me, criticized me. Truly, how can anyone be so mean?"

Eleanor raised her hand. "Please don't disrespect the dead. I can see you've been awake for most of the night. It must've been difficult, but you can't let tiredness cloud your judgment now." She spoke so calmly, so reasonably, that there was no way for Alice to protest.

I signed to Griffin that I needed him to stay behind and explain to Rose and Dennis what had happened. It was like he didn't even see me. Still, as long as he was around, they would know we hadn't abandoned them.

We picked up Lora's body together, one of us at each limb. Ananias was stronger than me—with powerful arms and wide shoulders—but not much taller, so he and I took her legs. Lora was so light that none of us struggled. Hard to imagine such a frail body could have endured year after year of storms.

We carried Lora up the worn stone steps and along the road to the shore. To the east, the sun was rising above Hatteras Island. I couldn't see through the glare, but I knew the Guardians would be coming for us soon.

How would I explain to them what had happened during the night?

We waded into the sound and let Lora's body float beside us. Eleanor offered thanks for Lora's years of companionship, and expressed hope for the afterlife. Ananias didn't speak, but he held Eleanor's hand throughout, and pulled her close when she choked on her words. Alice just stared at her grandmother, eyes dulled by anger and distrust.

Eleanor finished, and we let Lora go. Her body bobbed gently in the post-storm calm.

While the others headed for shore, I stayed and watched her drift farther into the sound. I studied her closed eyes, the way the lines etched into her forehead had smoothed out, making her seem younger again. She had indeed tested me, but it was a matter of life and death, not a trap.

Why hadn't I woken the others?

I heard someone pushing against the water, rejoining me. "Did you get any sleep at all?" Ananias asked gently.

"No."

"I'm sorry." He stood beside me, completely still. The

loose sleeves of our tunics flapped together. "Do you know what happened to her?"

I could have told him. It would have felt good to get it off my chest. Instead, I said nothing.

He sighed. "Alice is right: Lora was a miserable woman." He caught my look of surprise. "You know it's true. Every time we've come to Roanoke, Father's told me to look after her. But she never once thanked me." He turned to face the body once more. "Go ahead and mourn her if you want, but I'm glad she's dead. You should be too."

Even when Ananias left me, I stayed where I was, watching Lora float away. How could I be glad, when I was the one who let her die?

I got back to the shelter as Rose and Dennis were waking. Griffin sat with his back against the wall, hunkered down in his silent world. I thought maybe he'd fallen asleep, but his hand was moving. He was completing his drawing from the night before: a perfect image of Guardian Lora, her eyes closed and face relaxed.

The image seemed to shift before my eyes. Griffin hadn't drawn Lora sleeping. He'd foreseen her death.

I knew I should ask him if he was feeling all right. Perhaps even find out more about the drawing. But in that moment, everything seemed to have changed. A catastrophe had occurred, exactly as Griffin had predicted the previous afternoon—only the victim was Lora. Did that mean that when the Guardians arrived, my father would be among them, alive and well? Surely her death couldn't have been a coincidence. Perhaps it wasn't even my fault.

Ananias joined us then. When he gasped, I knew he'd made the connection too. After that, neither of us looked at the others. We couldn't afford to show our relief while Eleanor was busy explaining to Rose and Dennis why they'd never see Guardian Lora again.

CHAPTER 7

I awoke to the sound of muttering. Ananias and Eleanor sat on the steps, so I made my way over to them, past a sleeping Alice.

"How long did I sleep?" I asked.

Ananias glanced up. "A quarter day."

"Six strikes?" We measured time by placing a stick in the sand and watching its shadow trace an arc across strike marks in the ground. I pictured it passing six of them.

"You needed it. We just finished lunch, but we're running low on supplies. The Guardians still haven't come for us."

That was a surprise. After a storm, the Guardians' first priority was to take us back to the colony, or to bring us more food and water if we were going to need to stay longer in the shelter.

"Maybe something got damaged, and they're fixing it," I said.

"All of them?"

"Then maybe there's something wrong with the bridge."

Eleanor shook her head. "It was just a storm, not a hurricane. Besides, we've been checking the bridge. No one's been on it today."

"So we wait."

Ananias and Eleanor exchanged glances.

"Actually," began Ananias, "we're afraid there might be another reason the Guardians haven't come for us. And if it's important enough to keep them away, they could surely use our help."

I nodded. "I'll tell the others to pack their bags and head for the canoes."

They exchanged another awkward glance, and this time I knew what was coming.

"It'll be better if just the two of us go. Griffin and Dennis weren't feeling well last night. We really need someone to stay here and look after them."

"But I can . . ." *Help you,* I wanted to say. It's what Alice would have said—fiercely too. But they were right about Griffin and Dennis. The last thing I wanted to do was make them paddle over to Hatteras if there was a chance we'd have to return to the shelter for another night.

Ananias patted my shoulder, though his hand barely brushed my tunic. "Whether or not the Guardians need our help, one of us will return before supper. I promise."

Then they left, their strides long and determined, jaws set with the confidence brought on by well-honed elements. They held hands as they walked.

As soon as they were gone, Rose and Dennis joined me.

"Ananias says we're short on supplies," said Rose. "Unless you like wilted sea rocket stems." The ends of her hair blew about. Her hazel eyes shone.

"Would you catch us a fish?" I asked.

"Do I have to?"

"I haven't eaten yet today. Neither have Alice and Griffin. Please don't make us eat any more of that sea rocket."

She sighed. "All right. Fish it is."

We walked toward the sound. The sun was bright now, the air heavy and humid. At the water's edge, Rose rolled up the hem of her white tunic and waded in. When the water came to just below her waist, she closed her eyes and placed her palms flat against the surface. Her body was perfectly still, hands rising and falling with each gentle swell. Only her hair moved at all.

She'd stay that way as long as necessary—probably as long as half a strike—so Dennis and I collected kindling. It wasn't difficult; the storm had washed lots of driftwood ashore. There were dead fish too, even the remains of seagulls— their bloated white bodies still waiting for the vultures to arrive.

In the distance, Ananias and Eleanor's canoe was disappearing across the sound. The stillness of the afternoon reminded me how I tired I was. Dennis was working much faster than me.

"You seem better today," I told him.

He raised his face to the sky. The sun glowed upon his freckled cheeks. "Storm's passed," he said, like that explained everything. "Sorry about what I said last night, though." His expression grew tense. "It's the echo... makes me—"

"Don't worry about it," I interrupted. "You're fine now. That's what matters."

A flash of white pulled me around. Rose had already dropped to her knees. She bounced back up a moment later, a movement so fluid and quick that it caused barely a ripple. When she raised her hands, she clutched a trout as long as her forearm. It flapped desperately, silver scales glinting in the sun, but there was no escape.

Rose's tunic lay slick against her now, outlining the curves of her chest and hips. Water dripped from her hair. But she was oblivious to everything except the trout. As she lifted her left hand above her, she stared at the fish without blinking, even whispered something I couldn't hear. I would have sworn it heard her too, because it gave up fighting and grew still.

I held my breath. Waiting.

Rose brought her hand down with sickening force. She killed the trout instantly.

Then she was still again.

By the time Dennis and I finished gathering kindling, she was a hundred yards along the road. She held the trout horizontal in her arms, like an offering.

"That was so quick," I said as we caught up with her.

She nodded.

"Are you all right?"

"She's all right," said Dennis. "It's the echo. That's all."

As if she knew I was watching her, Rose tilted her head away. But not before I caught a glimpse of her tear-streaked face, half hidden behind disheveled hair. I wondered what her echo could be, and if she had any idea at all how beautiful she was.

Alice wasn't pleased that Ananias and Eleanor had left without us, or that I hadn't woken her. But most of all she wasn't pleased about having to start a fire to cook the fish.

"Why are you making me do this?" she hissed. "You know my element is weak."

"You can do as much as my father."

"No offense, but that's not saying much."

Alice was right. Neither she nor my father came close to Ananias's talent for manipulating fire. Griffin's control of the earth was also weak; but then, he had visions.

"Look. Ananias isn't here," I said. "You are."

"So? It's humiliating to struggle with an element."

"As humiliating as not having one at all?"

That quieted her momentarily. "Fine. I'll try. But I can't promise anything, and you know it. Do you have kindling?"

I pointed to the fire pit the Guardians had dug beside the exterior wall of the shelter. Dennis and I had filled it with driftwood. Alice knelt down and arranged the pieces so there were barely any gaps. Then she rolled up her sleeves, leaned back on her haunches, and pressed her palms together.

She rubbed her hands back and forth: slowly at first, then faster and faster, until the air was filled with the rush of friction and telltale wisps of smoke. Still she moved quicker, hands a blur as the first tiny flames licked at the edges of her fingertips. There were sparks too—they shot out in all directions, but disappeared before they hit the ground. And all the while the heat grew, rippling and warping the air, driving us back.

With yellow-orange flames radiating from her hands, Alice leaned forward and opened her palms toward the kindling. Sweat poured down her forehead, but she continued to rub the edges of her hands together, the fire growing as it drew oxygen from the open air. She didn't even stop when the first pieces of driftwood caught, but allowed her element to take over. Her head tipped backward and her shoulders relaxed. Thick smoke obscured her face.

I glanced at Rose and Dennis. They were clearly as surprised as me. We'd seen Alice produce smoke and sparks on Hatteras, but not much more. Now she was immersed in the fire she'd created. It didn't seem to affect her at all.

With the driftwood ablaze, Rose impaled the trout with a stake and balanced it on the makeshift spit. Alice drove her fingers into the flames and rearranged the sticks until the fish's black-and-silver skin began to sizzle. The kindling glowed like the sun and crackled angrily, but it gave off less smoke now, and I could see Alice clearly again: her smut-smeared face, and a single teardrop that traced a course through the grime.

"What's the matter?" I asked.

Alice pulled her sleeves down and wiped them across her

cheeks, erasing all signs of the tear-streak. "Nothing. It's just sweat."

She was lying, but I didn't call her on it. No need to make her feel bad.

"What does it feel like to have an element?" I asked Rose.

"Like nothing. An element just *is*. It's a part of you, like breathing."

"So what's the echo?"

"It's a side effect of the element."

"What's yours?"

She hesitated. "I make the fish come to me. And . . . I don't know how to explain this, but . . . it's like I reassure them. That everything is good. Which is a lie, because I kill them."

"So your echo is—what? That you feel sorry for the fish?"

She chuckled, but the sound got caught in her throat. "I know, it sounds stupid. But it gets to me. I make a promise, and then I break it. It takes a piece of me every time."

"What about you, Alice?"

Alice remained crouched by the fire. "I don't know what you're talking about."

"Your echo. Eleanor says everyone has an echo."

She grasped her hair. "Why are you doing this, Thom? You fixate on our elements, like they're all that matter. You just make it easy for Kyte and the others to bring you down."

Rose bristled. "My father works hard for the colony."

"Everyone works hard for the colony. Including Thomas. But all your father sees is a boy with no element. Whereas I see a carpenter and a tracker. I see someone who notices contours on the beach, channels in the sand, weakness in the cabins." She licked her lips and spat black residue into the fire. "Relying on our elements has made us careless—your father most of all." She looked up at last, and met my eyes. "I'm more than just my element; and if you had one, you would be too. Don't forget that."

Alice wiped her face again and stood. She left without a word. A moment later, the door to the shelter opened and closed.

Rose stared at the ground. Her lips were parted, but she didn't speak.

I was tongue-tied too. I knew that Alice hated Kyte, but I'd assumed it was because he was always punishing her. I never imagined it might have something to do with me.

Dennis shifted his weight from foot to foot, and finally turned away.

"I think your father just feels responsible for us," I said softly. Anything to break the awkward silence.

Rose smiled, but it was tinged with anger. "That's such a Thomas thing to say." She peered up and made eye contact; for once, neither of us broke it. "Alice is right, you know. It is unfair the way my father treats you. And I wish I could stand up to him, I really do, but . . ." She shrugged as the words ran out. "I just want you to know, she's not the only one who thinks you're special."

She lowered her eyes then, and twisted her bangle. Silence fell between us. But in my mind I heard the word over and over: *special*. I'd waited so long to hear her say it, to mirror what I felt for her.

I placed a finger on her bangle to stop the endless, nervous turning. She peered up again, eyebrows serious and straight, teeth biting her lower lip. She was breathing heavily. So was I.

I let my finger slide off, but before I could touch her wrist, she eased away. It was a tiny motion, but it told me everything I needed to know.

"Thomas, there's something—"

"I should go." I didn't need an explanation—didn't want one, either. "I'm still tired. Anyway, we'll all be busy once the Guardians arrive."

"You're going to join Alice."

Actually, Alice was the last thing on my mind right then. But it was obvious how much the thought bothered Rose.

I decided not to contradict her.

I'd been lying awake for half a strike when the door flew open and Dennis's footsteps pounded against the stairs. "Thomas, we need you," he shouted. "Something's wrong."

Alice was up in a flash, long legs flying across the shelter and onto the steps. I sprinted after her. Outside, I took a deep breath and followed their gazes across the sound to our colony on Hatteras Island.

"I can't see anything through the cloud," I said, rubbing my eyes.

Alice shook her head. "That's not a cloud. It's smoke." She took a hesitant step forward. "Our island is on fire."

CHAPTER 8

For a moment I figured I'd misheard her, but Alice was already shouting at us to grab our water canisters and head for the canoes. I ran back into the shelter to wake Griffin. When I shook him, he startled.

We go, I signed desperately, hands shaking.

He seemed to look straight through me.

"Leave him," shouted Alice from behind me. "We need to go!"

"No. He comes with us. He's strong in a canoe."

"You sure about that? He's barely moved all day."

I wouldn't leave him behind, though. Wouldn't make him spend the afternoon alone.

I grabbed Griffin's canister and threw it into my bag. Then I pulled his arm and half bullied, half dragged him out of his bed. He groaned in protest.

Out on the road, I scanned the sound for signs of Ananias and Eleanor's canoe, but saw only the wide expanse of blue-gray water. I checked the bridge, desperately hoping that the Guardians might be on it. But when I glanced at Griffin and saw the same ghostly expression he'd worn the day before, I knew they weren't coming for us.

My thoughts flew back to the previous afternoon, as my father had struggled to break free from Griffin's grasp. What if Griffin hadn't foreseen Guardian Lora's death at all? What if the terror he'd foreseen was our colony engulfed in smoke? What if our father was caught in the middle of it?

No one but Alice spoke as we drove our canoes through the water, her shouts of encouragement emphasized by the rhythmic splash of paddles and the sharp intake of breath that preceded each stroke. Halfway across, the remaining clouds dispersed, sunlight bursting through. The smoke from Hatteras Island changed direction too, whipped up and away by each gust. It made it easier for me to pinpoint the location of the fires, but also made it clear that they were still burning.

With every stroke, Rose and I lost ground on the other canoe. Having the element of water helped her to swim like a fish, but didn't extend to the brute force of propelling a canoe. Plus, we had Dennis's extra weight. Ahead of us, Alice gripped her paddle as if it were a weapon. Griffin followed her strokes mechanically.

I dug my paddle in and pushed harder. Little by little we closed the gap.

When we reached the marshy shore of Hatteras Island, Alice directed us along a winding creek that led to the center. We moved quickly on the calmer water. I'd half expected to see Ananias and Eleanor's canoe at the end, but they must have taken a different channel.

We dragged the canoes onto the bank. Just ahead of us, plumes of smoke were clear above the low tree line. Alice took off at a sprint, and we all followed. Griffin was slowest, his lurching strides made even more awkward by the uneven ground. I stayed with him, signing encouragement.

The acrid smoke grew thicker as we passed through trees and clambered over dunes, but we didn't stop until we could see the colony.

Or what remained of it.

The cabins were burnt-out shells, still crackling as the stilts were consumed by fire. Not a single structure had survived. There was no point in searching for possessions; there would be nothing left to salvage. As for the Guardians and Apprentices, they were nowhere in sight.

Our families had vanished.

"Mother! Father!" Dennis screamed.

Rose wrapped her arms around him, using her height to block his view of the destruction.

Alice stumbled toward the flames, eyes scanning the remains in search of something that might explain what had happened.

Griffin didn't react at all.

"They're probably just sheltering, right?" shouted Rose. Her voice sounded tight and shrill. "They'll come back once they know we're here."

I watched the flames lick the timber stilts. "It must have been a lightning strike."

"No. Not lightning," said Alice.

"How do you know?"

"The lightning ended last night. These fires are new."

"She's right," said Dennis. "This storm told me the lightning would pass early." He spoke with the same confidence as a Guardian of the Wind; more, even.

"But your element isn't fully developed yet. You could be wrong."

Dennis and Rose exchanged glances but said nothing.

"Look at this," said Alice.

Griffin was breathing heavily and massaging his right leg, so I left him sitting on the dune while the rest of us edged closer to her. She knelt beside a decimated cabin, prodding a piece of charred wood with a stick, conjuring sparks. She flinched from the searing heat.

"This wood got wet during the storm," she explained. "The wind and sun would've dried it, but . . . it burned so *quickly*." She grimaced again, and pulled back as though she was hurt.

"Are you all right?" I asked.

"Yes. It's just . . . the fire feels harsher on Hatteras."

Before I could ask her what she meant, Rose stepped forward. "What are we going to do?"

"We need to look for the Guardians," I said.

Alice narrowed her eyes. "I don't know. Everything about this feels wrong."

"So what do you suggest?"

"Until we can work out where the Guardians are, we need supplies — anything we can get. Do you know where your parents keep their dune box?"

"Of course not," said Rose. "Dune boxes are private. My father won't even let us talk about his."

"Well, he's not here now. So you'd better follow me."

"How do you know where it is?" I asked, surprised.

"Because I've explored every grain of sand on this island. It's about the only thing that's kept me from going crazy. Now, come on."

We clambered over dunes, the sand still damp from the recent storm. After two hundred yards, Alice knelt beside a large clump of dune grass and used her hands to measure away from the center. Then she cupped her hands and began digging.

"This one's quite deep," she said as she hit something solid. "Rose, Dennis, dig it out while I find the next."

Before they could ask how she was so certain about the location, Alice headed to a different part of the beach. I followed right behind. Here there were several smaller dunes, seemingly identical banks of sand and grass. When I looked back, I couldn't see Rose and Dennis at all.

Again Alice dove to the ground and measured with her hands to find the right place. She dug furiously, until even her elbows were below ground level. Then she pulled out a wooden box no longer than my forearm, decorated with sand dollars and sharks' teeth.

"Whose box is this?" I asked.

"Your father's."

"Have you opened it?"

"No! It's none of my business what your father put in there."

"So how do you know it's my father's box?"

She rested on her haunches and stared into the distance. "You should be grateful."

I *was* grateful, but that wasn't the point. She shouldn't have known the location of my father's box; not unless everyone was right, and she'd been spying on us all for years. And what other explanation was there? Alice *always* knew things she shouldn't.

"Check the contents, and bring the box with you," she said, leaving.

The box was unlocked, but the hinges had rusted. I wedged a stone into the seam where the two halves joined, and kicked it to open the box. A cloth parcel spilled onto the ground, along with a pair of binoculars that I slung around my neck. Inside the parcel was a small leather book. I fanned the yellow-brown pages, filled with intricate hand-written words in perfect straight lines.

Griffin would be pleased to have something new to read. Maybe it would perk him up.

There was something else too: a piece of paper, like the paper the Guardians had found in Skeleton Town. It was folded in quarters to fit in the box, but seemed newer than the pages in the journal. I unfolded it gently, careful not to tear it.

It was a drawing of a woman—long hair, high cheekbones, a tight-lipped smile. I'd never seen her before, as far as I could recall; but on the other hand, I'd seen her just that morning when I'd stared into the mirror-like water around Guardian Lora's dead body.

The woman looked just like me.

CHAPTER 9

I sprinted to where Griffin sat on the highest dune and dropped the box beside him. Although I couldn't imagine who had drawn such a fine portrait, I wanted him to see it. From her appearance, the woman had to be our mother. She had drowned the morning after Griffin was born. Now at last he'd know what she looked like.

Before I could unfold it, Griffin took the leather-bound book from the box. It was the first time he'd shown interest in anything since his seizure. It felt like progress.

Shouts from the water's edge pulled me around. I hoped it might be one of the Guardians or Apprentices, but it was Dennis. He was beside the smoldering remains of the colony's two sailboats, leaping up and down, waving his arms. He sounded excited, even exhilarated. When I glanced beyond him and saw what he was looking at, I understood why.

I flew down the dune and joined him. I shouted at the top of my lungs too, even though I knew no one on the distant sailing ship would be able to hear us. It was more than a mile to the southeast, and pulling away with every passing moment.

Rose and Alice came right after me. We all flailed our arms, willing someone on the ship to see us.

"A clan ship," cried Rose. I could hear the relief in her voice. "Can anyone see the flag?"

"It's yellow," said Alice.

"How can you tell?" I asked. I lifted my binoculars and focused on the ship. Sure enough, a beautiful yellow flag whipped atop the mast. "Alice is right. Which clan is yellow?"

No one answered, but it didn't matter. Clan ships passed by so rarely that we couldn't waste a moment.

"I'll grab one of the burning sticks from the cabins," announced Alice. "Use it as a torch. It'll make it easier for them to see us."

She took off up the beach as the rest of us jumped even higher, screamed even louder.

"It's not turning," said Dennis. "Why isn't it turning?"

"It's a long way away," answered Rose. "Keep going. Don't give up."

More yelling. More leaping on the spot, as sand slipped underfoot. But still no sign of Alice and her torch. I peered over my shoulder.

I couldn't see her at all.

"Alice?" The word came out quiet, but it was enough to make Rose and Dennis stop instantly. "Where is she?"

Rose spun around. "Alice," she shouted.

No response, but when the smoke cleared momentarily

I saw her. Alice stood behind the cabins, utterly still. With wisps of smoke coiling around her, she looked like a ghost.

My feet began to move, though I was barely aware of them. All I could think was that something had happened to her. Rose and Dennis followed right behind me.

When we reached her, Alice knelt in the sand, her eyes fixed on the entire row of cabins. "Fire is alive, like an animal," she murmured. "It eats and breathes . . . and moves. But it needs time." The way she spoke—quiet, methodical— sounded like she was explaining things to herself as much as to us. She wiped sweat off her brow, but she never blinked. "See these stilts? They've all burned to the same place. That means they burned at the same speed. The wind can't do that. Only way it can happen is if someone started them all at the same time."

"Who would start a fire deliberately?" asked Rose. "Who could've done that?"

No one answered, but I felt Dennis's eyes drift toward me. Apart from Alice, only two people had the element of fire.

"No," I said. "My father would never do it. Ananias neither. You know they wouldn't."

"I'm not saying . . ." began Rose. She stopped as Alice slid past us, eyes fixed on the clan ship out at sea. "What is it, Alice?"

I looked toward the horizon too. The ship wasn't sailing parallel to our island, I now realized, but at an angle, like it was in the process of leaving. I raised the binoculars and tried to make out what was happening on board.

"Put the binoculars down, Thom," said Alice. "They reflect the sun."

"So?"

"We need time to think."

"About what?"

"Put them *down*," she snarled. "The flag is black."

"What? That's ridiculous," said Rose. "Thomas saw it. It's yellow. Tell her, Thomas."

I heard every word, but I didn't respond. I was too busy watching the sailors on the deck of the ship, and noticing that there were no women or children at all. One of the men leaned against the ship's back rail and stared in our direction. Through the binoculars I could make out a mane of long dark hair that obscured his features. And I could see that his arms were covered in a variety of unnatural colors: red and green and blue. Most of all, I saw that when he raised his hand, all movement around him ceased. It was as though he'd frozen every person on board.

I felt frozen too.

Finally I forced myself to look away, to scan the rest of the ship. Halfway up the mast, fluttering wildly, there were now two flags: the yellow one being lowered . . . and a black one being raised.

"Black." I could barely get the word out. "They have a black flag."

"Put the binoculars down." Alice's voice was low and intense, like they could hear us somehow. "That's no clan ship."

64

I did as she said, and hoped that my eyes had deceived me. But I knew they hadn't.

It was a pirate ship.

"We need to go," said Alice. "Stay behind the cabins so the smoke will hide us. Then head for the dunes. Go *now*!"

I'd never run so fast in my life. When I reached the top of the dune, I dove over it and pulled Griffin down with me. He grunted angrily.

"What are they doing here?" Alice panted, once we were hidden. "They haven't passed this way in years."

Thirteen years, to be precise. I was too young to remember the details, but I knew the outcome all too well. They landed under the pretense of wanting to trade. But the following dawn they ransacked the colony, stole our food reserves, and threatened the Guardians with weapons that no element could withstand. By the time I was allowed to emerge from hiding later that morning, we had no food, no tools, and my mother was gone — drowned as she attempted to repel the pirates. The Guardians wouldn't say more, but over time other details emerged: how one of the pirates had struck her so hard that her blood darkened the waves crashing against the shore; how the Guardians would recognize him because of his colorful arms.

Everyone maintained a sympathetic silence. My mother's murder was one of the colony's greatest tragedies. But we couldn't dwell on that now.

"The Guardians must have used the contingency plan," I said, referring to the plan developed in the aftermath of the tragedy. "Does anyone know the details? Alice?"

Alice shook her head.

"Well, they have to be on Hatteras somewhere." I tried to keep my voice steady. "Come on, *think*. Where would they go?"

"I don't know," said Rose. "But even if you're right and they used the plan, what would've stopped them from coming to get us first?"

No one answered. We just lay flat against the dune, quiet and still, willing everything to make sense.

When the sound of my beating heart became as loud as the breaking waves and crying gulls, I took a deep breath and shimmied to the top of the dune. I lifted my head slowly and peered over it.

"Well?" Rose's voice still carried a hint of hope.

Without the binoculars, I could barely make out the rectangle of black cloth atop the mast. But I could see all too clearly the way the ship yawed as it turned to face its new target.

Us.

CHAPTER 10

slithered back down the dune. "We have to go."

Only Alice seemed to understand. Rose and Dennis just stared at me blankly.

"They're coming back," I tried again, louder.

"Let them," cried Dennis. "Maybe they've got our parents in that ship."

"I'm sure they do," said Alice. "There aren't any bodies on the beach, and they wouldn't drag the Guardians out to sea just to kill them there instead. But we can't let them take us prisoner too."

Rose reached for her brother's hand. "What if it's the only way to see our parents again?"

"What if it's not?" I shouted. "You know what the pirates did."

Silence. No one would look at me now.

"Look, they're coming back. So they must have seen us and they must want us," said Alice. "We can either wait for them or make them look for us. At least it'll give us time to think."

"How long have we got before they reach us?" I asked.

"The wind is northerly, twelve knots," Dennis said.

"The current's not helping them," added Rose.

We turned to Alice, whose dead-reckoning skills were the best in the colony. "They're almost two miles away. Probably be able to lower anchor and row ashore in less than one strike. Maybe half a strike."

"Half a strike? We'll never make it back to the shelter that quickly."

"We may not have to. We just need to make sure we're not here."

When Rose reached around Dennis and pulled him close, it was clear she agreed with Alice. Whether he wanted to or not, Dennis would be forced to run away from the only place he'd ever called home.

"Wait!" Alice scanned the ground. "The dune boxes . . ."

I pointed to the box in Griffin's hands.

Rose reddened. "I put ours down on the beach."

Alice tapped hers. "Two out of three. It'll have to do."

"I can run down and get it."

"No. We haven't got time. Anyway, I don't want the pirates getting another look at us. The less they know, the better."

Dennis furrowed his brow. "Is it true what they did?" he asked me. "To your mother, I mean."

I took a deep breath and nodded. It almost reduced him to tears.

Above us, smoke hung in the air. I could still hear the fire crackling and smell the burning frames of our cabins. I wanted to climb over the dune one last time and take in the sight of our former homes, but I knew I couldn't.

Besides, it wasn't home anymore.

Dennis was first to move. He crawled to the base of the dune and sprinted toward the trees. As we ran after him, I wondered how quickly the pirates would be able to chase us down. And whether they would be carrying the mysterious weapons that were such an awful part of their legend.

Halfway across the sound, Rose and I were lagging behind Alice and Griffin again. Rose's shoulders were shaking as though she was cold . . . or crying. I told her to stop paddling, and crawled around Dennis to the front of the canoe.

I tried to turn her hands over, but she pulled away. Slowly, reluctantly, she revealed her palms. Strips of skin had been torn back because she'd been gripping the paddle too tightly. Spots of blood pricked the exposed flesh. She wasn't used to all this paddling, not like Alice and me. Her skin was soft and smooth because she mostly stayed indoors, and ventured outside only when the colony needed her to. Now it would take days for her to heal.

"I'm sorry, Rose," I said. "Here, let me—"

She tucked her hands against her sides and shook her head. I wanted to help her, but she seemed miles away now. And when she looked at me, it wasn't at my eyes, but at my forehead—dripping with sweat—and my mouth. With each of my ragged breaths she seemed to shrink back farther.

"I . . . can't," she murmured.

Can't what? I wanted to ask. Her hands were shredded. Pirates were heading for the remains of our colony. She couldn't afford to turn down my help. There wasn't time for this.

"I'll take over for her," said Dennis as I leaned forward again. "We have to keep moving."

I went back to the stern as they swapped seats. As soon as Dennis was ready I thrust my paddle into the water and drove us onward. My arms burned and my chest ached. I hoped that the pain might block out the images plaguing my mind: Rose pulling away from me; my mother's murderer.

It didn't.

I leaped onto the platform and tethered the canoe with a simple bowline knot. There wasn't time for anything more.

I placed the strap of Rose's bag over her shoulder and gathered my own bag and dune box. I wanted us to travel through Skeleton Town together—it might have felt comforting—but Griffin and Alice were already a hundred yards ahead. Dennis didn't know whether to race after them or wait for his sister. Somehow our tiny group had already splintered.

Back at the shelter, everyone rushed inside. I couldn't stop thinking about the approaching pirates, though, so I raised the binoculars and focused on the fuzzy distance. The tip of the ship's mast peeked above the trees on Hatteras Island, its black flag still fluttering. Nearer, dark-clothed figures emerged from the trees that bordered the marsh, led by the man with long dark hair and colorful arms. As soon as he had a clear view of the sound, he raised a telescope to his eye. It seemed to be pointed directly at me.

I jumped through the doorway and pressed my back against the wall. "They're here!" I yelled.

Alice raced up the steps. "Here? In Skeleton Town?"

"No. On Hatteras. One of them has a telescope."

She glanced at the binoculars in my hands. "Did he see you?"

"No."

"Why were you looking?"

"I needed to know if they were coming."

"Why else would they turn the ship around?" She pounded downstairs to where the others stood still and silent. "What? This isn't a mystery. By now the pirates are probably crawling all over Hatteras, trying to find us. Eventually they'll cross the bridge. They won't stop until they get us."

Rose frowned. "How do you know? Anyway, who put you in charge?"

"No one. Just like no one put your father in charge of the colony. Seems he did it himself, and look how that's turned out."

"Enough!" I stepped between them. "We need to work together. Listen, Hatteras is narrow, but it's also several miles long. If they think we're there, they won't cross the bridge until they've searched it. That gives us time."

"Who says they'll cross the bridge at all?" asked Rose. "They might just paddle over like us."

"No. Their ship is moored on the ocean side of Hatteras.

71

The only way they can get smaller boats into the sound is to drag them across the island. I can't see them doing that."

"What about Ananias and Eleanor's canoe?"

"Even if they find it, it's only good for three people."

"I suppose so. Still, someone should keep watch so we know when the pirates cross. We could watch from the water tower."

Alice shook her head. "Too exposed. They might see us. But there's a building halfway between here and the bridge. Used to have two floors, but the roof has gone completely and the top floor is mostly destroyed now. If we watch from there, we'll have a good view. Should be able to stay out of sight too."

"That's crazy," said Dennis. "Have you forgotten what happened to your grandfather? For all you know, that might've been the building where he died."

"It's not. I've searched it top to bottom, and it's safe. Anyway, we don't have to worry about keeping watch yet. It'll take the pirates a while to search Hatteras, like Thom said. For now, we need provisions."

"Where are we going to get provisions?" I asked.

Alice was gripping her dune box so tightly that her knuckles had turned white. "Just . . . explore this place, okay? If you find something useful, bring it back."

A silence descended over us. Rose fingered her tunic, which was smeared with blood.

"You've got to bandage your hands," I said. "Better clean them too."

She bit her lip. "We'll need water for that."

"There's a water tower right next to us," Alice reminded her. "I'll fill the canisters now before the pirates start watching."

"How will we know if the water's safe?" I asked.

"I'll know," replied Rose confidently.

I wanted to ask more. Catching fish barehanded and testing the purity of water were entirely different. Besides, she was still a full year from becoming an Apprentice. So why was she speaking with a Guardian's confidence? Had someone been working with her in secret too, the way Eleanor had with Dennis?

I wondered then if everyone knew things they shouldn't, and if I was the only one in the dark.

CHAPTER 11

Alice tucked our water canisters into her bag and slid the strap over her left shoulder. She climbed the ladder nimbly, and clambered onto the top of the tower's giant tank. It looked decrepit, but didn't shift at all under her weight.

We lost sight of her for a while. When she reappeared, she tossed full canisters over the side. I cushioned the fall with my own bag.

It was almost evening and we were hungry. The trout was inedible by now, its flesh burned so badly that it crumbled into pieces when Alice retrieved it from the spit. We couldn't afford to make another fire either—a plume of smoke would give us away.

Rose handed out the canisters. "It's all right to drink."

"How can you tell?" I asked.

"It's my element. I can see and smell the quality of water. I can taste the impurities in a single drop."

I took a long swig. The water tasted good. "Thanks. We'd be in trouble without you."

Rose stared at her hands. She'd used her cloth hair band as bandages for her palms, and now her hair draped across her face. "We're still in trouble. And I don't think water's going to change that."

In the silence that followed, I tried to think of something reassuring to say. But *what*? Rose was hurt. Dennis was scared. Even Griffin still seemed to be in shock, a full day after his seizure. I wondered yet again what he'd foreseen. Lora's death? Our father's death? The death of every Guardian? It seemed more important than ever to know, but I couldn't ask. How would I forgive him if he'd known everything that would happen, and hadn't warned me?

With maybe one strike of daylight remaining, we left the shelter to search for supplies. The air was still, the sky dotted with wisps of clouds. The fires on Hatteras must have been extinguished, because the smoke was gone. Through the binoculars I saw only one or two men walking the shore. They clearly didn't know we were on Roanoke, which was a relief.

Rose announced that she'd scout the land just beyond Skeleton Town. Alice said she'd forage for food in the area around the shelter. Dennis and I joined her.

We passed battered buildings on either side of the main road. While Alice and Dennis pressed on, I stopped to peer into each one. Most were only one floor, just like our cabins. They were large, though, and made of a smooth rock-like material that seemed immensely strong. The shells were fairly intact—about half the buildings still had roofs—but the guts had been destroyed when the windows had broken. It was hard to see the floor through all the debris.

Finally I stood beside a doorway that looked eerily familiar: the shattered glass, the handle locked fast. Memories from the previous night flooded back. I ran my fingertips over the itchy scabs that dotted my forearms.

I couldn't go back into that building. Not yet.

To the right of the door, something glinted. It was a small, tarnished metal sign, so faded I could barely read it. As I ran my hand across the surface, I felt the indentations of letters spelling out the word *clinic*. It was the same word that Guardian Lora had used.

"Thomas, look!" Dennis shouted. He stood in front of a gray building across the road from me. His arms were full.

"What have you got?"

"Clothes. Lots of them." He held them up. "Can you believe it? If only the Guardians had known about this place."

He was right. Fabric was always in short supply. When clothes were damaged, they were repaired, or the material was saved for future repairs. Rose was already expert at crafting new clothes from worn-out pieces of material that the Apprentices gave her. She also worked harder than any of us to make sure those clothes lasted. Nothing was thrown away.

But if Lora knew about the clinic, how had she not realized there were clothes just across the road?

"Where's Alice?" I asked.

"She's gone. Showed me this place and then ran off."

Dennis hurried back inside. I didn't want to return empty-handed, so I walked to the next building. It had no door at all, just a hole where one used to be. Inside, the walls were bloodred. Row upon row of shelves were piled high with objects I didn't recognize, all of them broken. The floors were dusted with the crushed remains of colored glass bottles.

I thought of Lora's dead husband as I shuffled across the floor, first one foot, then the other. It felt firm, but I kept my weight behind me, just in case.

In the far left corner, a plain white door had been left ajar. The handle had been destroyed. I figured that if someone was willing to break the door to get inside, I should take a look.

It was a small storage area with a single narrow window high up the wall near the ceiling. But where the room outside was cluttered, here everything had been carefully organized into piles. There were plates and bowls of various sizes; small wooden boxes; even shoes. A container of metal knives, forks, and spoons caught my eye. There was more in there than we had possessed in our entire colony. The Guardians would be staggered by my discovery, if they ever got to see it.

I threw a handful of cutlery into my bag and kept looking. On the shelf above was a row of dusty water canisters. I added them too.

There was a small black object on the next shelf. I couldn't see it clearly, so I tried to turn it over. Before I'd even lifted it, it made a sound—a low buzzing that made me step back. It rolled onto the floor and broke into several pieces.

I nudged the scattered pieces with my shoe. They were tiny, in shapes I'd never seen before. I wanted to inspect them, but the sun was setting and I could barely see anymore.

I raised my arm and ran my hand across the top shelf. Dust coated my fingers. Halfway along, I brushed against several round, smooth objects. I held one up to the window. There, in the waning light, I saw a piece of smooth red glass, attached to a strip of leather. It was identical to the one that Eleanor had been wearing around her neck for as long as I could remember.

Did Eleanor know about this room?

I remembered Alice calling the object a pendant. I dropped it in my pocket to show her later.

I stepped out of the room and retraced my path through the building. Outside, my thoughts returned to the pirates. I sprinted back to the shelter.

Alice arrived at the same time as I did, and we joined the others in a circle on the grassy area beside the shelter, away from prying eyes on Hatteras Island.

"They're not coming yet," said Rose. "We've been checking."

"Where's Griffin?" I asked.

"In the shelter. I gave him some food, but he wouldn't even look at me." She seemed frustrated. "I figured he was feeling better after he paddled across the sound earlier."

I could tell the others were concerned too. It would be hard enough for us to survive, without having to look after Griffin.

"Look, I don't know what he saw yesterday," I said, "but it must've been terrible. Think about it, though—if he could paddle earlier, it's only a matter of time before he can do even more."

"Are you sure we have that much time?" asked Rose.

"I'm sure we need him. Griffin's smart. He sees things the rest of us don't. Trust me: He'll be all right."

I sat down and emptied my bag, mostly as a way to change the subject. The canisters and rusted cutlery paled in comparison to Dennis's bundle of clothes, but Alice seemed fascinated.

She reached for a fork and studied it. "Where did you get this?"

"A storeroom in one of the buildings. Why?"

"There's something familiar about it. I've seen this before," she explained, pointing to an emblem on the handle.

Rose didn't wait for Alice to continue before revealing her discovery: a bag full of pawpaws. I hadn't eaten one of the delicious, succulent fruits since the previous year. Just the feel of the smooth green skin in my hand made my mouth water.

"Are there more?" asked Alice as we all helped ourselves.

"No. There were lots on the ground, but they were rotting. Must've been the storm."

"One piece each, then. We have to ration ourselves until we know how much we have."

Before anyone could complain, Alice unwrapped a blanket and laid her discoveries before us. Then there was a different kind of silence.

There were pecans, blackberries, huckleberries, figs, and elderberries. She'd even found grapes. We hadn't eaten so well since Ananias and Eleanor became Apprentices.

While the others cracked the nuts and gorged on berries,

I watched Alice. Food wasn't all she'd found. She pulled a length of rope from her bag, and a canvas sheet.

"Where did you find all this?" I asked.

"Just . . . around. Go ahead and eat. I've had my fill."

I didn't eat, though. I couldn't, until I knew the truth. "How did you know about the building with the clothes? You took Dennis straight there."

"Got lucky, I guess."

I had to stifle a laugh. "And the fruit and nuts were just lucky too, right? Come on, Alice. We're in this together."

Alice pursed her lips and pulled something from her dune box. She laid it gently on the ground, and carefully unfolded it until it filled the space between us.

It was a map, but unlike any I'd seen — impossibly large and precise. It might have been even bigger once, but now a tear ran vertically along the left-hand side where the mainland ought to have been. Everything about Roanoke Island was indicated on it: elevations, forests, even roads and buildings that surely didn't exist anymore. The island filled the center of the map, with Hatteras Island pushed to the far right-hand side like an afterthought.

No one in our colony could have created anything so perfect, I was sure of that. But then, where had it come from? Surely not Skeleton Town. The state of the buildings suggested a terrible past. How could a flimsy paper map have survived if stone couldn't?

Something didn't make sense. As I looked at the expressions on everyone's faces, it was clear they knew it too.

CHAPTER 12

I found the map in the dune box," explained Alice.

We scanned it together. The Guardians had taught us how to visualize the land and water since we were young. It was important to get our bearings, they'd say—necessary for tracking animals and planting seeds. But who could have compiled all this information?

"Some of these words have been added," I said, pointing. "The handwriting is different."

"It may have been one of the Guardians. This is where I found the rope," said Alice, placing a finger beside the word *store*. She moved it to the left a little, where the word *grove* had been scrawled. "And here's where I found the fruit."

"Why keep this map from us?"

Alice shrugged. "I didn't find much at these places. I picked all the fruit and nuts. I figure they kept it a secret because supplies were short. Same with the clothes, maybe."

"You don't seem surprised," said Rose.

"I've always wondered about this place. Something just doesn't add up."

My mind was racing. What Alice said made sense, but our lives could have been so different with extra clothes and food. Yes, Skeleton Town was hazardous—unstable buildings and a sea of broken glass—but we'd survived so far. There was even a functioning water tower.

"Eat up, Thomas," said Alice, interrupting my thoughts. "We'll save the leftovers for breakfast."

Rose stood. "I'll take first lookout. Just switch places with me whenever you wake up."

"You don't know where it is."

"So show me."

I pictured Rose all alone. What if she missed the pirates' approach? What if something happened to her? "I'll go too."

Alice raised her eyebrows. "How will you see across the sound?"

"Same as you. Binoculars."

"Aren't you tired?"

"I'll be fine."

Alice looked at me, and then at Rose. "Of course you will."

We climbed the rickety stairs to the lookout and chose an area beside the crumbling east-facing wall. Through one of the bigger holes I saw bonfires burning on Hatteras Island. The pirates were planning to stay.

When Rose and I were settled, Alice walked down the stairs, her eyes flitting between us the whole way.

Rose spoke first. "I'm glad you're here."

I watched her from the corner of my eye. The moon was behind her, and her face was in silhouette—her gently sloping nose, lips parted by the smallest degree. I could hear her breathing. "Me too."

I was sure she wanted to say more. So did I—how much I liked talking to her, even though it felt more awkward every day; how I started each morning by watching her walk along the beach before the sun grew too strong; how I thought about her even when she wasn't around. How I wanted to touch her so much it was killing me.

Instead, the silence sat between us, thick and heavy. Rose stared into the distance. I continued to watch her, her chest rising and falling with every breath.

"How are your hands?" I asked. "Can I see?"

I reached for her bandaged left hand, but she pulled back suddenly, even leaned away from me. My hand hung in mid-air.

"I'm sorry," she whispered. She stared at her hands. "I—"

"It's okay. They hurt. I shouldn't have tried to touch them."

"No. It's . . ." Her mouth was open as though she were about to explain. Or better yet, change her mind. Finally she shrugged. "I'm sorry," she said again.

I felt bad for her injuries, but hurt was mixed in too. Every word she spoke told me how much she liked me; every action said the opposite. The distance between us seemed to shrink every day, then grow larger than ever in the blink of an eye. What was I supposed to think?

"I guess I should go to sleep," I said. "Promise you'll wake me when you get tired?"

"I will."

I lay down and stretched out. At first, I heard nothing but the wind as it brushed the late summer marsh grass. But then there was another sound: short, ragged breaths . . . sobbing.

I closed my eyes and thought of all the things I wanted to say to Rose. All the ways I wanted to comfort her. But really, what could I say or do for a girl who kept me at arm's length?

I woke abruptly as Rose's elbow connected with my nose. She grunted once, loudly, but after that her breathing was quiet and even. Her tunic rose and fell with each breath. With her blond hair draped loosely across her arm, she looked beautiful.

My breath caught. How long had she been asleep?

I shuffled over so that I could see across the sound. The bonfires in the distance were still burning. But so was another, much closer than before.

I grabbed the binoculars and pressed them to my eyes. I wasn't imagining it—the pirates had advanced to Pond Island in the middle of the sound. They stood in a group at the far end of the bridge. They'd halved the distance between us.

Did they already know we were here?

A part of me wanted to wake Rose, remind her what was at stake. Alice would never have fallen asleep on watch. But what good would it do?

"You planning to watch her all night?"

I hadn't heard Alice approaching—not even a footstep on the stairs. Who knew how long she'd been there? "I wasn't watching her. I was just—"

"You don't need to explain." She knelt beside Rose and shook her awake. "You can go now."

Rose turned to face us, bleary-eyed and confused. "Oh."

She sloped away, dragging her blanket behind her.

Alice took her place. She pulled her knees up and wrapped her arms around them. She was wearing different clothes than before: a black vest that left her shoulders bare, and black shorts that made her legs seem longer than ever. I was about to mention the clothes, but hesitated. I wasn't sure why.

"Pond Island already," Alice announced, all business. "Just a small group, though." She pointed. "How many men can you count in the firelight?"

I focused the binoculars on the fire. "Four, maybe."

"Right. Means they don't know we're here, but they've put a sentry post there just in case. They'll be watching Roanoke for sure. We need to be careful."

"What if they cross the bridge?"

"They will, but not yet. Crossing the gap wouldn't be safe at night. It's not even safe during the day."

Hearing her mention the gap in the bridge reminded me of the map. "Did you see that the word *gap* was written beside the bridge in the same handwriting as *grove* and *store*?"

"I thought you'd missed that."

"No. I'm just not sure what it means. I can imagine the

85

Guardians planting fruit trees, but there's no way they could make holes in a bridge, right?"

"I don't think so, but I'm not sure about anything anymore." She puffed out her cheeks and exhaled slowly. "Did you notice there weren't any birds or animals on Hatteras when we crossed earlier?"

"No. I wasn't really paying attention to that."

"Hmm. I looked around for the horses, but I couldn't see them." She snorted. "Listen to me, worrying about wild horses. Weird, isn't it? With everything that's happened, it's the horses I can't forget."

Weird, yes—but not surprising. Alice had always loved watching the wild horses on Hatteras. She'd managed to get one to eat from her hand once. After that, they'd ventured closer to the colony, taking the food we left out for them.

It dawned on me then that we'd all miss the colony in different ways.

"The horses probably ran away when the pirates set fire to the cabins," I said.

"I suppose so." She didn't sound reassured. "Listen, I found something else today."

"Here on Roanoke?"

"Yes. Two sailboats. Inside a covered boathouse." She was breathing faster than usual. "Some of the cleats have rusted. I don't know if they'll still float, let alone if they're seaworthy. But they look good."

"What about sails?"

"They're there—folded in bags. I didn't have a chance to

look at them, but I want to go back. If we need to escape, a sailboat might be our best chance."

I wasn't sure about that. It had been a struggle to convince Dennis not to surrender to the pirates immediately, so escape was surely the last thing on his mind—at least until we knew what had happened to our families.

"Where's the boathouse?" I asked.

"A mile and a half to the southwest."

"That's all? So the Guardians must've known about them."

"Yes."

"Why would they hide two extra sailboats from us?"

"I don't know."

I focused on the bonfire a mile away. It was true—the pirates would cross eventually. Which meant that we were running out of time to explore Roanoke Island. Alice had unearthed pieces of the past, but what if there was still more? The pirates had weapons; maybe there were some here as well. Skeleton Town was full of secrets, and it was time for answers.

Alice watched me stand. "What are you doing?"

"Going to explore. There's stuff here we can't explain. The sooner we know what we have to work with, the sooner we can make a plan."

She handed me my bag. "In that case, bring everything. It's not like we're saving it for anyone."

I ran along the road into town. Occasionally the animal noises of night drifted on the breeze, but otherwise I could have been the only person in the world.

I figured I'd start by heading for the storeroom I'd found

earlier. I was sure I could find it in the dark, and fill my bag with what remained on the shelves. But as I was about to enter the building, I heard a sound behind me.

It stopped me dead.

It was between a rustle and a scrape, like a branch dragged across the ground. I spun around, but saw nothing. It could have been a bird or an animal—I didn't know. Now the world was hushed again.

I held my breath and honed my senses to the whispers of sound around me. Animal or not, something about the sound had felt out of place—just like the noises I'd heard during the storm the night before, though clearer without wind and rain drumming in my ears.

I heard it again, this time from the building next door.

The clinic.

I crept along the street and slid through the clinic's glass door. I'd only taken one step when something flashed before me: a sleek animal with striped fur. In the moonlight that filtered through the glass I thought I recognized it too; from its size, and movements, and coloring, I was sure it was a *cat*—the first one I'd seen in years. It paused momentarily, but seemed wary of me and padded away. I stayed close and tried not to lose sight of it.

To my surprise, it became clearer the farther it went. Around us, darkness gave way to a faint amber glow that seemed to come from the back of the clinic. I pressed forward. I shut out everything except the light before me, growing steadily brighter.

The cat slid around a corner and didn't return. I barely noticed. Now I was transfixed by something far more remarkable.

A lantern not much bigger than my hand sat on an otherwise empty table. Watching it, I felt as though a wildfire had been caught and tamed especially for me. Only there was no flame.

I took a deep breath and reached forward, touched the glass dome on top. I expected to feel heat and pain, but felt neither. As the beams slid around my fingers and danced against the ceiling and walls, a single thought filled my mind: *Is this how it feels to have an element?*

Slowly, cautiously, I picked the lantern up. A thin black cord connected it to a wall, but fell away when I moved. After that, I stood still, mesmerized by the experience of directing my own personal sun. True, it felt uncomfortable in my hand—there was a dull ache that I hadn't noticed before— but I was too exhilarated to care. I'd discovered something that might really help us.

I made my way back through the clinic, and ran along the road, desperate to show my prize to Alice. I almost tripped, so I held the lantern in front of me to illuminate the ground. My breathing, already heavy, accelerated until it kept pace with my footsteps.

But I wasn't alone.

One moment I was surging toward the intersection. The next, something knocked the lantern from my grasp. It clattered loudly as it hit the ground, already extinguished. Blind and off-balance, I tumbled after it, elbows and knees scraped and torn.

I swallowed the pain and fought to keep quiet.

A shadowy figure appeared beside me. From the corner of my eye I saw a knife blade reflecting in the moonlight.

CHAPTER 13

rolled away. Leaped up. Raised my fists. But the lamp's afterglow remained in the center of my vision, blinding me.

"What are you doing, Thom?"

"Alice?" I squinted as her figure became clear. "What am *I* doing? You attacked me."

"I didn't know it was you."

"I was carrying a lantern. Couldn't you see me?"

"No. I just heard footsteps. I saw a glow above the buildings. I knew you didn't have a lantern, so I thought . . ." She hung her head as she slid the knife back into its sheaf.

"Well, I don't have one anymore! It was amazing, like ten candles all in one, but no flame. I've never seen anything like it." I wiped blood from my knees. "Did you see where it went?"

"No. Sorry." She waited for me to forgive her, but I couldn't. Not yet. "Follow me," she said.

I hobbled after her. A few yards later the buildings ended at the intersection. Just across the road to our right was the shelter. To our left, the road led to the sound.

She pointed toward the water. "What do you see?"

"Nothing. Just the outline of the bridge. And the pirates' bonfire." As soon as I said it, I had to look away. I knew what was coming.

"Light carries. The pirates are watching Roanoke Island. If you'd made it this far they'd have seen the light. They'd know we're here."

She was right, of course. I'd been too excited to think of anything but the lantern.

"I'm sorry," I said. "I wasn't thinking."

"It's all right."

"No, it's not. I could've given us away. I need to be smarter than that."

She hesitated. "Well, I'm sorry too. I didn't mean to hurt you. You're the last person I'd want to hurt."

Our eyes met for a moment and then she stared across the sound again. "Why don't you go back to the shelter? Get some sleep."

"No. I'm fine. Really." I began limping toward the lookout. "How did you get to me so quickly, anyway?"

"I told you: I heard your footsteps."

"But you were all the way at the lookout."

"Sound carries almost as well as light around here. Anyway, I'm a fast runner."

"You can say that again." I rubbed more blood from my knees. "My goal for tomorrow is not to get sliced up in Skeleton Town."

Alice laughed. "That's too bad."

92

"Why?"

"Scars look good on you—remind me we're not so different after all."

Back at the lookout we sat side by side. Alice rubbed her bare arms, so I draped my blanket over her shoulders. "You're wearing new clothes."

She smiled. "I thought you only paid attention to girls in white."

I was glad for the darkness. At least she wouldn't see me redden.

"I just figured we might as well use what Dennis found," she continued. "And these fit much better than my old tunic. Plus, it'll be harder for them to see me if I'm in black."

I didn't need to ask who *they* were.

"I keep imagining they're already here," she said. "I think I hear things."

"I know what you mean. I hope the Guardians are all right. Ananias and Eleanor too."

"I just hope they're alive."

"What? But you told Rose—"

"What she needed to hear to keep going. Her and Dennis both. I do think everyone's alive, but I wish we knew for sure. It'd be a real shame to risk getting captured if they're already dead." She glanced at me, and quickly added: "I miss them too, Thom. Eleanor and my mom, at least."

Hearing Eleanor's name reminded me what I'd found in the storeroom. I took the pendant from my pocket and handed it to her.

Alice held it up to the full moon. A panicked look fell across her face. "It's Eleanor's pendant."

"No. I found it in a storeroom."

She looked closer. "Oh, I see. It's darker." Her eyes flicked back to me. She swallowed hard. "Can you help me put it on?"

I hadn't meant for her to wear it, but it seemed right somehow. So I took the ends of the cord and brought them together behind her neck. My fingers brushed against her bare skin and she gasped, followed by a long, slow exhale. Her shoulders relaxed. Her entire body seemed to melt.

I finished with a sheet bend knot. It was a poor choice—complex and hard to undo—but I wasn't concentrating on the knot anymore. Besides, Alice didn't know, and she didn't seem to care. She just held the glass pendant in front of her and turned it around in her fingers.

"Thank you," she said, peering over her shoulder. "It's lovely."

"You're welcome."

She turned to face me, eyes narrow and intense. "What are you thinking?"

"I'm thinking that you're like a storm," I answered honestly.

Her eyes grew wide, and her entire face seemed to open up too—a rare unguarded moment. "How so?"

"It's just . . . everything about you. The black clothes. The way your hair sweeps across your face like a wave breaking. And your eyebrows—so dark and heavy, like thunderclouds."

She was still watching me, but her breathing had grown

94

faster, shallower. There was a tension between us that felt new. I kind of liked it.

"That probably sounds stupid," I said.

"Not at all. I like storms." She smiled awkwardly. "Don't you?"

I shrugged. "Depends. Sometimes I do. The ones that clear the air, leave everything feeling fresh and alive. But sometimes they can be kind of scary, you know?"

"Scary?"

"Intimidating."

Her mouth opened in an O shape, and she nodded. Another smile, and this one seemed genuine. "I don't mean to be intimidating. Just direct. There's something weird about the way the Guardians treat you and me, and I don't like it. Never have."

I felt my mouth go dry. "What do you mean?"

"Oh, come on. The way they keep us apart. Every time I'm alone with you, someone interrupts us. It's like they're spying on us."

"Why would they do that?"

"Why do you think? Because they don't trust us. Or maybe it's just me they don't trust. Anyway, they've already decided you should be with Rose."

I didn't know what to say.

Alice picked at a callus on her thumb. Now her eyes were on everything but me. "Don't tell me you haven't thought about it. And if that's what you want, then fine. I just don't like the Guardians telling me how *I* should feel."

"How do you feel?"

"About you?" She raised her eyes, kept them fixed on me as she stretched out her hand. Her fingertips glanced across my palm like whispers, each tiny movement sending shock waves through my body. I felt every muscle, every bone come alive. Felt the warmth of her skin radiating through me. Felt her gazing at me with an intensity that was exhilarating and exhausting.

I counted twenty heartbeats before she stopped. She was panting like she'd run a mile, face caught in the memory of a smile. I couldn't seem to breathe at all.

"That's how I feel," she said, fingering the pendant swinging loosely across her chest. "How about you?"

CHAPTER 14

I woke at first light, bones aching, elbows and knees itching. Alice had thrown her blanket over me, but the wind had picked up and the air felt damp. It wasn't cold, but I shivered anyway.

I heard shuffling beside me. Griffin stared at the dense mist swirling over the sound, even though there was nothing to see. When he realized I was awake, he smiled.

You. All right, I signed, unable to hide my relief that he'd emerged from his shell.

He nodded unconvincingly. *All right.*

"We couldn't sleep," came a voice from behind me: Rose. She wrapped her arms tightly around her brother and didn't look at me. "They're gathering on Pond Island."

Alice nodded. "Yes, but it'll be difficult for them to cross the bridge. That narrow plank is dangerous in strong winds. We'll have time to react." She spoke gently, reassuringly. I'd never heard her talk to Rose like that before.

The blurred outline of the sun peeked over the trees on

Hatteras Island. The mist began to burn off and I could make out the tiny silhouettes on Pond Island. But there weren't four of them anymore. "That's got to be a dozen men, at least."

"Fifteen," said Alice without looking.

"I'm hungry," complained Dennis, teeth chattering. "Can we eat now?"

Alice pulled a small bundle from her bag: a cloth containing the remaining nuts and berries. There wasn't much. "There are a few pawpaws in the shelter too."

Dennis dove in. Rose licked her lips, but she didn't take any. She just stroked her brother's hair as juice dripped down his chin.

I couldn't eat either—not if Rose wasn't going to. But maybe we could do something about that now that Griffin was feeling better. *Need. Food*, I signed.

Griffin stared at his hands. *Difficult.*

That much was true. Like Alice, his element—earth—had never blossomed the way it was supposed to. On a good day, he'd find root vegetables hidden just below the surface of the ground. On a bad day, nothing at all. But what other choice did we have? What was the point in hiding from the pirates only to starve? Anyway, I knew everyone saw him as a weak link. This would remind them that he had an element too.

Please, I signed.

Griffin looked at the meager offering of berries and nuts, and at Dennis as he gobbled them down. *All right. I. Look.*

I wanted him to eat too. He hadn't touched food in two days. His skin was sallow, cheeks pressed against his teeth. But he didn't seem hungry. Or maybe he just couldn't face eating yet. Perhaps he wasn't fully recovered after all. If so, it was touching that he was willing to search for food for everyone else.

"Why are the pirates here?" I asked. I signed for Griffin too. Even if he was just pretending to feel better, involving him in the discussion might distract him from the nightmare of the previous days.

"I've been thinking about that," said Rose. She paused a moment to find the right signs. "Maybe it's all an accident. Maybe the pirates got caught in the storm and this was the nearest land."

"Then why not just lower anchor and move on later? Why destroy our colony?"

"They probably wanted to steal our possessions. They've done it before."

"No," said Alice. She leaned forward and, like Rose, concentrated on finding the correct signs. "I saw the remains of the cabins. There was more than timber there. I think they destroyed the contents too."

I mulled this over. I was certain the pirates' landing wasn't an accident, but I couldn't say why.

Flags, signed Griffin. *Flags*.

It took me a moment to catch on, but then I understood. "The ship's flags!" Suddenly my mind was racing. I pictured us all on the beach, and Griffin sitting atop the dune, staring into the distance. I thought he'd been too overwhelmed to notice what was happening around him. Instead, he'd been watching the ship as closely as any of us.

"What about the flags?" asked Rose.

I struggled to sign and speak at the same time. "They were switching from yellow to black as they sailed away. Think: If the pirates had been flying a black flag when they arrived, the Guardians would have begun the contingency plan. But they didn't. So it must've been yellow. And if it was yellow, then the pirates clearly planned this. It was no accident at all."

There was silence after that. It was a lot to process, the thought that we'd been carefully targeted.

Rose cleared her throat. "You're sure they have our parents on board?"

I glanced at Alice and nodded. "Yes. Ananias and Eleanor too. When they left us at the shelter, they wouldn't have known the pirates were on Hatteras. They'd have been captured as soon as they got there."

"So why'd the pirates leave without *us*?" Dennis's voice was small, barely more than a whisper. "The Guardians must've told them we're here. They wouldn't have come back otherwise."

I took a deep breath. "The pirates only came back after they saw us. Maybe the Guardians didn't tell them we were left behind because it's *us* the pirates are after."

Dennis lifted a berry to his mouth, but then lowered it again. "Why? What have we got?" He stared at his lap. "Anyway, I don't believe you. Our parents would never leave us all alone."

"They didn't," I reminded him. "They thought Guardian Lora was here."

Rose furrowed her brow. "Ananias would have told the Guardians what happened to Lora."

I pictured my brother and Eleanor crossing the dunes as the pirates torched our cabins. "What if they never got the chance? Maybe the Guardians had already been taken onto the ship."

Dennis seemed to be on the verge of tears now. Rose pulled him closer. "What are we going to do when they come for us?" she asked.

"Hide. There must be four miles of island each way to the north and south."

"No hiding," said Alice. "They'll find us, even if it takes them days. And I don't think we have enough food to outlast them." She flicked hair from her eyes. In the morning's first rays, they matched the sky—almost translucent. "No. We'll use the boats to get away."

Rose raised her bandaged hands. "I don't think canoes are an option."

"I'm talking about sailboats, not canoes. There are two in a boathouse southwest of here. I want to see if they're seaworthy."

"You found two sailboats? When were you planning on telling us?"

"Thom already knows."

Rose's eyes narrowed, but remained fixed on Alice. "I see. And if the boats sail, then what?"

"I'm not sure. But I figure as long as we can sail, we can escape."

"Escape where?"

"I don't know, all right? But we don't stand a chance on foot, so if you want to see your parents again, I suggest you start thinking."

"And what are the rest of us supposed to do while you're checking out these mysterious boats?"

"Griffin's looking for food," I said quickly, playing peacemaker. "It'd be really helpful if you could make sure the water canisters are full. And Dennis should stay here and keep watch. You all right with that?" I asked him.

He nodded.

"Good. Just remember: If the pirates begin to cross, shout real loud."

For the first time all morning, Rose looked at me. "And what about you? What'll you be doing?"

Before I could reply, Alice shifted position and her fingertip brushed across my leg. It seemed accidental, but my face flared at her touch.

Alice stood. She was at least three inches taller than Rose. "Thom's coming with me," she said. "I thought you knew."

CHAPTER 15

We left Skeleton Town and passed from grass to marsh. Once we entered the woods it was almost impossible to know that we were on an island. If not for the sun, I'd have had no idea what direction we were running in.

"We won't be able to hear Dennis from here," I said.

Alice didn't slow down. "Don't worry. We won't be gone long."

I did worry, though. Just as I worried about Dennis, alone in the lookout. If there was one person who couldn't afford to fall asleep, it was Dennis. Not only that, but I'd forgotten to give him my binoculars—they still hung from a cord around my neck.

We emerged from the woods onto a cracked road, narrower than the ones in Skeleton Town. In the distance I saw water again, and the Plague-ridden mainland beyond. As we followed the road, I spotted something else as well: dirty wooden planks peeking through suffocating foliage. It had to be the boathouse.

"Hard to believe it's still here," said Alice, reading my thoughts. "The bushes are probably all that's holding it up."

We pushed branches aside as we rounded the old building. At the front, a battered wooden dock led inside the boathouse. Two sailboats leaned against the rear wall, smothered in canvas sheets. Even from several yards away I could see that they were tethered with strong rope and expert knots. Whoever stowed them had been far more interested in preserving the boats than using them.

A cloud of dust filled the air as we untied the knots and pulled off the covers. What lay beneath was unlike any sailboat I'd seen. The hull was bone white and rock hard. The mast seemed to be made from an extraordinarily long piece of thick metal. The Guardians had shared metal nails and cutlery with us, but never anything like this.

Alice raised an eyebrow and rapped her knuckles against the mast. The sound resonated even after she stopped. "Incredible, isn't it?"

I nodded. Whoever the Skeleton Town colonists had been, their inventions were the stuff of dreams.

I knocked the mast as well. It felt hard against my knuckles. I wrapped my fingers around it. It was cool to the touch and perfectly smooth.

Alice gripped it too and tried to shake it. It didn't move at all. But the mast felt different now, as if energy was running through my palm. It wasn't even an uncomfortable sensation, just strange. I breathed quicker, gripped tighter.

Alice let go and the energy stopped. For a moment she

seemed confused. Then her expression shifted, like a dark cloud lifting. She stared at me, and I stared right back. Roanoke Island was full of mysteries, and I looked forward to hearing her explain this one. It was clear that she'd caused the energy somehow—it started and stopped with her—but how? Did she even know?

Evidently not, because she seemed as surprised as me. She flushed red too, so I looked away to spare her any embarrassment.

"Come on," I said. "Let's test the boats."

We eased the boats across the dock and into the water. Each one took on a little water as it splashed down, but then no more. They were seaworthy.

Alice crouched on the dock, elbows resting on her knees, hands pressed against her cheeks. When she caught me looking at her, she broke out in a wide smile. "It's been eight years."

It took me a moment to realize what she meant. "Yes. Eight years."

Back when we were very young, the Guardians had taught us to sail in the four wooden sailboats they'd discovered on Hatteras Island when they first arrived. I'd enjoyed sailing, but only in calm seas. In strong winds I wasn't heavy enough to hold the boat down, so I'd release the rope connected to the mainsail, wasting the most powerful gusts. Alice weighed even less than me, and her arms were so short she could barely hold the rope and tiller at the same time. But she was fearless. She'd rein in the sail and lean out of the boat until the only thing stopping her from falling in was the canvas strap securing her feet. Her hair was longer back then, and sometimes, as the wind dropped, she'd lower it into the water so that it trailed behind her in a blur.

She'd never seemed happier than in those moments. But when Rose and Dennis's grandparents had capsized in the squall, and another boat was lost to a hurricane, everything had changed. From then on, the sailboats were to be used only as fishing vessels, the Guardians had told us. I think they simply didn't want to entrust one of their two remaining boats to a child as anxious as me, or as reckless as Alice.

All along, there had been two more boats just a short distance away.

"Here," said Alice, rolling a canvas bag toward me. "Now for the sails."

I leaned back as I opened the bag, braced for more dust. Somehow it was clean. I spread the mainsail across the dock and inspected every part of it, knowing that the smallest tear might render it useless. It was intact. More than that, it seemed almost new.

"This one looks like it's hardly been used," I said.

"Nor this one. You remember how to rig one of these things?" There was the hint of a challenge in her voice.

"I think I'll work it out."

Side by side we rigged the boats. I was surprised at how much I remembered of booms and daggerboards, shackles and winches. We worked carefully at first, and then quicker, racing against each other. I knew I'd never win, but at the hint of competition, Alice's eyes took on a delighted glint.

As she leaned forward and raised the mainsail, her vest rode up, revealing a sliver of skin. It was spotless and tan, divided in half by the bumps of her spine. Would it feel the same as the skin on her fingertips?

She turned around so suddenly I didn't have time to look away. "Everything all right?"

I swallowed hard. "Yes."

She reached for the pendant and twisted it around her fingers playfully. "Nice view, isn't it?"

"Huh?"

She pointed toward the water, and the mainland beyond.

"Oh. Right. Yes."

She was trying to hide a smile, I could tell. "I want to take the boats out," she said wistfully. She ran her fingers across the rough canvas, watched it ripple with each touch. When a breath of wind entered the boathouse, the sail fluttered.

I faced the mainland again. I almost convinced myself I might be able to see the Plague-carrying rats that had engulfed the land since before I was born. But to the naked eye it seemed indistinguishable from Roanoke Island: a mixture of trees and tall grass.

Or maybe not. When I raised my binoculars I spied the shell of a small building. It looked wooden, but I couldn't be sure. Bushes had mostly consumed it, but that didn't make it any less remarkable. For the first time, here was evidence that someone had inhabited the mainland.

"You need to see this." I handed Alice the binoculars. "Look at the far shore."

She didn't raise the binoculars, but seemed to lock in on the building all the same. "Do you think it was built before or after Skeleton Town?"

"Before, I guess. It's wooden, right? That's got to be easier to come by than stone."

We stared at this relic of a world we could never know. It was fascinating, but alarming too. Plague to the west. Pirates to the east. How long could we really hope to survive?

Alice's eyes remained locked on the building. Slowly, she raised the binoculars. Then she gasped.

"What is it?"

She pressed the binoculars into my hands. "Check out the right side."

I located the building again, and followed the greenery to the right. This time I noticed something else. Peeking through were three large letters: CRO.

They looked as though they'd been daubed on with blood.

CHAPTER 16

s that blood?" I asked.

"Sure looks like it." Alice shivered, but recovered with a deep breath.

Returning her attention to the boat, she lowered the sails and rolled them tightly around the beams. It was how we'd been taught to leave boats that we planned to use again soon.

Would we really be sailing to escape the pirates? Where would we sail?

"Come on," she said finally. "We should head back."

We fought through shrubbery and rejoined the road. After a couple hundred yards, she veered off into the woods. There was no path, no sign that this is where we'd emerged earlier. She seemed certain, though.

I looked back at the boathouse but I couldn't see it.

"Are you coming?" Alice called out.

Finally I located a couple of the planks. "How did you find this place?"

"It was on the map."

"Show me."

She stopped, but she didn't turn around. "Why?"

"When you left Dennis yesterday, you knew exactly where you were going, didn't you?"

"I don't know what you mean."

"I can read a map, Alice. This boathouse wasn't marked on the one you showed us. It's also a three-mile round trip, and you did it in less than one strike. You knew it was here. How?"

I waited for her expression to change, a flicker that I was onto something. But she didn't react at all, just fixed me with her blazing blue eyes.

"The boat was dusty, but the sails weren't," I continued. "You must've already checked them yesterday. I'm guessing you would've checked the boats too, only you couldn't move them by yourself. That's why you needed me to come along. Right?"

She leaned against a tree, the hint of a smile on her lips. "Funny, isn't it? The more cynical you get—the more you doubt everything—the closer you get to the truth. You sound so much smarter when you're angry."

The words caught me off guard. She seemed to take pleasure in them too, and I didn't know how to respond. Had I imagined holding her hand the night before?

"All right," she said. "Since we're asking questions: Why did my father hide the map in the first place?"

"So we wouldn't know about the stores of clothes and food."

"Why?"

"I don't know." I thought about it. "Maybe the Guardians were afraid we'd help ourselves to whatever we wanted."

"Or maybe they didn't want us to realize how well they know this place. Lora said their first colony was on Roanoke. What if they were here years instead of months?"

"Until your grandfather died, you mean."

She paused. "If he died here at all."

"What?"

"Think about it. Every year the Guardians remind us what happened to my grandfather, but I haven't seen a single building with weak floors. Have you?"

I shook my head.

"Anyway, Eleanor told me that every time she comes here it brings back memories she can't place."

"Ananias said something like that once."

"Hmm. I think the real question is why the Guardians left Roanoke Island. And why they don't want us knowing what's here."

My mind flashed back to the night that Lora died—the way she'd described the clinic, and given me precise directions. Now it all made sense.

Or did it? If the Guardians knew Skeleton Town was safe, why lie to us? Why send Lora at all?

"Lora wasn't looking after us," I said as the pieces fell into place. "She was here to make sure we didn't leave the shelter and explore the town. She was here to keep the Guardians' secrets."

Alice didn't say a word, but her silence spoke volumes.

111

"Why are you smiling?"

"Like I say, you seem much smarter when you're angry."

Her words stung again, and this time it wasn't just the Guardians I was angry at. "If you already know everything, then tell me what they've been hiding from us. What's so important about this place?"

She pursed her lips. "I'm not sure yet. But I'll tell you one thing: They were so worried we'd find the boathouse they didn't even mark it on the map. That has to mean something."

She began walking away, and I hurried to catch up. "So how did you find it?"

"Isn't it obvious?" She waited for me to make the connection; sighed when I didn't. "I've explored this island eight times."

I felt my breath catch. "You can't expect me to believe that."

"Why not? Because you couldn't do it?" She flicked a stray tendril of hair from her eyes. "I know more about Skeleton Town than you can imagine."

"How did you do it?"

"I waited till nightfall, and took a canoe."

"By yourself?"

"Yes. It's hard, but doable."

"When? When did you start exploring?"

She cast her eyes down, and her steps slowed. "The day of your Apprenticeship."

"My sixteenth birthday?"

"Yes. I'd really tried to be good until then—listening to the

Guardians, helping any way I could. Not that my father ever noticed, but I tried. After that day, though, I knew I couldn't stay forever—not after the way they treated you. I'd prefer to spend my life sailing around on a clan ship than be stuck in that colony."

Alice picked up her pace, and this time I didn't try to keep up. The thought that she had been exploring Roanoke Island alone made me feel—*what?* Betrayed, maybe. Or naïve. I'd always figured I was too open to keep secrets. Now I realized it was simply because I had no secrets to keep.

But it was more than that. When I saw myself through her eyes, I felt as though I'd let everyone down—me, most of all. The night of my sixteenth birthday, I'd lain on my bed wondering what the future held. Meanwhile, Alice had dedicated herself to creating an entirely different future for herself.

Alice sensed me lagging behind, and stopped. She didn't seem as defiant anymore. "Why do you think the Guardians work so hard to keep us apart?"

I shrugged.

"My father caught me returning from my eighth trip. Said the next time I took a canoe, he'd make sure I was exiled to the mainland. Said I could die alone of the Plague, for all he cared. Said it was no wonder your father and the other Guardians didn't want me going anywhere near you. Then he said I was a plague too—different, but just as destructive. I think they keep us apart because they're afraid I'll influence you."

"Why?"

"Because you're the most trusting person in the colony,

Thom. And I'm the least. They can handle me alone. But if you joined me, they'd have their hands full." The thought seemed to amuse her. "I have to escape from this colony. There's nothing here for me. Never has been. You can see that, can't you?"

"What about me?"

"I'm not saying it's not hard for you too—"

"No. I mean, what about *me*? I'm here for you. Isn't that..." I was about to say *enough*, but stopped myself. "Something?"

Alice didn't speak, but she raised her left hand until it was hovering beside mine. Her finger brushed against me, skin on skin, as faintly beautiful as a warm breath. My entire body responded to her touch, a glance with all the power of a gaze.

"You're not just *something*, Thom. Not to me. But I need you to be even more."

She didn't wait for me to ask what that meant. She just began jogging through the trees, knowing that I'd follow.

To be honest, I knew what she was saying: The time for trusting was over. The Guardians had lied. They'd left us unprepared and unprotected. Lora's refusal to answer our questions had been a calculated measure all along. And what of Ananias and Eleanor? Did they already know everything we'd worked out? I hoped not. It would be hard to forgive them.

Alice peered over her shoulder. "We should hurry."

I didn't want to hurry, though. In spite of everything, being alone with Alice in the boathouse had been a distraction—a place without pirates and the imminent threat of attack. All the way to the edge of Skeleton Town, I felt a peacefulness I hadn't known in days.

Then the sound of yelling split the air.

Dennis.

We broke into a sprint. There was only one reason for him to be shouting.

He stood beside the shelter, pacing in tiny circles.

Rose arrived at the same moment. "What's the matter? Are the pirates coming?"

Dennis wouldn't look at any of us. "No, but . . . I couldn't see them," he said, his words punctuated by rapid breaths. "One moment they were on Pond Island, the next they were gone."

"Gone where?"

"I don't know. I think they just moved to the end of the bridge. But I thought they were crossing. So I climbed the water tower to get a better view."

"What did you see?"

"A man." Dennis swallowed hard. His lips trembled. "He had long hair that blew about. And he . . . had a telescope. I'm sure he was pointing it right at me."

I pictured the man stopping an entire ship full of pirates with a single raised hand. "When did it happen?"

Dennis shuddered. "Just now."

I scanned the bridge with my binoculars. There was no one there. Then I surveyed Pond Island. It seemed empty too.

"Looks like they went back to Hatteras. I guess he didn't see you." I smiled, hoping it would cheer him up.

"No. He definitely saw me."

"You can't know that," said Rose.

"Yes, I can." Dennis tugged at the ends of his sleeves. "When he lowered the telescope, he looked straight at me… and waved."

CHAPTER 17

For a moment, there was silence. Now that the pirates knew we were here, what hope did we have?

Rose pointed toward Hatteras. "More smoke," she murmured. "What's left to burn?"

No one answered. It wasn't really a question.

"We'll be all right," I said. "We'll think of something."

Dennis looked desolate. "Like what? A plan to get our parents back? Make the pirates leave? Rebuild our cabins?"

"We need to go back to Hatteras," said Rose.

Alice snorted. "No way."

"Why not? Why shouldn't we surrender? They've got our parents. You said so yourself." Her eyes flickered toward me, and left me just as quickly. "Anyway, what else is there to stay for?"

"They killed my mother," I said. "If we go back, what's to stop them from hurting us too?"

"If that's their plan, why aren't they crossing the bridge right now?"

More silence, and this time I didn't have an answer. Truthfully, it made no sense. Were they trying to starve us out? Was something else going on? Something involving the Guardians that we couldn't hope to understand?

"I'm not asking you to go back with us," continued Rose. "I'm just saying, we can't keep doing this. Dennis wants to see our parents again, and so do I."

"It's not safe," I protested.

"I don't care. Not anymore."

I hated hearing the defeat in her voice. I didn't want Rose to leave. I didn't want to stay on without her either.

"Before you leave, let's eat," I said. I pointed to the grassy square. "Just one more strike. There are still pawpaws, right, Alice?"

Alice nodded, and headed inside to get them.

Rose, Dennis, and I turned off the road together. She kept Dennis between us, like a shield. Was she angry with me? Jealous of Alice? Surely not. I'd spent almost as much time with Rose as I had with Griffin over the past couple of years. I'd tried to tell her over and over how much she meant to me, but she pulled away every time I got close. If anyone had a right to feel hurt, it was me.

"What's that?" she said, shaking me from my thoughts.

She pointed to a pile of food that lay on a cloth at the foot of a cypress tree: vegetables and roots. Before I could reply, Griffin walked past us and deposited more food.

How? I signed.

His eyes seemed especially bright. His hands shook with excitement. *I. Touch. Earth.*

It was how Guardians of the Earth always uncovered food. But Griffin had never come close to unearthing this quantity on Hatteras. Was there really so much food on Roanoke?

Where? I asked.

He raised his eyebrows and pointed to a grassy area near the woods, at least a quarter mile away. *I. Feel. Here.* He pointed to the ground at his feet, then the woods again. *Food. There.*

I was amazed. How could he possibly sense food from a quarter mile away? I'd never heard of such a thing, not even from the Guardians.

But the vegetables and roots still lay before me.

Earth. Here. Good, he added, though I knew he really meant it was better than on Hatteras. *Why. We. Not. Live. Here?*

"Did he say this came from a quarter mile away?" asked Rose, before I could respond.

"Yes."

"Interesting." She sat down and began rinsing the food with water from a canister. It spilled onto her bandages. Strips of cloth hung down apologetically; she tucked them in. Somehow she didn't seem surprised by Griffin's announcement.

Griffin tried to get my attention again. *Something. Else,* he began. *Cat. There.* He pointed toward the road with the clinic, but I couldn't see a cat.

I. Know, I signed back. *I. See. Yesterday.*

How. Is. Here?

When we were younger, there had been many cats on Hatteras Island. The Guardians had bred them in case rats ever crossed from the mainland. We'd given them names, fed them fish scraps, and let them sleep in our cabins. But one summer, a few of the cats had become sick. Before the season was over, they'd all died.

So how had this one survived?

Cat. Here. How? signed Griffin when I didn't respond.

I'd forgotten about the cat once I found the lantern, but Griffin had a good point. How could a cat travel from Hatteras to Roanoke Island? Swim two miles? Unlikely. Jump the gap in the bridge? Even more unlikely.

I. Look, he continued. *Cat. Alone.*

Someone. Put. Here, I suggested.

He weighed my words. *Maybe.* But he seemed doubtful.

"Thom!" shouted Alice.

I ran back onto the street as Griffin took off in search of more food.

Alice was pointing at the sound. To the southeast, the water seemed ablaze with reflected sunlight. But nearer to us, in line with Pond Island, something was floating. It looked like one of our canoes.

I peered through the binoculars. It was ours, all right—Ananias and Eleanor's, I guessed. "It's empty. Must've gone adrift at high tide."

"Adrift? I don't think so. The pirates wouldn't waste a canoe."

"Well, no one's paddling."

"Look closer."

I felt a flash of annoyance, but did as she asked. Something glinted inside. "There's something in it. I can't make it out."

Rose stood beside us now. "Are they coming?"

"No. But something in the canoe just caught the light."

"What are we going to do?" asked Dennis. "The wind's pushing it this way."

I tried to locate the pirates, but couldn't see anyone. Meanwhile, the canoe continued its slow, steady progress toward us. Something inside glinted again, and I tried to hone in on it.

That's when I realized the canoe wasn't empty at all. "There's someone inside."

"Who?" demanded Rose.

"I can't see."

She began to run toward the shore, with Dennis right behind.

"It could be a trap," I shouted, but they didn't stop.

Alice bent down and picked up two chunks of stone. She handed one to me. "If it's a trap, use this. Aim for the head. Don't hesitate."

We caught up to Rose and Dennis near the water's edge. The canoe was still a hundred yards away. As I raised the binoculars, Rose waded in and disappeared beneath the water. When she resurfaced, she was already forty yards away.

"Come back!" I shouted.

"She can't hear you," said Alice.

Rose ducked underwater again and halved the distance between her and canoe. One more plunge and she surfaced alongside it.

I watched for signs of a trap. Rose would have been completely silent in the water, I was sure of that, but as soon as she touched the canoe, anything might happen.

She seemed to know it too, and circled twice. Content that she was safe, she placed her fingers gently on the rim of the canoe.

In a sudden motion she pulled the canoe down and glanced over the side. Then she ducked under the water again. But not before she screamed.

"What happened?" cried Dennis.

"I don't know." She hadn't tipped the canoe toward us, so I hadn't seen anything at all. "I'm going in."

"No," Alice snapped. "Her element is water. You can't help her out there."

Rose surfaced again beside the bow of the canoe. She'd been under a long time. Had something kept her down? Was she struggling?

It certainly didn't look that way. As I focused on her once more, I noticed that the canoe was moving with her now. She was dragging it to shore.

So why did she look distraught?

Still no pirates, but something told me we were being watched. Why go to the trouble of launching a canoe unless they were going to watch?

I ran into the water as Rose drew closer to the shore. I gripped the rock in my hand, ready to strike anything. Or anyone. But there was no need for that. The canoe contained no pirates, no traps—just Guardian Walt.

His throat had been slit in a perfectly straight line.

I turned away and gagged. Dennis did too.

Alice helped Rose out of the water and held her as she sobbed. But her eyes never left the corpse.

In his hands, Walt held a piece of broken glass. It's what had reflected the light, brought us to him in the first place. I pried it from his cold fingers and held it up to the light. On one sharp end was a smear of blood.

It was the weapon they'd used to kill him.

Rose was crying, but she was alone. The rest of us were relieved it was old Walt—who'd never recovered after his family had contracted the Plague and returned to Roanoke Island to die quietly. From that day, it had always seemed as though he was waiting for an opportunity to join them.

Had he volunteered for this? Pleaded with the pirates to take his life instead of someone else's? My father's, maybe?

Rose broke from Alice and grasped Dennis's hand. Together, they walked to the shore. When she looked back, it wasn't at Walt, but at Hatteras Island. They couldn't return now. Not after this. They were stuck on Roanoke Island, come what may.

We all were.

CHAPTER 18

Alice and I released Walt to the sound. I offered blessing for safe passage. When the words caught in my throat, Alice took over. We spoke kindly and thoughtfully, but it meant nothing. Walt had lost his family and died savagely, knife-like glass slashed across his neck. It was impossible to believe that in his final moments there had been any peace at all.

Back in the shelter, Griffin was slicing vegetables and roots with a swift, efficient motion. He obviously sensed something strange had happened, but trusted me to tell him about it when the time was right. It was part of the unspoken under-standing between us.

For once, I doubted there'd ever be a right time.

He put the food in cloths for each of us, but still wouldn't eat any himself. Instead, he retreated to a corner and began rifling through our dune box.

No one complained about the texture or the taste of the food. Unless Griffin could find more, worse lay ahead.

Afterward, Alice handed each of us a pawpaw, along with a spoon from the stash I'd discovered. Dennis sliced his and Rose's in half, to save her from having to use her injured hands.

The knife made its way to me next, but before I could cut the fruit, I saw Alice slide her pawpaw behind her back. When she realized I'd seen her, she shook her head, a warning to me to keep quiet. She wore an odd expression too: fierce, determined. It worried me.

Though I was hungry, I followed her lead and saved my fruit. If Alice knew something the rest of us didn't, I couldn't afford to ignore her.

My stomach rumbled in displeasure.

"They're taunting us," she muttered finally. "Trying to break us. They could be here in less than a strike, but they refuse to cross the bridge. Something strange is going on. We need to find out what it is."

"How?" I asked.

She flared her nostrils. "I'm going to spy on them tonight."

"*What?* You saw what they did to Walt."

"They won't catch me. I'm invisible. Always have been."

"But there are guards at the end of the bridge."

"I'll stay away from the bridge. And when I get to Hatteras, I'll hide the canoe."

"You can't paddle a canoe alone!"

She shot me a determined smile. "I've done it before, remember?"

Rose narrowed her eyes. It was obvious she didn't believe Alice, but equally clear that she saw us as a team now.

I waited for her to tell Alice that the plan was madness, but she didn't. Maybe she figured all was lost already, so what harm could it do? At least, I hoped that was the meaning of her silence.

I couldn't bear the thought of Alice crossing the sound alone. Facing the pirates alone. No one doubted her bravery, but courage didn't guarantee safety. If anything, her fearlessness might put her at even greater risk.

I closed my eyes. "I'm going too."

When I opened them, Alice was staring at me, eyebrows raised. I expected her to say no, that she preferred to work alone.

For once, she didn't.

Griffin woke me from a deep sleep. He tugged my blanket hard, as if he'd been trying for a while. Through the small windows near the ceiling the sunset glowed orange and purple. The shelter was almost dark, except for a candle that flickered against the far wall.

Across the shelter, Dennis was already asleep. Rose sat beside him, eyes closed, humming.

Griffin placed something before me: the leather book from our father's dune box. He removed a piece of paper and handed it to me. It felt like dead leaves, yellow-brown and brittle. I was afraid it would disintegrate when I touched it.

I knew immediately why Griffin wanted me to see this page. It showed a very young girl—so lifelike, finer than any drawing I'd ever seen. Even more surprising, she was colorful.

A brown cloth tied around her waist covered her yellow skin, while her neck was adorned with a row of pale pink shells. From the condition of the picture, she must have lived a long time ago.

Beneath the picture were two letters—*J. W.*—and a single word. It was faint—barely there at all—but after a moment I deciphered the letters: *VIRGINIA.* I'd heard the word before, though I couldn't remember when or where. Perhaps it was the name of one of the clan ships, or another colony.

Griffin took the page from me and reinserted it into the journal. Then he removed a different one. It was the same girl, same age, same clothes, same word *VIRGINIA* written carefully underneath. Her bold eyes seemed to stare right at me. But what made my heart beat wildly were her hands, raised skyward, and the tall flames shooting from every fingertip.

One of my earliest memories was of Ananias using his element: the sparks spitting from his fingers while my father held me back so that I wouldn't be burned. I'd watched his element grow, marveled at his ability, his tolerance to heat. But I'd never seen him produce flames like these.

Now that Griffin had shared this picture with me, I considered showing him the one of our mother. But then I thought of Walt. Had the pirates killed her as easily as they'd dispatched him? Had they cast her adrift too, her body bloated by the sun, gulls feasting on her remains?

A hand brushed my tunic and I snapped back to the present. *You. Be. Strong,* signed Griffin. His expression told me it was a statement, not an instruction. I wondered if any of us could be as strong as him.

"You're awake," called Rose. She picked up a pile of black clothes and brought them over to me. By then, Griffin had tucked the pictures safely away. In our world of long-kept secrets, he was saving one for us.

"Alice says you need to wear these," she explained.

"What are they?"

"Some of the clothes Dennis found. I tried to find the best fit, but you'll need to tie this around you." She handed me a length of rope. "Go ahead. I won't watch."

I retreated to a dark corner and changed into the clothes. The tunic was too big, but the length was perfect; it ended just below my waist. I tied the extra material down with the rope. The trousers were perfect too. "How did you guess my size?"

"I know you. And I'm observant." She bit her lip, hesitated. "Like that pendant you gave Alice—it's really pretty."

I felt the weight of her words. "It was just something I found. I figured . . . because of the one Eleanor has—"

"You don't need to explain. I understand."

She inspected her handiwork. When she was satisfied, she looked right at me. "I want you to know, the way the Guardians always keep you and Alice apart . . . it's not my fault. I never asked them to do that."

"I believe you."

"I just want you to be happy. I hope you are . . . happy." Her eyes welled with tears, but she didn't cry.

I took in her matted hair and her dirty tunic. She was falling apart. Broken. And she was still beautiful. "Rose, I—"

"Shh. You should go. Alice is waiting near the canoe."

"Already? It's not dark yet."

"Are you afraid she'll be seen?" Rose flashed a smile—
somehow it looked genuine. "This is Alice we're talking
about, remember."

Yes, Alice was different. She hadn't even turned four before
everyone stopped playing hide-and-seek with her. The game
just wasn't any fun when she could never be found.

Rose covered her mouth with her hand. "One more thing
before you go. Dennis thinks . . . no, he *knows* there's a storm
coming."

"Another?" I glanced at Dennis's slender body, the rise and
fall of his blanket. "But he might be wrong, right?"

"I don't think so. Before he went to sleep he was complain-
ing that his head hurts. His echo is very sensitive." She looked
at him pityingly. "His whole element is extraordinary."

I remembered what Eleanor had said two nights ago, about
his element being *special*. "When is it coming?"

"Tomorrow, he thinks. And it'll be big."

"How big?"

"Biggest he's ever felt." Fear weighed heavily on her features. "It's like he's already in it. Feeling it. He's told me about
the swell, and fallen trees, and the sheer size of it."

She broke off with a shrug, and I could tell she was holding
something back. "What is it, Rose?"

"His element has always been special. More advanced

than it should be. But ever since we got to Roanoke, he's been telling me things I've never heard my father say. It's like he knows so much more here—the kind of detail you can't believe. It's all true, though; you can tell by the way he says it. Thing is, the headaches have been much worse too. It's all just . . . impossible."

Except that it wasn't impossible at all. Without her saying it, I knew she was thinking of Griffin finding vegetables a quarter mile away, and Alice creating full flames for the first time. Perhaps she was even reliving the moment she'd caught the trout—how it had happened so quickly that even she seemed surprised.

Is this why the Guardians were anxious to keep us away from Roanoke Island? Perhaps the danger wasn't Skeleton Town itself, but our elements.

Those of us who had one.

"I'm just saying," she continued, "please get back quickly. I don't know when the storm's coming, but I want you here with us. I have to know you're safe."

I glanced around the shelter at the empty spaces where, only two nights earlier, eight of us had lain down to sleep. Tonight there would be only three. "You should light another candle."

"There aren't many left." She smoothed out her tattered tunic to distract herself. "We'll be all right, though."

I thought of Dennis, nestled in a pile of blankets. And Griffin, confused by everything that was happening. What would happen to them if Alice and I didn't make it back?

"You should go, Thomas. Paddle evenly. Conserve—" Her voice caught.

I picked up the bag I'd packed earlier and checked the contents: the knife, the blanket, the pawpaw . . .

As I ran a finger over the fruit's soft green skin, I pictured Dennis nibbling his pawpaw earlier that afternoon. He'd cried at first, still blaming himself for a situation he couldn't hope to control, but by the time he finished, he'd seemed calmer. Eating the fruit hadn't just staved off hunger; it had reassured him that some things remained the same, even in a world turned upside down.

"Here, take this." I handed the pawpaw to Rose.

"Why?"

"Just in case."

"In case what?"

Truthfully, I didn't know the answer.

Rose reached into her pocket and pulled out another untouched pawpaw. The two pieces of fruit rested in the palms of her bandaged hands.

"You saved yours too."

She shook her head. "Alice gave it to me." She swallowed hard, and her voice cracked a little. "Just in case."

CHAPTER 19

I found Alice near the water's edge, hidden behind a sprawling plant. She wore trousers instead of shorts, a black tunic instead of her vest. It covered her shoulders and arms, seemed to hide the gentle curve of her neck and shoulders. Even though the clothes fit perfectly, she looked uncomfortable.

"Rose knows your size well," I said.

"Hmm. Yours too." She raised an eyebrow. "No surprise there."

There was a bowl in her lap, filled with something gray I couldn't make out. She stirred the contents rhythmically.

"Does it taste good?".

She laughed. "I doubt it. It's ash, for camouflage. If you're hungry, there are nuts in my bag."

"I don't think I can eat anything. I'm scared."

"It's natural. Helps you stay alert."

"Aren't you scared?"

She peered up at me. "Of course I am. But you've still got to eat. You need energy."

"I'm fine," I said, pacing back and forth beside her.

"No, you're not. I watched you earlier. You didn't eat or drink enough. Try sipping from the canister."

"I'll be all right."

"No." Alice narrowed her eyes. "I don't care if you have to pee over the side of the canoe when we're halfway across the sound. Once we get to Hatteras we won't be carrying anything."

I felt the bag strap pressing into my shoulder. "Why not?"

"We've got to travel light, stay silent. Right now, our only advantage is the pirates don't know we're coming. We can't risk giving ourselves away."

"You've thought about this a lot." I forced down a swig from my canister.

"Trust me, I've learned the hard way. The first time I sneaked over to Roanoke Island I carried everything I'd need. But it was dark, see, and when I stopped for a snack, I left my water canister behind. The next day I woke up late because I was so tired—paddling the canoe by myself was torture—and my father asked where my canister was. It was such a small thing, but he wouldn't let it go. It was like he suspected something, and wanted to punish me. But it taught me a lesson: Only carry what you need, and plan for everything."

"Have you? Planned for everything?"

She stirred the bowl again, but this time the movement

was irregular. "I'm prepared," she said finally. "I'm always prepared."

I tugged at my sleeves nervously. Was I prepared? Could I ever be prepared for something like this? "Why didn't you tell me you were sneaking over to Roanoke Island?"

"Would you have gone with me?" She didn't look up, but her smile teased me, made it clear she already knew the answer. "I didn't want you to have to lie for me, Thom. You shouldn't get into trouble because of me."

She stopped stirring, and tapped the handle of the fork against the side of the bowl. "All right, I need you to sit down and face me. Do what I do."

I sat. The sun had finally set, and the wispy clouds that had been stretched across the sky were gathering into something more ominous. In the almost dark, Alice dabbed ash onto her cheeks, a look of intense concentration on her face. Strands of black hair fell across her forehead. She rubbed the powder onto her chin, across her cheekbones, and up around her forehead and ears. My fingers shook as I mimicked her every movement.

She leaned back and studied me. "Not bad. You just need a little more around the temples."

I loaded up two fingers and applied the ash in slow circles.

"You missed a bit." I could feel her breath as she pointed to a spot on my face that I couldn't see. Her pendant swung between us. "Right there."

"Here?"

"No." She leaned forward, took hold of a flap of my sleeve,

and guided my hand to the right spot. But I was aware of nothing but her lips, slightly parted, and her tongue touching the space between her teeth. "Right there," she whispered.

I imagined I could feel the warmth of her hand where she still held my sleeve, her fingers glancing the hairs on my arm. I let my arm sink, just enough that we could touch again, like yesterday. Make the connection.

Alice pulled back suddenly. I froze, and so did she.

"I-I'm sorry," she said. "You surprised me."

I tried to nod—something vaguely reassuring—but the look in her eyes wasn't one of surprise. It was worse than that. It was the same expression Rose wore whenever I tried to get close—appalled, disgusted. I'd come to expect it from Rose now, but Alice had *touched* me. She'd let our hands connect, and sighed contentedly when my fingers brushed her neck.

Had I just imagined it?

No. Alice always knew exactly what she was doing.

"Why did you touch me yesterday?" I asked, struggling to stay calm.

"Because I wanted to."

"And now?"

"It's complicated."

I wanted to laugh, but couldn't. "Complicated?"

"Yes." She studied her blackened hands. "I'm sorry. I'll understand if you don't want to come with me anymore."

Now I was just plain angry. "I'm not doing this for *you*. We all need answers, right? Especially Rose." I threw in the name out of spite, and was pleased when Alice flinched.

"Fine. Well, just remember that I've explored Roanoke Island by myself and didn't get caught. I know a lot of the Guardians' secrets, and they don't even realize it. What we're about to do . . . it's something I'm very good at."

"This is different. Even if we make it across without being seen, we might not get close enough to hear anything."

"Don't worry. I'll hear them." She sounded amused.

"What do you mean, *you'll* hear them? We're not splitting up."

"No, we're not. But you've got to trust me, okay? Even when you're not sure . . . promise you'll trust me."

She wore a look I hadn't seen before: sincere and earnest, but also vulnerable, as though my response carried enormous weight.

"I do."

She began to apply the remaining ash to her hands. I did the same, until not even the smallest piece of skin was showing. As the world around us was plunged into darkness, I could barely see her at all.

"I won't let the pirates win, Thom. I never let anyone win. I'm just not a good loser."

CHAPTER 20

The first paddle strokes were the worst. Every muscle in my arms protested, but I blocked out the pain. I couldn't afford to be weak. Not with the others back in the shelter, waiting for news and reassurance. And not with Alice before me—her strokes barely a whisper, shoulders rocking back and forth, tunic shifting like the water beneath us.

We headed south and hugged the Roanoke Island shore-line before we set out across the sound. Then we paddled due east past the southern edge of Pond Island. The pirates were dangerously close here—a couple hundred yards away—and I imagined I could hear their voices carried on the breeze.

We paused just long enough to force down some nuts and drink some more water. I wanted to break the silence and tension, but we couldn't take that risk. Besides, what use would words be? Clouds still blanketed the sky, and the water still lapped against our canoe, and the pirates still had all the answers.

Alice pushed harder as we entered open water. Bonfires

dotted the Hatteras Island shoreline less than a mile away, their angry orange flames contorted by the freshening breeze. Occasionally I saw pirates too—resting and waiting. I tried to make out their faces, but couldn't.

After several strokes, I realized I was looking for one in particular: the man with long dark hair and colorful arms. The one with the telescope. My mother's murderer. *Who is he?* I thought. *What does he want with us? What do we have that's worth sacrificing so much? Why hasn't he captured us already?*

At Hatteras Island, Alice directed us toward one of the narrow channels through the marsh. We took fewer strokes now, just glided forward. Instead of running aground, we stopped a few yards short, where the canoe would be less likely to be found. Alice wrapped a length of rope around several blades of tall needlerush and tethered the canoe.

"Will it hold?" I whispered.

"Should. We're sheltered here. Not much swell to loosen the knot." She sounded like she'd done it a hundred times before. "Have some nuts, and drink some more water. Remember, we carry nothing."

I did as she said. By the time I was done, I felt sick to my stomach, but my mouth was still dry.

Alice closed her bag and stuffed it under her seat, so I did too. She removed her shoes and eased her legs over the side of the canoe, her feet sliding into the marsh. Again I followed her lead. Together we pressed onward until the marsh dried out and we felt solid ground beneath our bare feet.

Sitting on the dirt bank, I used the edge of my tunic to dry my feet, and put my shoes back on. Once we were ready, we kept low and sprinted toward a line of pine trees, where Alice dropped to a crouch on a bed of needles. Mosquitoes filled the air around us and feasted on every piece of uncovered skin.

We took several moments to scan the island and get our bearings. I knew this place well—the wooded area was narrow and sparse—and as we crept through it I made out the glow of bonfires to the north and east. I imagined I could feel the heat as sweat dripped down my forehead.

"Do you smell that?" whispered Alice urgently as we emerged the other side.

I sniffed the air. Sure enough, there was a faint odor of cooking meat blowing from the direction of one of the fires. "What is it?"

Alice looked horrified, but then she shook her head ambivalently. "I-I can't be sure."

I waited for her to tell me what she suspected, but she wore her stoic face again.

"We'll head for the largest fire, over there," she said, pointing to one just beyond the ridge of dunes.

"The one where the smell is coming from?"

"Yes. If they're cooking, they'll be distracted. They're probably not keeping watch either. Anyway, the fire's not close to the water's edge, so I don't think it's a lookout."

That made sense, though I was still puzzled by *what* they were cooking. I'd never smelled anything like it before. It certainly wasn't fish, though what else could they have caught?

We dropped to all fours as pine needles and dirt gave way to sand. There wasn't much vegetation to hide us here, so we shuffled forward, one eye fixed on our surroundings. Finally we shimmied up one of the dunes and settled in behind a large clump of grass.

The bonfire was barely twenty yards in front of us. Through the grass fronds I counted eleven pirates. They sat around the perimeter of the fire and stared intently at a makeshift spit. Cooking slowly, its body severed and rearranged to fit on the spit, was one of Alice's beloved wild horses.

I turned to her instinctively. She closed her eyes, but she didn't seem shocked, just resigned. I wanted to tell her I was sorry, but we were too close to the pirates to risk speaking now.

I faced the fire again. Horse fat glistened in the flames, body parts spitting and crackling in the heat. The smell was powerful, pushed toward us by the ocean breeze. The sight was so horrific that it took me a while to tune in to the men's voices. Even then I struggled to hear them until their conversation became louder and more hostile.

"Well, I say we eat our fill while we're here," complained one pirate, a strong-looking man perhaps ten years older than me.

"Forget it, Jossi," replied a much older man. "There's a reason we've survived this long, and it isn't 'cause we eat everything in sight."

"Then who we saving the other horses for, huh? I ain't sticking around here 'til I starve."

This announcement was met by a murmur of agreement.

"How many of them kids are there, anyway?" demanded another pirate.

The old pirate produced a hacking cough. "Dare isn't sure."

Jossi whistled through holes where his teeth should have been. "Ain't sure? Last I heard, this mission was *destined*. It don't exactly fill me with confidence that he ain't even sure how many of them there are."

"He said it looked like four or five. Maybe six."

Angry laughter rippled around the circle. Jossi spat into the fire. "You know what I say, old man? I say it looks like Dare's lost his edge. I think y'all know it too. We gave up a good life to follow him here. During hurricane season."

"No one forced you."

Everyone was muttering now, but Jossi shouted, "That ain't the point. We're trusting our lives to him. The way you say it, thirteen years ago Dare didn't need no damned telescope just to count kids on a beach."

Alice tilted her head toward me. It was oddly comforting to discover they didn't know everything about us yet.

The old man was silent now, but another pirate spoke up. "If you're so smart, Jossi, how 'bout you explain what them kids is doing on Roanoke Island in the first place."

Jossi shrugged. "Who cares? It's been two days. I say we grab 'em."

"Well, someone's changed his tune, eh?" growled the old man. "Two days ago you called that girl a liar for saying the kids were on Roanoke. Beat her bad too, till she sent us south

141

instead. Well, now look—damn, if she wasn't telling the truth all along. And you're ready to head over to Roanoke just as quick as you can."

"Why not?"

"They may've been lucky, is why not. Or it hasn't taken effect yet. Plague can take days, remember?" He brushed sand from his hands. "Either way, we wait. You think them Guardians would've set up camp on this godforsaken sandbar if they could've lived safely in that town?"

"But them kids *are* living safely."

"You sure about that? You volunteering to be first across the bridge?"

For a moment Jossi was silent. "Dare should've let me take that canoe we found. Get me within two hundred yards, I could've taken down every last one of 'em."

"We need the kids alive. At first, anyway."

"I wouldn't kill them, old man. Just a single shot to the leg. Something to slow 'em down. Instead, we're waiting to see who dies first: us or them."

"Quit your whining. They can't hold out forever. Anyway, they won't *all* be dying, will they? Least, not until we get them. That's the whole point."

Jossi let out a single laugh. "So says the mighty Dare. But what if he's wrong? What if they're just fine over there?"

The old man took his time before answering. "Then I'd say the solution is not only real, but more powerful than we ever imagined."

"Pah! The other explanation is there ain't no Plague any-

142

more. What if Dare's precious *solution* ain't even real . . . just something to distract us—"

Suddenly Alice drove my head against the dune. Sand scraped my face and crept into my open mouth. Terrified, she clenched her teeth and jammed a finger against her lips.

I didn't react because I didn't need to. I could hear the footsteps too now, the slow grinding of sand that grew closer every moment.

I closed my eyes and waited for the sound to die away, but it didn't. Whoever it was, was still headed our way. Clenching my fist, I made a decision right then: I'd fight back. If not for me, for our families. And my mother.

Finally, I opened an eye. A few yards behind Alice, illuminated by the distant fire, I glimpsed someone.

He had long dark hair and colorful arms.

CHAPTER 21

Dare.

He was no more than five yards away, breathing heavily. When he stopped moving, I was certain he'd seen us.

Instead he crouched down and eavesdropped on the pirates' conversation. A moment later he strode confidently around the dune, his footsteps finally, mercifully, growing quieter.

I looked at Alice as I stole several deep breaths. She mouthed the word *sorry* to me, but I shook my head. She didn't need to apologize. If not for her, we'd have been caught for sure.

I peered through the grass again and in the dancing firelight saw the man who had come so close to discovering us. He was as tall as I'd thought, though thin and wiry. His sinewy arms bore images I still couldn't make out, in a rainbow of colors—most of all red, like spilled blood that wouldn't wash off.

"Well, well, if it ain't Dare," said the pirate named Jossi. "Thought we'd lost you."

"I'm sure you missed me." Dare's rich voice oozed sarcasm. "Where you been?"

With exaggerated slowness, Dare removed something from his left trouser pocket. It was clear that he was used to having everyone's attention, and enjoyed the power. "I visited Bodie Lighthouse."

"Why? We know the children ain't been there."

"Agreed."

"Anyways," added the old man, "you and I went there thirteen years ago. The door was locked . . . hadn't been opened in years. Probably rusted shut by now."

In his hand Dare held what looked like a piece of paper. "Actually, the door wasn't rusted shut. It opened easily. And the lantern room is filled with newspapers, photographs, and enough food and water for a siege."

This announcement was met with silence. I turned to Alice to see if the words meant anything to her, but she shook her head. Beside the fire, Dare smiled at the pirates' stunned expressions.

"Oh, yes. Someone has been living there, all right. But there's only bedding for one person. And from the freshness of the water, I'd say whoever it is left when they saw us coming." He allowed the silence to linger. When he spoke again, his voice was tinged with venom. "All of which gets me thinking those kids have themselves an ally now."

"Dare, I—"

"Shut up! I gave an order to inspect the lighthouse. But none of you went, and now we've wasted a day." He took a deep breath, struggling to remain calm. "You really think they'll surrender just 'cause we destroyed their miserable little colony once before? You think that seeing us on Pond Island is giving them nightmares? 'Cause I don't. I bet right now they're laughing at us."

Another pirate spoke up, his voice shaky. "But . . . we questioned them older children. They swore they ain't seen or heard of no Guardians 'cept the ones we captured."

Dare sat down and crossed his legs. "Then I'd say we have an even bigger problem. That lighthouse is only six miles away from their colony. But someone has been living there in secret. Now, who would be able to do that?"

The man rubbed his forehead. "You don't mean . . . the *seer*."

"Who else?"

"But she'd been exiled last time we was here."

"Yes, she had. And she'd left—just like they told her to. But what if she came back?"

"Why would she?"

"Why do you think? Homesickness. Maybe she wanted to watch her grandchildren grow. It doesn't exactly matter why."

Jossi stood and brushed sand from his trousers. "Let me get this straight. She weren't around thirteen years ago, but now she's back?"

"So it would seem," agreed Dare.

"Well, that's one explanation. Or it might just be these so-called visions of yours are make-believe."

The men fell into complete silence. No one moved.

"My visions are more accurate than you can imagine. Thirteen years ago, I said the solution was here. Now it seems I was right. Believe me, the solution is on Roanoke Island."

Jossi began to circle around the perimeter of the bonfire. "Ah, the *solution*. Course, you also said them kids would come to us."

"And they did. Just not the *right* one."

"Hmm. That must be mighty disappointing for you, Dare. To think you burned down their colony just to get them Guardians to talk, and they still lied." Jossi laughed. "But I guess you missed that one, huh?"

Dare remained still, his face unreadable.

Jossi finally drew alongside him. "You know what I think? I think—"

There was a flash of movement, and a cry pierced the air.

I held my breath as I tried to work out what had happened, but an eternity passed before Jossi collapsed to his knees. Still screaming, he held his right hand in front of his face.

In the firelight that glowed behind him, I saw the space where his pointer finger used to be.

Dare was standing now, their positions reversed. "Yes, Jossi, I know *precisely* what you think. You think it's time for a new leader. You think I can't hear the click as you pull back the trigger on your gun. You think I didn't foresee this from the moment the plan crossed your tiny mind twelve days ago. You think I wouldn't notice you were supposed to be on the ship guarding the prisoners tonight." Dare shook his head. "Even now, you're thinking it's pure

147

coincidence that I waited for you to get within striking distance before I severed your trigger finger."

Jossi was scrabbling around in the sand, presumably trying to find his finger. The thought was so sickening that it took me a moment to realize what Dare had just said: Someone was guarding the prisoners. Our families were *alive*. It was the news we had come to hear. I should have been relieved, but instead they seemed as far away as ever. I couldn't even make out the ship anchored offshore.

There was another sudden movement as Dare picked up the finger and tossed it into the fire. Jossi crawled after it on all fours. He stabbed a hand toward the flames, but he was tentative, afraid. When he sat back on his haunches, it was obvious he'd given up.

Dare grunted in disgust. He joined Jossi, and plunged his own hands into the fire. As he roared from the pain, I closed my eyes. I imagined I could hear his flesh crackling, smell the burning. When I opened my eyes again, Jossi's finger rested in his palm.

"This what you're looking for?" Dare dropped the finger contemptuously into Jossi's outstretched hand.

Jossi's whimpering twisted into something even more tortured.

"Now let me tell you what *I* think," spat Dare. He removed something metal and shiny from Jossi's pocket and tossed it to the old pirate. "I think you're a snake, hissing ideas into weak men's minds when you think I can't hear." He leaned closer. "But I don't need to *hear*, Jossi. I already *know*."

148

"I'm sorry," Jossi choked. "I'm sorry. Please forgive me."

"Forgive you?" Dare laughed. "You should be begging for your *life*, not forgiveness."

Jossi bowed his head. "I-I'm—" His voice cracked. "I'm sorry."

"No, you're not. But I'm still not going to kill you. Unlike you, I see the value of keeping people alive. Everyone has a purpose. Yes, even the prisoners. Of course, once we have our solution, well . . . things change. But for now they live. Just like you."

"Thank you," mumbled Jossi.

Dare paused to wipe the blood from his blade. "Don't thank me yet. Your night has barely begun."

Still kneeling, Jossi shivered violently. He pressed his shirt against the wound, the agony alive in his eyes.

"See this?" muttered Dare, thrusting the piece of paper before him. "This was in the lighthouse. And there's more. Much more. Best of all, there's a map. I left it spread out for you, so you couldn't miss it when you go there later. I think it's only fitting that my would-be assassin should be the first to see it."

Jossi hesitated. "W-what's on—"

"No, no!" cried Dare. "I wouldn't want to spoil the surprise. Go study it for yourself. When you're done, bring it back here along with everything you can carry. And be sure to return before daybreak. Tomorrow I plan to send a group across the bridge to Roanoke Island. Can you guess who'll be leading the way?"

Jossi didn't say anything, but his mangled hand trembled.

"Enough, Dare." The old man's husky voice broke the silence. "No one should cross that bridge. We can't take the chance."

"If that's what it takes to capture the boy, we have no choice," replied Dare firmly. "Anyway, I have a hunch that when Jossi returns, he'll assure us that *chance* isn't involved at all."

A murmur grew amongst the pirates, but no one dared ask what Dare meant. Clearly he was used to playing mind games. What's more, he was evidently used to winning.

"You're certain this boy is the solution?"

"Yes, I am. And if I'd been thinking clearly thirteen years ago, we'd have captured him then."

The old man bowed his head. "How will you know when you find him?"

"Oh, I'll know." Dare folded the blade back into the shaft of his knife. "And so will you, just as soon as I call his name."

With some difficulty, the old man stood and approached the horse roasting on the spit. He stabbed the flesh with his knife and pulled a hunk away. He gobbled it up, still steaming, and chewed it with mouth wide open. A moment later he nodded, and the other pirates nudged closer and helped themselves. After that there was nothing in the air but the sound of chewing, and a rare smell of fresh-cooked animal that left me light-headed with hunger even as it broke my heart.

I rested my head against the dune. In the distance I heard

the waves breaking, brushing a million tiny grains of sand up and down the beach. I wanted to believe that the familiar sound was the same as it had always been. But nothing felt the same anymore.

Finally I pointed back down the dune to signal that we should leave. Side by side, Alice and I crawled away until we were out of sight. Then we ran toward the cover of trees.

For once, I led the way, adrenaline coursing through my body. With each step my mind replayed what Dare had said. I tried to give his words a different meaning, but it was hopeless.

When we slowed down, I sensed that Alice's eyes were fixed on me. She knew as well as I did what those words meant: The boy Dare sought was still at large. But Dennis hadn't even been born thirteen years ago, so it couldn't be him. No, the pirates had returned to Hatteras, destroyed our homes, and decimated our lives for the chance to capture one specific boy.

Whatever the *solution* was, it could only be Griffin or me.

CHAPTER 22

lice watched me. I would have understood if she'd hated me in light of everything we'd learned, but instead she just looked sad. Finally she bit her lip and reached out as though she were going to hug me. But she didn't.

Of course she didn't.

"Thom, is there something I should know about you and Griffin?"

"Like what?"

"I don't know. Just . . . anything."

"No. I don't know what Dare wants with us."

Her silence reeked of doubt.

"If there was anything, I'd tell you. I don't keep secrets from you, remember? I promise."

Reluctantly, she nodded.

"We need to go to the lighthouse," I said.

"It's six miles. We don't have any water."

"By morning they'll have ransacked it. We need to know what's there—who's been living there."

Alice stared into the darkness. "The woman they were talking about . . . they made it sound like she was from our colony."

"Yes. And she's a seer, like Griffin. Do you know who she is?"

"No." Alice sighed. "I wish I could see the moon. I think we're at least two strikes into the night. We have to get away before daybreak."

"We will."

She didn't say another word, just took off running south toward the lighthouse. When the terrain shifted from hard ground to marsh, we headed onto the beach and half ran, half walked through powdery sand.

After a couple miles we spied a lone sentry, dozing beside a small fire. We couldn't risk being seen, so Alice led us up the beach and around the dunes. She was sure-footed and lithe, and with each step she disturbed sea-sparkle, so that the sand around her seemed to glisten blue-green. Just as well, because I was struggling to see her. When she spoke, it was only to warn me of some unforeseen hazard, or far-off groups of sentries I couldn't even make out.

It felt like we'd been running forever when the clouds finally parted and a sliver of moonlight illuminated the grass-land before us. I'd begun to wonder if we were lost, but now the distinctive black-and-white stripes of Bodie Lighthouse loomed a hundred yards ahead of us.

"How did you find it?" I asked as we reached the massive iron door at the base.

"I have a good sense of direction." She grasped the door handle and pulled it open. "Come on."

We walked along a corridor, our footsteps loud and intrusive. I ran my fingers along the walls on either side of us, and though there were doorways, I couldn't see what lay beyond them. At the end of the corridor, we entered the main shaft. I could tell by the way sound reverberated how high up it must reach.

It took us a moment to find the staircase in the darkness. Then we began to climb, the metal stairs echoing until it seemed there were a hundred of us in there. My feet were invisible beneath me, but once I found a rhythm, I climbed faster. I counted the stairs as we went: two hundred and five. My thighs throbbed.

As we neared the top I began to make out the gray walls and the iron grating on each stair. I figured my eyes were growing accustomed to the darkness, but then we came upon the lantern room itself, surrounded by large windows that admitted every bit of moonlight that could penetrate the clouds.

In the center of the octagonal room was a massive glass lantern. The Guardians had said the lighthouse was probably designed to prevent ships from grounding. Certainly it might have spared their ship from being wrecked. But no one had ever seen the lantern working, and the door had been sealed when the building was first discovered.

At least, that's what they'd told us. Now, it seemed, the room's purpose was to house the mysterious seer, whose belongings were spread across oak tables pressed tightly against the walls.

Alice stared at a piece of paper that looked oddly familiar.

"It's the map you found in your father's dune box," I exclaimed.

"Yes . . . and no."

I looked closer. Sure enough, this map was even bigger. Where the mainland had been torn off her father's map, here it remained. Words were written across various parts of it, although I couldn't read them because of the low light and the fact that vast swathes had been shaded over with what looked like one of Griffin's burnt twigs. Not just one twig either, but several, the shading applied in stages.

"Why was Dare so fascinated by this?" I could tell that Alice was asking herself, not me. "Everyone kept talking about the Plague, but what difference does this map make? What did it reveal to him?"

The edge of another piece of paper protruded from underneath the map. I tugged it out. It was the same size as the map, even looked like a map, but it was entirely foreign to me. As was the small piece of paper on top of it, covered in tiny words that might have been legible if not for the lack of light.

Time was precious, so I began to inspect the rest of the cluttered room. The next table was stacked with battered tin containers. I opened the top one and removed a piece of paper; it felt strangely slick to the touch, but as the moon disappeared again, I couldn't make out what was on it at all. The way the light fluctuated, we'd be hard-pressed to learn anything.

"You have to make a flame," I said.

"In here? No way. What if someone sees it?"

"I'm not talking about a fire—just a small flame. It's going to take forever to see what's here if we keep waiting for the moon to come out."

Reluctantly, Alice rubbed her hands together. Her movements grew faster and faster, the friction palpable, the heat emanating like an invisible glow. I was closer to it all than ever before. I *felt* it all.

Then she slowed down.

"What's the matter?"

"I don't know. I just can't make a spark. It's like . . . there's nothing there."

"But yesterday—"

"I know what I did yesterday! I don't understand it either. My element isn't very strong, remember."

"Can you try again?"

With a deep sigh, she brought her hands together. Everything was the same: the hands flying back and forth, the sound, the heat. But still—

A spark flew from her left hand and landed on the corner of the map. The paper ignited at once. Alice launched herself at it, patted it with her palms until nothing remained but the odor of smoke. "Enough," she whispered. "No more."

She wasn't watching me, but I nodded anyway. From the way she leaned across the map, head hung low, I knew she was embarrassed. I didn't understand why her element was so unreliable, but I already regretted forcing her to experience it.

With no other option, I lifted my piece of paper to the

window and waited impatiently for the moon to reappear. Several moments passed before a dull light reflected off the shiny surface, though I still couldn't make anything out until the moon emerged completely.

The paper bore an image of five people: three adults and two children. Only this was no ordinary image. Something so lifelike could not have been hand-drawn. It looked as though its subjects had been caught and frozen.

Worst of all, one of them was my father.

CHAPTER 23

'd have recognized my father's eyes anywhere. Even his formerly long hair couldn't disguise them. But that meant that the two children in front of him were . . .

Alice appeared beside me. When she breathed in sharply, I knew she'd seen it too. "What is that?"

"I don't know."

"Do you remember it?"

"No."

"Is that your mother, then?" Her finger hovered beside the young woman in the picture.

"I'm not sure," I said, though it wasn't true. This woman was same as the one on the portrait I'd found when I first opened my father's dune box. It had to be my mother.

I gazed at her bright eyes and wide smile. She had her arms wrapped tightly around Ananias. Beside them, my father held me close. I was just a baby. The third adult was an older woman, though I didn't recognize her.

Alice smiled, but she seemed tense. I was too. How could such a picture exist?

"Your mother was beautiful," said Alice finally.

Yes, she was. And Ananias looked so comfortable in her arms. Only, I was totally separate from her, not even connected by a finger. I hated feeling jealous—especially after so many years—but I couldn't help wishing that she had been holding me instead.

"Who's the older woman?" asked Alice.

"I don't remember her."

"Do you think she's the seer Dare was talking about?"

"Could be. Who else would keep this picture?"

Alice studied the image. I could tell she wanted to ask something, and I guessed what it was.

"You think she's my grandmother, don't you?"

"Your grandmother died years ago."

"Yes." That's what the Guardians had told us, anyway. Once, I'd asked my father what had happened to her. He said she had been lost at sea. It wasn't a long explanation, but the way he'd said it had deterred me from bringing up the matter again.

"Did they ever explain . . ." Alice began. Then she saw my face. "I'm sorry."

"Don't be. If my grandmother is the seer, that means she's alive. And Dare thinks she's our ally."

"Then where is she now?"

I shook my head and looked at the image again: the happy

family of five. Then I noticed something else. We were standing in front of a stone building, its large glass windows clean and intact. "This looks like Skeleton Town. I think they *were* living there, just like you said. But this building is still perfect. You don't think . . . they lived there *before* the town was destroyed?"

Alice narrowed her eyes. "It looks that way. But then, who destroyed it? And why did the Guardians leave? Even the pirates said they wouldn't be living on Hatteras if they could've been on Roanoke."

"None of this makes sense."

Alice peered out the window and scanned the surrounding area. "We should hurry. I have a bad feeling."

I heard her, but I couldn't take my eyes off the picture. I finally had something to remember my mother by, but the very same image made a lie of everything we'd been told. Everything I thought I knew. In the end, Alice—the doubter, the cynic—was right.

I spied something else in the picture too, coiled around the older woman's feet. It was small, and relegated to the corner, but I could still make out its striped brown fur and two yellow eyes. "Wait. I've seen this cat."

Alice rejoined me. "Where?"

"In Skeleton Town."

"You're sure it was this one?"

"Yes. It's the first one I've seen in years. It ran into the clinic the night I found the lantern. I got a good look at its markings in the lamplight. Griffin's seen it too."

I recalled the mysterious sounds I'd heard in Skeleton Town—the ones I'd never been able to place. But if the seer had traveled to Skeleton Town, why was she hiding from us?

I was about to ask Alice what she thought, but she was looking outside again. Knowing that Dare's men would take everything by morning, I stole a final look at my mother and placed the image inside my pocket. When I looked up, Alice was completely still, her mouth open in surprise.

"What is it?"

She didn't even hesitate. "They're coming."

"Already?" I stared out the window. The moonlight waxed and waned with each passing cloud, but I could make out the area immediately before us. "I don't see anyone."

"We need to go."

"What are you talking about? Think about the map, the image. We need to search this place, get some answers. By tomorrow Dare will—"

"You're not listening!" Her words punched the air. "Three men are heading this way. I don't know for sure they're coming to the lighthouse, but I think it's likely, don't you?"

"There's no one there, Alice."

"You promised to trust me."

"There's no one out there. I'm not blind."

"But you can't see like me!" When she turned to the window once more, her eyes filled with tears. "Please, let's go."

She went to leave, but I touched her arm to stop her. She flinched and pulled away, but stayed. I couldn't remember the last time I'd seen her cry.

"How exactly *do* you see, Alice?"

I wanted her to look at me, but she wouldn't. So I stared out the window at the emptiness. The tall grass around the lighthouse swished back and forth in the stiffening breeze.

There was no one out there. No one at all.

"What did you mean?" I asked again.

Alice slid to the floor. "I'm going to tell you something, and I don't want you to hate me."

I was confused. More than that, I was scared.

She pulled up her knees and hugged them. "It's not an accident that I know the Guardians' secrets. Or that I knew where the dune boxes were. Or that I can disappear and never be found."

A part of me wanted her to stop right there. I'd known Alice ever since she was born. Knew her as well as anyone. Perhaps better than anyone.

"I have . . . *something*. It's not an element, but I see and hear more than you. I don't spy on people. I don't eavesdrop, either. Honestly. I don't need to."

I could barely breathe. "How?"

"I don't know. It's like your binoculars. When I focus on a small point I can bring it closer, make it clearer. Even sounds rise above the noise around me. Same with my other senses."

"I don't believe you. That pirate ship was a mile from the shore when we got to Hatteras and you never even saw it."

"I wasn't *looking* for it. I was focused on the fires, and the dune boxes. I just never looked at the ocean. But when I did—"

"You saw the flag was yellow," I said, finishing her thought.

162

"Then you said it was black. The rest of us couldn't see that."
I took deep breaths, tried to make sense of everything. "How long . . ."

"Since I was born. That's why you could never find me at hide-and-seek. I always knew when you were coming, so I'd move." She tried to laugh, but it sounded wrong.

"You have another element."

"It's not an element," she whispered.

"You never told me."

"I didn't know what to say."

"How come no one else can do this?"

She paused. "I think my mother can."

"You *think*?"

"She tells me things—things she shouldn't know. I think it's her way of reassuring me I'm not alone."

"And what about *fire*?"

"That's the point. My real element is weak, like Griffin's. It's like having this other ability has diluted it."

"That's not what I mean. Everyone else's element comes from a parent. Has your mother been keeping fire a secret too?"

From the corner of my eye, I saw her rub the ends of her hair between her fingertips. Invincible Alice suddenly looked vulnerable. "No. She says the fire came from my grand-mother—skipped a generation."

I continued to stare at the grass outside—saw nothing there. "Why are the Guardians keeping this . . . whatever it is, a secret?"

"They're not. My mother and I are the ones keeping it a secret."

"Why?"

"Don't you see? This isn't like an ordinary element. It's not even like Griffin's visions. It doesn't do the colony any good. I see and hear things I shouldn't. Things that happen in secret. Things said in private. The Guardians have always hated me. My own father hates me. What do you think they'd do if they knew about this?"

She reached out to take my hand, to reassure me perhaps, but at the last moment she pulled back.

"Will you stop doing that?" My words came out fierce and hurt. "Pretending to touch me. It's cruel."

She shrunk back. "You're right. It's not fair. I'm sorry."

I nodded sharply, but inside, her apology grieved me. I hadn't wanted her to say sorry—I'd wanted her to touch me again. It might have made up for all the years she'd been lying to me. It might have made me forget that she was even more different from me than I could've imagined. It would have given me the chance to say that I was sorry too—that she'd had to hide who she really was.

Instead, I just stared out the window, my mind swimming with a thousand thoughts. I was so confused that it took me a while to notice the scene had changed.

We were no longer alone.

Three men lumbered through the grass, their silhouettes clear. They were probably no more than a couple hundred yards away. And they were headed straight for us.

Alice dried her eyes. "They're getting close, aren't they?"

I didn't answer.

"We need to run now," she said with quiet urgency.

I didn't move. Not at first. I felt frozen, weighed down by the realization that after all these years I'd barely known Alice at all.

She stood and rolled up the maps spread out across the table, the small piece of paper caught between them. Then she stuffed them into her tunic pocket and took off.

Even when my legs began moving, pulling me down two hundred stairs in Alice's wake, my mind stayed in the lantern room. Instead of focusing on escape, I was wondering if anything or anyone was real anymore.

How could I ever know?

CHAPTER 24

Our footsteps sounded deafening on the staircase, relentless and rhythmic. I brushed my fingertips along the wall as we descended and hoped it was thick enough to hide the noise.

When we reached the bottom, Alice stopped suddenly. I almost slammed into her.

"Listen," she said.

At first, I heard nothing but the dying echoes of our hasty descent. Then voices, soft and distant. The men couldn't be far away.

"Quick. Follow me." She dropped to all fours and shuffled across the floor toward the corridor. Then she stopped. I could see the half-open door so close by, but the men's voices were growing louder. Even if we could have reached the door, there would have been nowhere to hide.

"Back," she spat. "Under the stairwell."

I slid over to the staircase and wedged myself into the space under the iron stairs. They were reassuringly heavy, but

I could feel the holes in the grating. "They'll see us," I said.

"It's our only chance." Alice pressed herself next to me, yet still managed to make sure we weren't touching.

The three men spoke over each other, their words garbled. I knew when they'd entered because their angry voices ran along the corridor and echoed around the lighthouse shaft.

"There's rooms here," said one. "We should check 'em. See if there's anything worth taking."

"You reckon Dare would send us to get a map if there was something better down here?" said another.

"Maybe Dare don't know everything—"

"And maybe he does. Let's ask Jossi what he thinks."

A grunt from a third man.

"I'll take that as you agreeing with me, Jossi."

"Then explain why he ain't known nothing for months until now," demanded the first man.

"I don't know. But he sure knew what he was doing when he sliced off Jossi's finger."

"Maybe."

"*Maybe?* Don't be so damned stupid. Why do you think Dare sent the three of us out here?"

"What do you—" The first man hesitated. "No. He can't know about that. It was two weeks ago. We was alone, the three of us. Hell, we didn't even promise Jossi we'd back him up. We was just listening to him, is all."

"But we both *thought* the same as Jossi, right? And I say the fact we're here right now, just the three of us, is 'cause Dare read our minds as clear as he read Jossi's. The only reason we still have our trigger fingers is 'cause he can't afford to waste three riflemen. So how 'bout we find that map and get back. 'Cause if he exiles us, we'll be dead within a week, and you both know it."

"Not if we've got the solution."

"That's a big *if* right now."

Jossi spoke up again: "What's he going to do to the kid, anyway?"

"Whatever it takes. This is bigger than any of us. One dead boy is a small price to pay."

That silenced them. They approached the staircase quickly. I willed them to keep moving, and held my breath as the first man placed his foot on the step above us.

Then he stopped.

"Why was the door open?" he called out. The two men behind him stopped moving. "You know what Dare says about sealing doorways."

"There ain't no problem on Hatteras."

"Don't matter. It's one of the rules. *His* rules."

"He must've forgotten."

"Dare?" The man snorted. "I don't think so." He paused. "Where are the sentries for this part of the island?"

"Half a mile northwest of here. Why? You think they came in here to check it out?"

"No, I don't," said the man, voice even quieter than before, almost as though he was listening for something. "They'd have been as careful as Dare himself; unless they wanted to feel the tip of his blade, that is." He climbed another stair and took a deep breath. "I'm just saying—keep your eyes and ears open."

The men continued their climb, hands fumbling for the stair rail, feet agonizingly close to Alice's arm. I counted each step. When I got to one hundred, I began to breathe easier.

Alice leaned toward me. "Go," she said, more breath than word.

We slid across the floor and into the corridor. I slipped through the half-open door, and pressed myself against the rough exterior wall. Alice was right beside me. The night breeze ruffled her tunic.

She pointed to the northwest. "We'll head for the woods over there."

"That's where the sentries are."

"Don't worry about them. We'll steer clear. Right now we've got to keep the moon behind us so we can't be seen from the lantern room. Move quickly. We'll pause at the tree line."

I nodded once, but before I could take a step a whistle blasted high above us. It cut through the air like a knife.

I peered up at the top of the lighthouse. A lantern swung back and forth in the window. "They've raised an alarm. How do they know we're here?"

"I don't know. We didn't—" Her right hand snapped against the pocket in her tunic. "It's the map. I took the map."

I ran to the door. "They're coming. I hear footsteps. We can't outrun them."

Alice spun around like she was looking for something. "We may not need to. Follow me."

She took off at a sprint, legs flying across the grass. We were heading south now, away from our canoe and toward the moonlight. A voice from high above us rang clear through the air: "To the south. Head south!"

I looked over my shoulder and saw two figures emerging from the lighthouse. They spied us immediately, and gave chase. We had at most two hundred yards' head start.

"Come on," yelled Alice.

She led us onto a stony trail, wide but overgrown with weeds. I never took my eyes off her.

Another couple hundred yards and we left the path and headed into reeds. A few more steps and the ground became marshy. Then we were knee-deep in a creek.

"Put your hands in the water," she whispered furiously. "Feel around."

"For what?"

"Something solid."

I didn't ask any more questions—there wasn't time. I just plunged my hands down and moved them around aimlessly. My feet slipped on the muddy bottom of the creek. The men grew closer.

My knee hit it first: something hard and smooth. "Here."

Alice dove under the water. A moment later she resurfaced, pulling something with her. "Help me."

I grabbed an edge and pulled too. The object floated to the surface.

"Take the other end. Flip it over."

I stood opposite her and we turned it. Even in the dark-

170

ness, I could tell that it was a small canoe. But not like any I'd seen before. It wasn't even made of wood.

Alice jumped into the bow seat, and I took the stern. We each grabbed one of the paddles tethered to the sides, but these were different too, with blades at either end. The shaft was metal. Everything about the situation felt unreal.

She paddled alternating left and right strokes as though she'd done it a million times before. I copied her. The desperate strokes drove us forward, but gave away our position entirely.

"They're on the water!" The words were followed by two loud footsteps and an enormous splash.

"Keep paddling," Alice screamed.

I glanced behind me. The man was trying to run through the water, but soon it came above his knees. He was losing ground. Finally he climbed out and dove into the reeds. "This way," he shouted to the other man. "Get back on the path."

We had momentum now, and our strokes were efficient. Whatever it was, the vessel moved much faster than a canoe. The water slid under us, and the creek grew wider. "Twenty yards to open water," panted Alice.

No sooner had she spoken than the footsteps grew louder again. It was as if they'd been running away from us, and now the path had diverted them back toward us. When one of them tripped and fell, screaming, the other didn't stop for him.

"Ten yards." Alice's voice sounded different. That's how I knew we were in trouble.

I saw the mouth of the creek and the open water beyond. It

was so close, but so were the man's steps. Worse than that, the path was carrying him ahead of us. His breathing was labored, but there was something eerie about those breaths, like he was laughing at us.

Three more paddle strokes and the footsteps and breathing stopped. There was no other sound than our paddles.

"Watch out!"

At the last moment, I saw the reeds part, but there was nothing I could do as he leaped at me.

I swung the paddle up and back. The edge caught his left temple cleanly. By the time I raised the paddle again, he had fallen behind us, floating on his back, not moving.

I never saw the second man, so I couldn't protect myself. He launched himself from the path and landed with both hands on the edge of the canoe. We tipped to the side, so Alice threw herself to the right to counterbalance his weight. We took on water.

Before I could raise the paddle, he grasped the shaft with his left hand, yanked it free, and tossed it into the creek. Alice tried to keep paddling, but he was dead weight, as strong as an anchor. The bow tracked left toward the bank.

I pummeled his hands with my fists, but he pulled himself up and grabbed my arm instead. I used my free hand to try to get him off me, but he had a vise-like grip.

One dead boy is a small price to pay. The words were seared on my mind. How many others would die once I was caught? What if Griffin was the solution, not me? Would they kill him too?

I slashed at his face and grabbed a fistful of hair. I tore my fingernails across his forehead, felt his skin coated in blood. He gritted his teeth, lips pulled back tight, and roared—an animal sound unlike anything I'd ever heard.

I raised my foot to kick at him, but he pulled me so hard I slipped onto my back. For a moment he loosened his grip, and I kept scratching and clawing, every part of me focused on hurting him. My heart pounded, alive with uncontrolled anger.

He took hold of me again, and this time, I latched on to his arm too. His grip was tight and painful, but so was mine. He groaned—quiet at first, but then louder. His eyes grew wide. Again he loosened his grip, but I held tight as his head began to shake. The groan shifted to a guttural cry. In the moment before he let go, his eyes rolled back suddenly, so there was nothing but ghostly white.

Alice was paddling again—left, right, left, right. I scrabbled around, looking for my paddle, forgetting it was behind us in the creek. I tried to remember what had brought us to this place, but couldn't. I could barely remember the man who'd wanted to kill me. Was there one man, or two? Already the details felt like distant memories I couldn't recall. Before me, Alice's strokes blurred together.

I felt exhausted. I wouldn't have been able to paddle if my life had depended on it. Now I was the dead weight.

I looked over my shoulder at the path. Four men were running along it—or was it five?—but they were too far back to catch us. They didn't even seem interested in giving chase.

They just jumped into the water and dragged the bodies of their fallen comrades from the creek.

"We're clear," I tried to say, but the words came out garbled. "They're not . . . they . . ." I tried to focus, but I couldn't find the words. My mouth wasn't working anymore.

In the next moment, I passed out.

CHAPTER 25

hen I came to, a stiff breeze brushed against the waters of the sound, kicking up waves. Images flashed back, brought on by the pain flaring in my left arm: a man grabbing me, hurting me. And then that sound he made . . . his eyes rolling back . . .

I tried to shake off the thought, but couldn't. I'd wanted to hurt him, but was I really that strong? Had Alice seen it? She hadn't said anything at the time.

"What happened?" I asked.

"You fell asleep," she croaked.

Her arms still circled, dragging the paddle through the water. I noticed the blades at both ends—another discovery I couldn't explain. The only predictable part of this was how natural she looked, even though the double-sided motion must have been new to her.

I looked around, tried to get my bearings. I had no idea where we were. I felt guilty for having left her to navigate the sound alone. "How far to go?"

"Three miles. We'll be lucky to arrive before dawn." As she said it, she picked up the pace.

I was going to ask her how she could be so sure, but then I remembered what she'd told me in the lighthouse. No wonder her dead-reckoning skills were more accurate than everyone else's—she was seeing her target in an entirely different way.

Still she paddled faster, strokes like hammer blows against the water. When she stopped, she leaned over the side and dry-heaved.

"Are you all right?" A stupid question, but I didn't know what else to say.

She retched again. "I'm so thirsty."

"We could drink sound water. Just a tiny amount."

"No. Rose said not to."

She ran the back of her hand across her forehead and licked the sweat off it.

"Why don't you let me take over?"

For once, she didn't hesitate. She placed the paddle between us and curled up in the bow of the canoe, eyes shut tight.

I grasped the metal shaft and pushed the paddle blades into the water—first one side, then the other. It felt strange at first, but soon I was alternating strokes smoothly. Even with just me paddling, the canoe slid through the water. Had the Guardians known about this too?

I followed the contour of Roanoke Island, heading north. Waves lapped the sides and spilled into the bottom. The water sloshed around Alice, but she didn't seem to care. She had nothing left, whereas I felt stronger after my rest. Or whatever it had been.

"I'm sorry," she murmured. "For not helping, I mean."

"You don't need to apologize. You saved us."

"What about the thing I told you in the lighthouse? I guess you want me to apologize for not telling you before, right?"

I didn't answer. I'd need far more than an apology for that. The girl who'd dedicated her life to revealing the Guardians' lies was a liar too. Even when we'd touched each other's hands—shared that connection—she'd made a lie of it. How much of the Alice I thought I knew was real at all?

I paddled harder. If it had been my secret, I would've trusted Alice. Told her everything I was. How could you care about someone and not share who you really are? How could you take several trips to Roanoke Island without telling your only true friend? How could you suspect the colony was built on lies, and not share that?

Rose would've trusted me. Rose would've told me everything.

I was angry. I needed to slow down. I wouldn't have the energy to make it back otherwise.

"How did you know this canoe was hidden in the creek?" I asked.

"I've told you. I know every grain of sand on Hatteras."

"Every drop of water too?"

"More or less."

She was tired. I should have let her rest, but I was sick of lies. "Why can't you just tell me the truth for a change?"

Her eyes snapped open, jaw tense. Then, just as suddenly, she relaxed. "All right. A couple years ago I started exploring all the inlets on Hatteras, so I could make my own map of the island. I noticed the channel we just used near Bodie Lighthouse. Halfway along, there was a small bridge made of stone, like the buildings in Skeleton Town. I couldn't paddle my canoe under it, so I got out. That's when I stepped on this. I knew it was a canoe—or something like it—tethered underwater with rope. But it didn't make any sense to me, so I left it be."

"Did you tell the Guardians?"

"No. I thought they'd put it there. I knew there was a contingency plan, and I figured this must be part of it." She sighed. "That's what I thought, anyway."

"But not anymore."

"No. For one thing, they've had the contingency plan ever since your mother was killed. If this had stayed underwater for thirteen years, it'd be covered in silt. Plus, it was the only hidden canoe I ever found—trust me, I looked everywhere— and look at it. It's not made of wood, and the paddles are so different. A lot faster too. Now that we know the seer has been living in the lighthouse, I figure it must be hers."

"Then where is she? And why did she leave it behind?"

"I don't know."

"And why haven't you ever seen or heard her? You've had this element all your life—"

"It's *not* an element!" She closed her eyes again. "It's not, all right? And I already told you—I can make objects appear closer, but only when I'm already looking at them. How should I have known she was in Bodie Lighthouse when no one else did? She's obviously worked hard to stay hidden."

"True."

There was silence after that. Alice's breathing became slow and even. In spite of my frustration, I hoped she wouldn't be too cold. She seemed too exhausted to feel much of anything.

As I paddled on, my thoughts returned to the pirates' conversation. They honestly believed that either Griffin or I could be a solution to the Plague. But how could a disease be solved? What did that even mean?

And why did they think the Plague had reached Roanoke Island? We'd been sheltering there during hurricanes for my entire life. There was no question that the island was Plague-free. And what difference would a map make?

The sun was almost rising as the bridge emerged from behind a shroud of mist. My body felt numb, arms and hands and back worn out. Alice was still sprawled across the floor of the canoe, legs jutting out at awkward angles. She looked half-dead, but woke suddenly when I stopped paddling.

She rested on her elbow and took in her surroundings. Then she pulled the rolled-up maps from her pocket and spread out the top one. "We should head in here," she said, pointing to the left.

"This isn't the channel that leads to Skeleton Town."

"No. It's part of this channel system called The Maze. If we get in there we'll be out of sight of the pirates. We can hide the canoe as well, so they won't find it." She lay back down. "It gives us another escape option."

As I pulled into the creek, I took a final look at distant Pond Island. Fires still burned, and the figures beside them were visible too now. There were even more men than before. To the left was the soaring bridge, its span interrupted by a single large gap.

Two more strokes and the bridge disappeared from view, hidden behind reeds. But my mind remained locked on the gap. I wasn't paddling anymore.

Alice sat up. "What is it? What did you see?"

I pointed to the map, still open in her hands. "I know why Dare wanted that. I know why the map changes everything."

CHAPTER 26

We grounded the canoe and dragged it onto land. Alice was right: With needlerush on three sides, no one would find it unless they knew exactly where to look.

"So what's on the map?" she asked again as we headed toward Skeleton Town.

I was about to tell her when she flapped it in front of me impatiently. "We're wasting time, Thom."

I didn't respond. I hated that she kept so many secrets and yet assumed I'd share everything. It felt good to be the one with answers for a change.

She raised an eyebrow. "Oh, I get it. You really do want me to apologize for not telling you what I can do, right? Well, I'm not going to. Because I'm *not* sorry."

"You sure about that? You seemed plenty guilty in the lighthouse."

She looked confused for a moment, but then her expression cleared. "Because I cried, you mean? That's because I didn't want to tell you. From now on I have to count on you not to tell anyone. *Anyone*. And if you want to know the truth, I don't trust you to keep your mouth shut." Her smile felt venomous. "If I'm sorry about anything, it's that you know my secret. Believe me, every single person in this colony has one just as big."

"You're wrong. I have no secrets."

"If you say so."

She brushed the needlerush aside and pressed ahead. She didn't stop until we were on the edge of Skeleton Town. "You really don't get it, do you? You think you're going to walk into the shelter and solve the puzzle for us. But it won't work like that."

"Everyone deserves to know what's going on."

"Everyone? Or Rose?" She tilted her head to the side. "You sure you want to tell her that Bodie Lighthouse is open, and your grandmother is alive, and there are identical maps, and—oh, yes—a picture of your family that defies explanation? If you're smart, you'll keep quiet about the map, and you'll hide that picture where no one will see it. Because it's *your* family—not mine, not Rose's. And something tells me she'd choose to shut you out before she'll accept her family's as mixed up in all this as yours is."

I hated how confident she was in every word. Even more, I hated that she was right.

I hesitated, but it was just for show. Alice was prepared to wait. "All right, fine. The reason your father tore the mainland section off his map is because it's uninhabitable; the Plague is there. It's like it no longer exists to him. I think the seer did the same thing, except she crossed out the mainland instead. She did it in stages too, like she was tracking the Plague's progress. But she never crossed out Roanoke Island."

Alice's eyes grew wide. "Of course—because the Plague never got there. And because he saw the map, Dare knows it too." She nodded. "But what does it have to do with the bridge? That's what you were looking at when you realized all this."

Did she miss *anything*?

"There are gaps in both bridges leading from Roanoke Island," I explained. "It makes sense to have a gap in the mainland bridge—stops rats from crossing and bringing the Plague. What doesn't make sense is for the Guardians to put a hole in the bridge between Roanoke and Hatteras."

"Hold on. You think the *Guardians* did that?"

"Yes. On your father's map, the gaps are marked in the same handwriting as the grove and the store. Plus, the picture I found in the lighthouse shows that Skeleton Town was destroyed *after* I was born."

"But how would they do that?"

"I don't know. But I think I know *why* they did it: They wanted to make it look like the Plague was on Roanoke Island. It worked too. The pirates still believe it. At least, they did until Dare saw the map."

Alice began pacing in circles. I could tell she wasn't convinced.

"Look, the pirates landed on Hatteras thirteen years ago and stole everything, right?" I continued. "Well, what if we'd

183

still been living on Roanoke Island now? They'd have taken everything—the boats, food, clothes. All these things we don't have the materials to make. What I'm saying is, maybe it wasn't us the Guardians were worried about. Maybe it was the pirates."

With every word, I grew more certain that I was right; and that Alice was coming around too. All the same, it was a while before she stopped pacing. "It's true, the hole in the bridge has kept the pirates away. But you're forgetting two things."

I tried to hide my irritation. "What?"

"The Guardians have been keeping *us* away too. Why? Why not just tell us the truth? It doesn't add up." She continued walking.

I hurried to catch up. "What's the other thing?"

"The Guardians gave up an easy life on Roanoke for a harder and more dangerous one on Hatteras. Who moves their colony and destroys a bridge just in case pirates decide to visit?" She paused to let me answer, but probably knew I wouldn't. "No, I think the Guardians must've been absolutely certain the pirates would come back. Now, how on earth would they know that?"

Rose was kneeling on the grass beside the shelter. I almost called out to her, but then remembered that Alice was with me. The situation felt strange and uncomfortable.

As soon as she saw me, Rose's face brightened. "You're back!" She sounded relieved, as though our arrival could undo all the other problems we had yet to face. There were dark circles under her eyes.

Dennis lay on the ground beside her, deathly pale. Rose dipped a cloth into a bowl of water and wrung it out. She laid it carefully across her brother's forehead.

It wasn't until Alice walked past us and into the shelter that I felt comfortable joining her. "What happened to Dennis?"

"It started last night. He woke up a few strikes after you left. At first he was just moaning, but he got louder and louder. And then he threw up. I gave him sips of water, but he couldn't keep them down. I've never seen anything like it. I swear, I thought he was going to die."

She dunked the cloth in the water again, and this time I could see that it was a strip of her tunic that she'd torn off. It made her appear even more ragged.

"You should take some of the new clothes," I said.

She followed my eyes to her tunic. Then she folded her arms across her chest like she was trying to hide. I felt bad for saying anything. She'd been too busy tending to her brother to worry about how she looked.

"Where's Griffin?" I asked.

"In the shelter. He didn't sleep much either. Spent most of the night reading that book from your dune box. Something has him excited, but I couldn't follow what he was trying to tell me." She pinched the bridge of her nose and closed her eyes. One deep breath, and she opened them again, ready to continue—ready to be pretend she wasn't really suffering. "Griffin was sweet—wanted to help me, but I couldn't let

185

him touch Dennis in case . . ." She bit her lip. "You know."

Yes, I knew. In case he foresaw Dennis's death.

"I saw that picture he drew of Guardian Lora," she continued.

"It's good, isn't it?"

"Hmm. Why did he draw her after she'd died?"

"He didn't. She was still alive. He drew it the evening we got here."

"I don't think so."

"Trust me. I was with him when he drew it."

Rose shook her head. "There's just something creepy about it. The way he has these visions."

"It's not his fault. You can see what it does to him."

"I didn't mean . . ." She turned red. "I'm sorry. It must be hard for you too—when it happens."

I shrugged.

"It's okay to say it, Thomas. I know you like to be strong for Alice, but you can be honest with me. You must realize how alike we are—devoting ourselves to our younger brothers."

It was true—I had always devoted myself to Griffin—but not for the reasons she thought. I did it because I wanted others to see him the way I did. I wanted the Guardians to acknowledge his intelligence and determination. His self-sufficiency. Instead, most of them couldn't see past his limp, and had learned barely a handful of our signs.

Rose dabbed Dennis's face with the cloth and shivered.

"Do you want a blanket?" I asked.

"No. We haven't been out here long. I just needed some

186

fresh air. It was so stuffy in the shelter." She draped the cloth across Dennis's forehead. He didn't respond at all.

"Is he going to get better?"

"I don't know. Normally the echo is worst as the storm approaches, so maybe he's over the hardest part. Then again, the storm's not here yet. It could be approaching for the rest of the day. In which case . . ." She took a steadying breath. "He was muttering during the night. Things about the wind and clouds, and where the storm will make landfall."

"Like your father."

"No." She faced me then, eyes bright and earnest. "My father would tell us within a hundred miles where the eye of the storm would pass. Dennis told me to within a mile. *One mile*. There's something strange going on here, Thomas. I don't know if Roanoke Island is cursed, or what. But no one is the same here."

As soon as she'd said the words, she looked away. At least it saved me having to state the obvious: One of us was still the same.

She returned her attention to Dennis. With his eyes closed and face ghostly white, it was as though the hurricane had already passed through, and he was its first victim.

CHAPTER 27

I wanted to see Griffin. If he'd spent most of the night reading the journal, it must be important. But Alice was leaning against the shelter door, staring at the sound.

Had she been spying on Rose and me? Given what I knew about her now, it wouldn't have been difficult.

Without turning around, she passed a small piece of paper over her shoulder. "This is what was stuck between the maps. I think you should read it."

I studied the tiny words, so perfectly formed. It didn't look like any handwriting I'd ever seen.

PLAGUE FEARS INTENSIFY AS EXODUS NEARS COMPLETION

Mandatory evacuations of east and west seaboards almost complete. 92 percent of population relocated to central states.

All coastal cities shut down pending biohazard clearance.

Government sources dismiss reports of new strain of Plague in three refugee camps as scaremongering.

Food and water rationing remains in effect as drought conditions persist.

Fuel restricted to government and emergency use only.

The paper was torn at the bottom, so I read it again. It made no more sense than before. "What does this mean? Fuel. Water rationing. Biohazard. I've never heard of these things."

"I know one thing it means: The Plague didn't come first. Whatever the *exodus* was, it came before everything else."

Alice had unrolled the two maps she'd taken from the lighthouse. She pointed to the bottom left-hand corner of the one I didn't recognize. "Look at this."

It was a scale, I knew that much. But instead of measuring fractions of miles, it measured hundreds of miles.

Alice watched me closely. "Now look over here." Her finger drifted to the far right-hand side, to what looked like a tiny island. But it wasn't the island she was pointing at. It was the word written beside it: *Hatteras.*

I knew what it must mean, but I couldn't comprehend it.

Alice's finger slid a tiny degree to the left. "If that's Hatteras—*our* Hatteras—then this is Roanoke." She stabbed the outline, barely larger than a dot. "Which means that everything else you see is the mainland."

I looked at the vast expanse of land. I'd always figured the mainland was bigger than either Hatteras or Roanoke. But this was unthinkable.

"Do you suppose the Guardians—"

"Know? Of course they know. But if that piece of paper is right and the Plague started in the center and spread out all the way to the coasts, then none of the mainland is inhabitable."

"Why keep it a secret, though?"

"Maybe the Guardians didn't want us to know that all this was lost," she said, sweeping her hand across the map.

"Do you honestly believe that?"

"Not at all. And neither do you, which is progress. But then, maybe we don't have all the information. If we ever see them again, I sure have a lot of questions I'd like to ask."

I studied the map, and tried to imagine what that much land would look like. Barely a moment passed before Alice inhaled sharply.

She pointed toward the bridge. "They're crossing."

"What?" I pressed the binoculars to my eyes and focused. The pirates weren't hard to see—there were about thirty of them on the bridge. They ambled along like they had all the time in the world. Maybe I was being paranoid, but it felt deliberate, as though Dare wanted us to know he was in no hurry because we had nowhere left to run. "There's so many of them!"

"Keep your voice down," snapped Alice. "There's no need to make Rose—"

Footsteps scuffed the road behind us. "No need to make me *what?*" demanded Rose.

190

Alice tilted her head toward the bridge. "The pirates are coming."

Rose didn't seem affected by the news at all. Instead she watched Alice and me, our arms almost touching, heads locked conspiratorially over a mysterious map we hadn't yet shared.

"We should head behind the shelter," I said. "Get out of sight."

Rose pursed her lips. "Why bother? They know we're here."

"Yes. But right now, we need to focus on us, not them." I pressed the issue by walking back toward the grass. I trusted the others to follow.

They did, and as they turned the corner, the shelter door opened and Griffin joined them. When he saw me, his face fell.

I. Wait. You. His signs were large and accusing. He didn't give me a chance to explain, though; just opened up our father's journal and stabbed the page.

Before I could tell him to look at the bridge, Alice pointed at his journal. "I've got one of those," she told me. "It's full of the same yellow pages. Lots of little writing."

"You should show it to Grif—"

My brother closed the book with a snap, and thrust an open palm in the air: *Sign.*

I hadn't seen him so angry in years. He'd spied the pirates now, and his eyes flitted back and forth between them and the journal. It was like he was still wasn't sure which was more important.

"We need to run," said Alice, taking charge. "The boats are ready to sail."

I relayed the words to Griffin as Rose shook her head vigorously. "Sail where?" She pointed at Dennis. "He can't move, let alone run. Anyway, what's the point?"

"The point is our families are still alive. But only as long as the pirates don't catch us."

"How do you know that?"

Every question felt like an accusation, and they were speaking too fast for me to sign now. I usually liked that about signing—it slowed conversation down, allowed us to linger on details. Now, as I floundered around for the correct word, I cursed myself.

Griffin stomped the ground and raised his palm again. *Sign!*

Alice stepped into the road. "The pirates are moving faster."

I raised my hands and tried to explain what Alice and I had found out. "Last night, we got close to the pirates. We saw them, and heard them talking. They said the Guardians are being held prisoner on the ship."

Why? Griffin responded.

"Their leader is after something . . . some*one*," I explained. "He says one of us is the solution to the Plague."

Rose furrowed her brows. "What does that mean? How can anyone *solve* the Plague?"

"We can't. It doesn't make any sense. But he's got a whole lot of men believing him, and they're heading this way. And when he captures us, the Guardians will die. He said so."

"They're almost at the gap," Alice shouted. "They can only cross one at a time, but after that they'll move quickly."

Rose turned to me. "Do you know which of us they want?"

I hadn't considered how I'd explain this part to Griffin. There wasn't time to think it through either, so I clasped my hands behind my back. "A boy. They said they've been looking for the solution for the past thirteen years, so . . . it can only be Griffin or me."

Griffin kicked at the ground. *Sign!*

Rose looked sorry that she'd asked at all. But there was no getting away from it now—he had to know. I relayed the information with shaking hands.

"Can we hide?" Rose asked. "All of us together."

"I don't think so. We'd just be delaying things. They'll find us. Eventually."

She crouched down and ran her fingers through her hair, tugged at the knots in it, but her eyes never left me. "Then you should both go. Alice too. I'll stay here with Dennis. Try to throw them off your trail."

"No, you can't stay."

Her eyes drifted to her brother. "I don't have any choice."

"Then we'll stay together."

"No, we won't, Thomas. I can't let you take that chance."

"They're at the gap!" I could feel Alice's desperation. She began to walk down the road like she was being drawn to the sound.

Griffin raised his right hand. *We. Fight,* he signed. I noticed

193

he only pointed to himself and me. He didn't want the others to get hurt.

Seeing his jaw muscles bulge, the fierce look in his eye, I knew he meant it. He must have known as well as me how hopeless it would be, but he was willing to risk everything. This was the Griffin the Guardians never bothered to know. This was my brother. And it was all I could do not to cry.

When I didn't respond, Griffin joined Alice. Was it because he knew that fighting was hopeless? Or because he wouldn't force me to risk my life?

I felt worn out, defeated, as though the pirates were already among us. There was no hiding from them, no hope of running. There was just us five, the survivors, staying together until the bitter end.

Rose stepped toward me. "Go, Thomas. I'll send them the wrong way. I promise."

"You, lie? I don't think you're very good at that." I meant it to sound funny, but regretted it as her face creased up.

"Please don't make this harder for me. In my heart I want to be with you, but you have to go. Because if anything happened to you, I swear I'd—"

I reached forward and rested my fingers on her wooden bangle. She froze, but didn't pull away. She just held her breath as I turned it slowly around her wrist. The wood was smeared with blood and dirt. We stood inches apart and watched the colors blend together.

"I hate that you're seeing me like this," she whispered.

"Like how?"

"A mess."

"You're not a mess. You're pretty."

"No, I'm not. I don't know how much longer we can hold out."

"Shh."

I slid my little finger underneath the bangle and touched the smooth pale skin inside her wrist. A part of me was waiting for her to pull away, though I hoped so much that she wouldn't. Rose closed her eyes and sighed. I immersed myself in the energy flooding through me. My finger felt hot. Alive.

Rose opened her mouth, furrowed her brows, and released a sound that was half sigh, half moan. Her energy surged.

Rapid footsteps from the road intruded on the silence. "You're not going to believe this!"

I pulled back immediately, but Alice was already there. It was obvious that she'd seen us.

"You need to come," she continued, all business.

Rose and I joined her on the road. I raised the binoculars and saw the pirates were still on the bridge. But they weren't moving. It looked like they'd stopped at the gap, and decided not to continue. Even stranger, they were talking—all of them at once, and most of them were facing Dare. They looked furious.

Dare didn't react at all. He was too busy training his telescope on me.

"What's he doing?" muttered Alice.

Suddenly a red-faced pirate knocked the telescope from Dare's eye. It fell to the ground. He yelled at Dare as the other pirates formed a group behind him. I didn't need to hear them to feel the tension.

Still Dare said nothing. He didn't flinch. He just waited calmly as the man continued his tirade. Then, as the pirate paused for breath, Dare grabbed his tunic and lifted him off the ground. In a fluid motion he swung the man around and let go.

The man didn't fall onto the road, though. There wasn't any road. He dropped like a stone eighty feet into the sound.

The whole time, Dare stared in our direction. Even when he signaled for the pirates to retreat, he kept his eyes fixed on us. But his expression had changed now. He looked crazed, demonic, as he raised his hands above his head and clapped them together.

Over and over again.

CHAPTER 28

didn't know what to say. It was too bizarre. Even Alice was lost for words.

"Are they . . . retreating?" asked Rose.

"Yes," replied Alice.

"Why?"

No one answered. We should have felt relieved—pleased, even—but it made no sense. I was certain it had nothing to do with us.

"What's happening?" pressed Rose. "For days they won't cross. When they finally do, they stop halfway."

"They didn't cross before now because they thought Roanoke Island was Plague-ridden," I said.

Alice flashed me a glance, but Rose didn't notice. "Why would they think that?"

"Because the colony was on Hatteras. And because there's a hole in the bridge, as though people were afraid rats would cross over from Roanoke."

"But they saw us here yesterday."

"The Plague needs time to take effect. They didn't want to cross until they were sure it was safe."

"How do they know it's safe now?"

Alice's eyes bored into me. The answers were right there, on her maps. Didn't Rose deserve to know the world she lived in?

Then I thought of her hands, covered in filthy bandages, and the shadows under her eyes. And Dennis, alone behind the shelter.

"The pirates gave us two days," I began, the half truth slipping out more easily than I would have imagined. "None of us seem affected, which gives them hope. Makes them think this solution is real."

Rose didn't respond at first. I worried that she'd seen through my hesitation and Alice's furtive glances. "You seem to have all the answers."

"We overheard the pirates—"

"So you say. Did the pirates say why they planned to stop halfway across the bridge, by any chance?"

I shook my head.

Rose ran a finger along my sleeve. "Pity. I hate secrets."

Rose said we needed food, and vegetable roots weren't enough. She said she'd catch a fish or two. After all, Alice could start a fire whenever she liked now that the pirates knew where we were.

I said I'd join her to collect kindling. I hoped she'd be pleased, but she didn't seem to care.

Alice wanted to come too, so that she could inspect the bridge, try to work out what might have happened with the pirates. First, I asked her to give Griffin the journal from her dune box. If anyone could piece together the information in those pages, it was Griffin. He offered to keep an eye on Dennis too. Still, Rose said nothing.

Rose and I walked in silence. I wanted her to touch my tunic again, to make a connection between us. But she seemed distracted. It was as if she knew I'd lied to her.

"I don't know what's going to happen to Dennis," she said finally. "His element is consuming him. It's like Griffin's visions—he doesn't control his element anymore; his element controls him." She paused. "I don't know why I'm telling you all this. I guess I just don't want there to be any secrets between us."

Alice pulled alongside us. I was grateful. Rose's remarks felt calculated, and I didn't know how to respond. But the farther we walked, the more it felt like a chasm separated the three of us. With every step, silence forced us apart.

When we reached the bridge, Alice headed for the gap, and Rose and I continued down to the water's edge.

"Did you see Lora die?" she asked.

The question caught me off guard. "What do you mean?"

"It's a yes-or-no question."

"Yes. Who told you?"

"No one. You and Alice and Griffin spent half the next day asleep, so I figured you'd been awake all night. Why didn't you tell me?"

She stepped backward into the water, waiting for my reply.

She didn't even bother to raise the hem of her tunic. It floated around her like a cloud.

I wanted to answer, but couldn't. Words would just confirm my guilt. But I was losing her. I had to say something. "I just . . . didn't think of it."

She wore a distant smile. "My father coddles me, Thomas. He thinks I don't notice the things that go on in our colony. Thinks I don't know there are lies." She drew a deep breath. When she placed her palms flat against the surface of the water, they shook. Not from fear, or from nerves, but from anger. I could see it in her rigid pose and hear it in her voice. "Do you coddle me too?"

"No."

She drew another breath, and let the air slide between her teeth in a hiss. "I hope that's true."

I barely recognized this version of Rose. Maybe it was sleep-deprivation, but every word had an edge that made her seem more like Alice. Only, I didn't want her to be like Alice. I wanted her to be Rose. I wanted her to be the person who saw the best in everyone.

"I'm sorry that you have to do this," I said, waving my hand across the water. "I know the echo hurts you."

"I don't care about the pain. I'll kill every fish in the sound if that's what it takes to keep us alive."

Her words chilled me. I knew I ought to be collecting driftwood, but I couldn't take my eyes off her. She looked different than I'd ever seen—stronger, as though she were summoning fish rather than coaxing them.

Something in the water brushed by her, but Rose didn't move. The fish had been spared. Oddly, it didn't swim away, though. It just continued toward the shore.

Straightaway, there was another fish, and another, circling around her and leaping out of the water as if they were trying to be caught.

Still Rose didn't move.

Before I could ask if she was all right, the first fish leaped out of the water and landed beside me. It flapped about uselessly, gills opening and closing in a desperate attempt to stay alive. I stood frozen to the spot as it died slowly before me.

There were more fish now. They came suddenly, darting toward Rose, slapping against her hands. The surface of the water turned white with their splashing. But Rose didn't move, and they continued onward, sacrificing themselves on the shore.

"Rose." I called her name, but she didn't answer. "Rose!"

She raised her head and closed her eyes. She seemed locked in place, unable to move or stop. The surface of the water was no longer visible. It shone like silver fire.

I ran into the sound, but tripped on the mass of slick bodies swarming around my legs. When I surfaced they pressed against me, furiously making their escape. I tried to forge a path through them, but I may as well have been fighting a wall. And Rose was sinking under them. She'd summoned them to her, and now they were claiming her.

"Rose!" The force of a hundred fish drove me back to the shore. "Rose!"

She didn't even struggle as her shoulders dipped below the surface; her head too. She was completely submerged. And no matter how loudly I shouted her name, she didn't respond.

Fish flew onto the shore. I held my arm up to protect myself. Through the glittering bodies I stared at the space where she'd been standing. Rose had disappeared completely, just as though she had offered to die too.

CHAPTER 29

ose!" I called her name, louder and louder. I tried to force my way through the wall of fish again. Failed.

There was nothing to see but a mirror-like mass of bodies fighting on the surface. They twisted and rippled like water. I couldn't even guess where Rose had gone under anymore.

Several yards away, something plummeted from the sky. It hit the water hard, shock waves scattering the fish. The swell pushed them straight to me.

Before I could work out what had happened, Alice rose from the water. She swam for a couple yards. When her feet touched the ground, she pushed toward the shore, dragging her hands beside her. Finally she stopped and ducked under. When she resurfaced, she held Rose's arm in her hands.

I forced my way back in and grabbed Rose's sleeve. Together, Alice and I pulled her onto the shore.

Rose collapsed on the ground, coughing up water. Reeds pierced her clothes, but it hardly mattered—they were ruined anyway. Once she caught her breath, she just lay there. With her eyes wide open, unblinking, she looked eerily similar to the fish dying all around her.

"What just happened?" cried Alice. She was shaking. Limping too. That's when it dawned on me what she'd just done: She'd jumped from the bridge towering over us.

I stared up at the giant arch. She'd leaped into the water beyond where Rose had been standing, but it may still have been only two yards deep. She could've killed herself.

"What happened, Rose?" Alice repeated, softer this time.

Rose swallowed hard. "I was angry. So I summoned every fish. I just wanted to be quick, get it over with. But they all came. It was like they needed to die."

"And what about you?" I asked. "What happened to *you*?"

Rose blinked at last. "I don't know. One moment I was in control, the next . . . it felt like my element controlled me."

Alice pulled back her right trouser leg. A gash ran across her knee and down the side of her lower leg. It was bleeding heavily.

"Thank you for saving me," said Rose.

"You're welcome," Alice replied. But it was me she was looking at.

Alice carried four fish back to the shelter. She hobbled the whole way, while Rose stopped periodically to rest. My arms were laden with wood, so I couldn't help either of them.

Alice arranged the wood carefully and prepared to create fire. She had barely begun to rub her hands together before a sliver of yellow flame sliced through the air. Moments later, the kindling was ablaze. Two days before, I'd assumed she'd never conjure an open flame. Now she resembled the young girl in Griffin's picture—confidently issuing flames like it was the most ordinary thing in the world.

So what had happened in the lighthouse? She'd barely managed a single errant spark there.

"This is why the Guardians kept us away from Roanoke," murmured Rose. "When we're here, we can make our elements do unthinkable things. But our elements can make us do unthinkable things too."

Alice placed two fish end to end on the spit. We watched the fire growing, steam and smoke mingling as the water evaporated from the fish, and the oils in their skin seeped out.

"Did it hurt, almost drowning?" I asked.

Rose shook her head slightly. "No. I wanted it. The power I was feeling . . . it was awesome. I've never felt anything like it." She paused. "I shouldn't have let it happen, though. When I felt the element growing, I should've pulled back. I let it consume me."

"Why?"

"Because I was angry at you. I wanted you to see how powerful I can be. I wanted you to know that we can all have secrets. Difference is, I choose to share mine."

She watched me, waited for me to tell her everything I knew. For a long moment, she didn't even blink. Finally, she glanced over my shoulder at Alice as if she'd found her answer there.

"You should get some sleep," she told me.

"So should you. You spent most of the night looking after Dennis. Go on. We'll switch in a couple strikes. I promise."

Rose stood uneasily and made her way toward the steps. When she was out of sight, Alice leaned back from the fire.

"Are you all right?" I asked.

She inspected the gash on her knee. "It'll heal."

"Did you find anything interesting on the bridge?"

A spark returned to her eyes. "Nothing at all. Not even the planks. No one can cross that bridge anymore."

"Where have the planks gone?"

"By the looks of it, someone moved them."

"Who?"

"I don't know. But the pirates have been watching that bridge for two days. So it must've happened before that."

My hand gravitated to the picture in my pocket. When I pulled it out, I looked at the woman with the cat at her heels. Perhaps the seer, my grandmother, had been even busier than we thought.

"Will the pirates get another plank?"

Alice thought about this. "I guess so. Why else would they retreat?"

The clouds were thickening behind Hatteras. Twisting. Merging. Normally there would have been lightning and thunder by now. Rain too. I almost wished the storm had been in full effect already. To see such clouds without rain and lightning felt even more threatening.

Griffin emerged from the shelter and joined us. Instinctively, I slid the picture back inside my pocket. Then I wished

I hadn't. Which secrets was I keeping, and from whom? Did I even know anymore?

Griffin didn't seem to notice. He clasped both journals to his chest, and strode confidently toward me, barely a hint of his usual limp. Even Alice must have noticed, because she left the fire and joined us.

Look, he signed before he'd even sat down. The gesture was large, like he couldn't hold it in.

He opened the journal from our father's dune box and flicked through until he found the picture of the girl with flames on her fingers. *VIRGINIA*. As before, I was struck by how old the yellowed pages looked, how strange the girl's appearance. Dennis had unearthed many clothes in Skeleton Town, but none that looked like hers.

On the reverse side of the page was the distinctive handwriting that filled the journal: tiny letters tied together with swirls and tails.

Griffin tapped the page. *Read.*

It told the story of a shipwreck in the channel connecting the sound to the ocean; presumably the Oregon Inlet. The turbulent water had claimed seven men. In spite of that, the writer had pressed on to Roanoke Island in search of his family. He was convinced they were there when he saw *"a great smoke rise in the Ile Roanoke near—"*

There the story ended.

I turned the page, but the words didn't follow. It made no sense. I was about to ask Griffin for an explanation when he placed Alice's open journal beside our father's.

I didn't need to read the new page twice to realize it continued mid-sentence from my father's page:

"—*the place where I left our Colony in the year 1587, which
smoke put us in good hope that some of the Colony were there
expecting my return out of England.*"

The pages had been mixed up—that much was clear. But
why?

Before I could ask, Griffin pointed to a passage farther
down the new page:

"*. . . before we were half way between our ships and the shore
we saw another great smoke to the Southwest . . . we therefore
thought good to go to that second smoke first: but it was much
further from the harbour where we landed, than we supposed
it to be, so that we were very fore tired before we came to the
smoke. But that which grieved us more was that when we came
to the smoke, we found no man nor sign that any had been
there lately—*"

I read the pages again, one after another. When I looked
up, Alice was staring at me. A part of me still wanted to believe
that the colony being referred to was Skeleton Town. But I
knew it wasn't.

Whoever had written this had done so long before the
foundations of Skeleton Town were laid.

CHAPTER 30

riffin closed the journals. He was the keeper of something inexplicable but undoubtedly precious, and from the way he held the books, I could tell he knew it.

Show. More, I signed.

He shook his head. *Not. Everything.* He watched my blank expression and used a sign I hadn't seen in months: *Incomplete.*

"What's he saying?" asked Alice.

"He says it's incomplete. There must still be pages missing." I turned to Griffin. *Where. Pages?*

Griffin pointed east, toward Hatteras. *Dune. Box*, he explained. *Rose.*

"The remaining pages must have been inside Kyte's dune box," I told Alice. "But why would they split the book up in the first place?"

"In case we ever found one of the dune boxes. Which means they really didn't want us knowing this." Alice used her sleeve to wipe away the blood streaming from her leg. "The Guardians sure do like their secrets, don't they?"

Griffin continued to stare into the distance. I guessed that he was thinking about the final dune box. Was it still there, lying on the beach? Had someone picked it up? Would it be washed away in the coming hurricane?

Would the story he held so gently in his hands ever be complete again?

That's when I realized something else too: Griffin was embracing this new version of our past. More than that, he was determined to piece it together, step by painstaking step.

I pulled the mysterious picture from my pocket and handed it to him. His eyes grew wide as he placed a finger beside our father's head. Then he pointed to the woman with the cat wrapped around her feet.

Our. Grandmother, I explained.

Again, he seemed surprised rather than shocked. His eyes moved to the other woman—our mother. She was taller than the older woman, but the family resemblance was striking.

I wished I'd shown him the portrait of our mother that I'd found. Now it would seem like I'd been keeping things from him too.

Something else caught my eye then—something I hadn't noticed before. There was a door behind my father, and beside it, a small rectangular object. From the look of it, it was metal. And though I couldn't read the word that was written on it, I was fairly certain I already knew.

Come, I signed.

"Where are you going?" asked Alice.

"To find our grandmother."

"Where?"

I held up the picture. "In the clinic."

The broken glass in the clinic door sparkled as the sun momentarily appeared behind us. Through it, I could see the imprint of my footsteps from previous visits.

I signaled to the others to follow me, and we headed inside. "This is where Lora sent me the night she died."

Alice wore a quizzical expression. "What did she want here?"

"A container. She called it 'aspirin.'"

"What's that?"

"I don't know. I never found it. She gave me precise directions, though." I walked over to the shelves on the right. "It should've been right here on the second shelf."

"Well, it's not. And that's hardly your fault."

I nodded absently, but I was still looking at the shelf. It was covered in a thick layer of dust—several years' worth, probably—except for one circle toward the middle. Something had been sitting there until very recently. But who would have taken the container? Who even knew I was looking for it?

A seer perhaps? Someone who was happy to see Lora die?

I tried to cast the thought aside. Toward the back of the

clinic, Alice was searching inside every cupboard, under every table. Griffin was running his hands along the interior walls, his face a picture of concentration.

"This is where I found the lantern," I said. "Right there on that table."

"Do you think the seer wanted you to find something?"

I glanced around. "It's possible. But I don't see anything obvious, do you?"

This part of the clinic was mostly bare: bright white walls and filthy white floor. A single beam of sunlight filtered in, illuminating the particles of dust that spun in eddies around the room. Chairs were toppled over. A rickety ladder rested uneasily against a wall of shelves.

Griffin clapped once, a sound that stopped us in our tracks. Once he had silence he pressed both palms against the wall and closed his eyes. It was the same preparation he had when he was about to use his element. But why now? Unless . . . was he trying to feel vibrations, a sign that we weren't alone?

He pursed his lips and huffed. When he turned to us and shook his head, I had my answer. On Roanoke his element was more sensitive than a Guardian's, it seemed. Was there no end to the island's mysteries?

"I'm going outside," said Alice. "See what's on the roof."

I followed her. There was no point in searching inside anymore. There were no more cupboards to check, and nowhere else to hide. I was certain that the seer had been in the clinic at some point, but equally sure she wasn't there now.

Outside, Alice had kicked off her shoes. She ran her hands across the sheer stone wall, and dug her fingertips into gaps so tiny that I could barely make them out. Then, somehow, she began to climb.

"How are you doing that?"

She stared down at me. "My senses," she answered quietly. "I can tell by touch if something will support my weight. And if I'm strong enough to climb."

As she said it, I felt a pang of jealousy. With every new talent she revealed, Alice went from having one weak element to being perhaps the most extraordinary of all of us.

"Can I help?"

"Yes. Keep Griffin away. If he sees me doing this, he'll have all sorts of questions."

She continued to climb, fingertips uncovering tiny indentations, a single toe pressed into a crack too small for me to see. When she reached the roof, she pulled herself onto it.

"Be careful," I said. "You're pretty high up."

"Hardly."

I peered through the broken glass. Griffin was still inside, running his palms along the wall; but higher up now, hands above his head. He was almost touching the ceiling.

I looked back at Alice, at least five yards off the ground.

Just like that, everything fell into place. "She's not on the roof," I shouted. "I know where she is."

I ran to the back of the clinic, placed my foot on the first rung of the ladder, and climbed to the ceiling. I prodded

213

around for signs of movement. One of the ceiling tiles lifted. I eased it to the side and stood up straight so I could see what was in the space between the ceiling and the roof.

It was dark, but I could still make out two yellow eyes. The animal hissed at me.

Then I detected another figure.

"You shouldn't have come looking," she said.

CHAPTER 31

The sound of her voice—deep and rich—shocked me. All I could think was that this was my grandmother. A woman who'd died when I was still an infant was not dead at all, but alive, and here in Skeleton Town.

"Cat got your tongue?" She shuffled forward and stroked the creature beside her. It purred gratefully in reply. "Never mind," she said, watching my confused expression. "It was a saying we used to have. In the old days."

As my eyes adjusted to the dark I took in the cramped space. Two cloth bags sat in a heap behind her. Even in the low light I could see that she was filthy.

"I thought it was your brother who didn't talk, not you."

"His name's Griffin. Anyway, how do you know that?"

"So he does speak!" She laughed without opening her mouth. "I've stayed hidden for thirteen years, and you're surprised I know about your brother?"

"Why are you hiding from us? Why did everyone tell me you were dead?"

She puffed out her cheeks and exhaled slowly. "Those are good questions. But if we're going to talk, I'd prefer not to stay cramped up here."

"I wasn't the one who made you hide out."

"No, you weren't. But neither was I, Thomas."

Hearing her say my name made me pause. Everything we'd taken for granted had gone; the things we knew had gone were inexplicably returning. The world had turned upside down, and somehow this woman—my grandmother—might know why. Suddenly her bedraggled appearance and over-powering odor filled me with sadness. How had she survived all these years?

I climbed down the ladder. Alice and Griffin were waiting, but they neither spoke nor signed. To be honest, I'm not sure any of us knew what to make of the old woman who followed me, straggly gray hair to her waist, frayed clothes, and quick eyes squinting against the light.

My mind filled with questions, but where should I begin? And what if her answers hurt me even more than the fact she'd been absent from our lives all those years?

It was Alice who broke the silence. "The pirates say you're an ally. So why aren't you helping us?"

The woman laughed, but it sounded strange, like she was out of practice. "Pirates, you say? I think they prefer to call themselves privateers. Though it means much the same thing, I suppose. Anyway, how do you know that?"

"We overheard a conversation last night. Dare said we had an ally now."

She frowned. "Really?"

"Are you an ally, or aren't you?" I asked. I signed for Griffin too.

She thought about this. "I'm here to reconcile you with your families. That's all."

"Doesn't seem that way," snapped Alice. "You've been watching us ever since the pirates landed, haven't you? You could've joined us."

"No. I don't exist."

"Of course you exist. You're here, with us."

"That's not what your Guardians have been telling you for the past thirteen years, though. Right?" She smiled again, but it seemed angry. "Tell me: Exactly how *did* I die? Was it sudden sickness? Drowning? Lost at sea? Really, I'm intrigued."

"Lost at sea."

"Of course. Not very original, but hard to disprove. And you all believed it, which is the main thing. Because whatever happens, we must always trust the Guardians, mustn't we?"

She leaned against the ladder. Beneath the grime, I could see that she wasn't so old after all; certainly younger than Guardian Lora.

I caught up signing to Griffin. When I was done, his eyes remained fixed on me, as if he wasn't comfortable looking at this woman. I could understand why. He'd been told she was dead. Now she was standing before him. Did anything make sense to him anymore?

I pulled the picture from my pocket and turned it toward her.

"Beautiful family." She snorted. "Too bad it's incomplete."

My breath caught. I couldn't believe she'd talk about her own daughter like that.

"I suppose this means you got all the way to the top of Bodie Lighthouse," she continued. "You must've been even busier last night than I realized—braver than I gave you credit for too. What made you want to visit my humble home?"

"Dare said it was important. He seems frightened of you. Is it because you're a seer like him?"

From above us, the cat let out another hiss. The woman responded by raising her arms. The animal obediently leaped into them.

"I doubt it. Not all seers glimpse the future the same way." She began stroking the cat. It nuzzled against her. "Many years ago, your Guardians claimed Dare had the ability to visualize his greatest future need. At the time, that need seemed to be me."

"Why?"

"Probably because I was a doctor. I could heal people."

"People with Plague, you mean?"

She flinched. "No, not that. None of us could cure that." She dug her fingers into the cat's fur and sighed. "What else did he say?"

"He said they'd be crossing the bridge today," said Alice. "Which reminds me: When did you get rid of the plank?"

She smiled. "When you first went back to Hatteras."

"And if we'd needed to cross the bridge, what then?"

"You had canoes. I was far more worried about the pirates crossing than you." She began to walk away.

"Where are you going?"

"Outside. I'd like some fresh air. Is that all right with you?"

She placed the cat on the ground and it trotted ahead of us. We followed in a line, and one by one crawled through the hole in the door.

Outside, the wind was strengthening, the air charged with the threat of weather to come.

"We still don't know your name," I said. "Father used to call you Grandma T, but he never told us your actual name."

"Everyone called me T, not just your father." She filled her lungs with the fresh salt air, and raised her face to the sky. "My name is Tessa."

Hearing that word—*Tessa*—dragged me back to the evening that Lora had died. I could still picture her wrinkled, sallow skin, and hear her rasping breaths. Why would Lora possibly have said my grandmother's name over and over as her life slipped away?

Suddenly that dust-free circle on the shelf inside felt very important indeed.

"I forgot something," I said quickly. "Carry on to the shelter. I'll catch up."

I slid back through the door and through the clinic. Once I was sure no one was following me, I made my way to the ladder, and climbed.

I crawled into the cramped attic space and saw the outline of the two sacks. As I pressed toward them, the ceiling below me shifted ominously.

I tried to spread my weight evenly as I dragged the sacks

back toward the ladder. I was about to throw them onto the ground below, but thought better of it. Better not risk breaking anything. Instead, I swung my legs onto the ladder and opened the first sack. The light was low, but I could make out blankets and a spare tunic. Between them was the lantern I'd found a couple nights earlier; she must have picked it up from the street after I dropped it.

The other sack was heavier. There was a large sheaved knife inside, and various objects I didn't recognize. It would be easier to see them in the light of the clinic.

I was about to close the sack when a white container caught my eye—hard and smooth, no larger than my hand. I removed it and held it close. ASPIRIN was written across it in large letters. Below, in similar but smaller letters, were two words: ARCHARD, LORA.

A faint sound from the clinic stopped me dead. I listened carefully, waiting for it to return, but there was only silence now. So I threw the container back inside the sack and pounded down the steps. I could see most of the building. It was empty.

I took a deep breath to collect myself. Before I could climb back up, I heard the sound again.

I spun around.

Tessa's smile was icy. "Find anything interesting?"

CHAPTER 32

tried to steady my breathing. "Where's Alice and Griffin?" I asked.

Tessa didn't even blink. "I told them to go on. Silly me, I forgot my sacks. Perhaps you'd hand them to me."

There was no point in pretending I didn't understand, so I turned and climbed. I felt her eyes on me with every step. I passed down one sack, then the other. Tessa took them without a word.

By the time I got down again, she was throwing more containers into the sacks. "It's medicine," she explained. "We'll need it for the Guardians."

"You're sure we'll see them again?" I asked hopefully.

"Aren't you?" she replied, avoiding the question.

I stole away and crawled through the door. Along the road, Alice stood at the intersection, staring toward Hatteras. I ran to join her, pleased to leave the clinic behind. "What are you looking at?" I asked.

"Use your binoculars."

I raised the binoculars and scanned the island. I couldn't see a single pirate. But something else was different too: The ship's mast that had been peeking over the trees for the past couple days was gone.

I swung the binoculars south. For a while I saw nothing but the tops of trees, and the ever-thickening clouds. But then I spied the ship's mast. "They're heading toward the Oregon Inlet."

"Yes. It's the only way for them to get·here, now the bridge is impassable. Guess we owe Tessa a thank-you. She's bringing the Guardians closer."

Except for the one she helped to kill, I thought, picturing Lora. I wanted to mention it too, but Tessa was only twenty yards away now.

It could wait.

Griffin sat inside the shelter, piecing together pages from the journals. He faced the wall, and didn't look around as we entered.

A part of me was surprised that he didn't have questions for this woman—she was his grandmother too. But then, she had disappeared before he was even born. There were no miraculous images of the pair of them together. Why should he feel anything for a relative who'd chosen to leave?

On the other side of the room, Rose sat beside Dennis. She had finally changed into some of the new clothes: white shorts and white sleeveless top. I'd never seen so much of her skin before—smooth as the sound, and white as a breaking wave.

When she looked up, I turned red. Then she did too. At least, until she saw Tessa.

"Not a pretty sight, am I," said Tessa, walking toward her. "But it's not me you need to worry about. How long has he been like this?"

"Since the middle of the night."

Tessa knelt beside Dennis and felt his forehead. She lifted the legs of his shorts to reveal his upper thighs. When she pulled them down again, she seemed relieved.

"It's not Plague," I told her.

"You're an expert, are you? What is it, then?"

"It's his echo."

"Ah." She nodded. "So his element is wind. How old is he?"

"Nine," said Rose. "But his element is amazing."

"Naturally." Tessa tried to get Dennis to open his eyes, but he wouldn't.

"He says the light hurts."

"That makes sense." Tessa pursed her lips. "He has a migraine—a kind of headache. It's common for anyone whose element is wind. We think it's linked to atmospheric pressure—as a storm moves in, pressure builds—but who knows? Anyway, I have medicine that'll help."

Tessa removed a container from one of her bags and opened it. She tilted the container and two tiny white discs fell into the palm of her hand. Gently, she lifted Dennis's head and popped them into his mouth. Rose leaned forward anxiously, but she didn't stop Tessa. It was only when

Dennis had swallowed the discs that I worried. There was still so much we didn't know about Tessa. If she'd had a hand in Lora's death, was it so impossible to think she'd do the same to us?

"We need to discuss a plan," said Alice, interrupting my thoughts.

"A *plan?*" Tessa seemed amused. "The way I see it, you have two options: surrender, or hide." She wound her hair behind her ears, but the ends still brushed against the floor. "Right now, Dare and his men are sailing south toward the Oregon Inlet. From there they'll head into the sound and across to the southern end of Roanoke Island. There's a ruined town called Wanchese down there. Dare will lock the Guardians up and then come for you."

"You seem to know a lot about his plans."

"I've lived in these parts my whole life. There are shallows off the southwest corner of Roanoke, and sailors avoid them. Besides, he'll want the Guardians to disembark as far from here as possible."

"Disembark?" repeated Rose hopefully. "You think he'll set the Guardians free?"

"No. I think he'll allow them to leave the ship, but he'll keep them prisoner until they agree to his demands."

"What demands?"

"Isn't it obvious?" groaned Alice. She grabbed a map of Roanoke Island and spread it across the floor. "Ever since the Plague started, the pirates have been stuck at sea just like the clan ships. Now they've discovered this entire island is safe." She waited for Rose to make the connection. "Dare intends to claim Roanoke Island for himself."

Rose flashed Tessa a confused look. "And you want us to *surrender?*"

Tessa clicked her tongue. "The pirates are coming. You can hide, fight, or surrender. The first will be pointless. The second, deadly. Right now, your parents are alive. Your only hope is to join with them. You can't imagine Dare is going to keep them prisoner forever."

"No. He'll kill us all instead."

"If that was his goal, he'd have done it already."

I stepped between them. "No. Rose is right. Dare said no one would be hurt until he found the solution."

Tessa's eyes grew wide, as though she recognized the word. It filled me with dread.

"You've heard of the solution," I said. "Is it Griffin, or me?"

"I don't know."

"How can anyone solve the Plague?"

Tessa hesitated. "Honestly, it makes no sense. Maybe it's a special immune system, or unusual metabolism. Even if you are both protected, I don't see how it could help anyone else. But it doesn't matter what I think. Dare's a seer. People have followed him for years. They don't do that unless they believe him."

Rose swallowed hard. "Once Dare takes over Roanoke, he'll just forget about the solution, right?"

Tessa shook her head.

"Why not?"

Alice reached for the other map—the one that showed the mainland stretching for thousands of miles. "These are Roanoke and Hatteras Islands," she explained, pointing to the tiny outlines. "And this is the mainland." She swept her hand across the map. "If Dare believes the solution can save him from the Plague, then the land is his. If he's willing to kill for Roanoke Island, just imagine what he'll do for all this."

CHAPTER 33

R ose stared at the new map. She'd suspected that we were keeping things from her, and now she had her proof.

Alice held up the piece of paper she'd found between the maps. "This was in the lighthouse too—says the Plague started in the central states."

"Yes," said Tessa. "About a thousand miles west of here, in the middle of the mainland. Killed almost everyone."

"Why didn't people get away? Go back to the coasts?"

"Because everyone from the coasts was still converging in the middle of the country."

"Was that the *exodus*?"

"Exactly. The focus was on getting people safely away from the coasts. Even when reports of the new strain of Plague started circulating, people still came to the refugee camps. But then the fuel ran out and they couldn't leave. The Plague spread. People tried to stop the rats with wildfires, but the land was dry and the fires got out of control. And the rats kept coming. They're scavengers, see—always searching for new sources of food. That's what led them here to the coast. It was the only place left."

"So what was the *exodus*?" I asked.

"An order for everyone living in coastal areas to head inland. It was a time of war—of terrible weapons and gases that turned the air to poison. We all knew such things could happen, and we ignored them. When the first attack came, it destroyed an entire region in half a day. So many dead. The next day, another city. After that, no one needed to be persuaded to leave."

"But you didn't leave."

"No." She looked at the map on the floor. "I'm a seer. I knew . . . things. That the future was here, on this island." She gave a tired smile. "I wish I could've made everyone stay. Saved everyone."

Rose wasn't looking at any of us now. This was so much for her to take on. The fact that Alice and I already knew some of it must have made it even harder to hear.

Meanwhile, Alice was nodding in agreement. The only kind of puzzles she liked were those that had been solved, and Tessa seemed to have all the answers. But there was still one puzzle Alice didn't know about.

"What about Lora?" I asked. "Do you wish you could've saved her too?"

"She was old. Everyone dies eventually."

"Some sooner than others." I walked over to her sacks and

emptied them onto the floor: the clothes, lantern, and containers. "You're a seer. You knew Lora sent me out that night,
and you knew why. Why did you hide the aspirin container?"

"What are you talking about, Thomas?" Rose asked softly.

"The night she died, Lora sent me into Skeleton Town to
find a container. But Tessa had hidden it."

Tessa's face hardened. "I also helped you find your way
back to the shelter in the storm. Or have you forgotten that?"

"But you killed Lora."

"Don't be ridiculous. A heart attack killed her. Nature
killed her. I just stopped her from using aspirin to slow the
process."

"Why?"

"Lora was a drain on all of you. She would've died one way
or another. It just would've taken longer."

"Your name was the last thing she said."

"Oh." Her mouth twisted into a smile. "Good. I'm glad to
think she may have had doubts at the end."

"Doubts about what?"

"Everything. Lying to you all. Exiling me because I
wouldn't promise to stay quiet about the past: the exodus,
Plague, pirates."

"That's why you left?"

"Of course. They'd constructed a perfect bubble for you.
Just you and Nature and the elements. Fairy tales of ship-
wrecks and a brand-new colony. But I wouldn't play along."

"If it was so important for us to know the truth, why didn't you tell us?" demanded Alice. "You've been living six miles away."

"I couldn't risk the Guardians finding out. There are worse fates than exile, you know."

"Like what you did to Lora," I suggested.

"Hmm. Something tells me nothing could've saved her."

"Why?"

Tessa flared her nostrils. "The pirates land under cover of a storm, and Lora dies the same night—quite a coincidence, don't you think? Every Guardian should've been in danger except her. Did something else happen that evening? Was someone else in trouble?"

"Griffin had a vision," said Alice. "Of his father, we thought."

"And how was Griffin afterward?"

"He was in shock . . . sat against the wall and drew."

Tessa began to return the containers to her sack. "And what exactly did Griffin draw?"

"A portrait of Guardian Lora," I said. "Why?"

"No reason." She closed the first sack and opened the second. "I'm sure it's a beautiful portrait. A tribute befitting a hero. Which is more than Lora deserved."

"Why did you hate her so much?"

Tessa looked up sharply. "That miserable woman made you risk your life, Thomas. How could she do that and still call herself a Guardian?"

I knew what she was saying, but I still felt guilty for having failed Lora that night. "She was sick. She didn't even seem awake."

"She was awake enough to choose you to run her errand."

"I was just nearest."

"No. You were the most dispensable."

I swallowed hard. "What are you talking about?"

"You think she couldn't have called out to Ananias or Alice?"

"She was suffering."

"She could've told you to wake them, then. Right?" She gave me a moment to respond. "Lora chose you because if someone was going to risk injury or death, she wanted it to be you."

"Why?"

"Isn't it obvious? Now that you know who you are, you must realize how hard she's worked to hide the truth from you. Her and all the Guardians."

"What truth? Are you talking about the solution?"

"No." Tessa scanned the room. As she did, the others cast their eyes down.

My stomach flipped. "What's going on?"

"You must know. How could you be here on Roanoke Island and not . . ." She shook her head in disbelief. "How can you still be nothing?"

That word again. I'd overlooked it in the past—it was part of being me—but not anymore. And certainly not from her.

My hands balled into fists and I couldn't unclench them. I felt more awake than I had in days. "You don't know anything about me."

"You think I haven't spied on you all these years? Seen you hiding behind dunes, in woods, instead of fighting every last one of them? And what of the lantern?" She lifted it from the ground.

"It broke when I dropped it."

"And when you picked it up?"

"I didn't pick it up."

"Why not?"

"Leave him alone," shouted Rose. "At least he's been here for us. Which is more than you can say."

Tessa turned to Rose and tilted her head. "You know, don't you?"

Rose opened her mouth but didn't respond.

"Know *what*?" I yelled.

Tessa's expression was full of pity. "That you're nothing."

Griffin turned around at last. Had I stamped my foot? Smacked my palm against a wall? I wasn't sure what had alerted him, but he looked frightened.

Rose buried her face in her hands. She was ashamed of me.

I glared at Tessa. "*You* don't get to say that."

"Why not? It's obviously true. Do you hear anyone disagree?"

Now I walked toward her. I didn't know what I was going to do, only that I couldn't hold my anger back anymore.

Alice ran between us. "No, Thom. Don't touch her!"

Before I could push her aside, Alice leaped back. She looked petrified.

She wasn't alone, either. Tessa grasped the lantern and shuffled back until she was pressed against the wall. Panicking, she held the lantern before her like a shield, and when I still didn't stop, finally threw it straight at me.

I raised my hands to defend myself, but it was a slow toss, and easy to catch. And once it was in my hands, I realized she hadn't been trying to hurt me at all.

The light was blinding.

CHAPTER 34

I couldn't look directly at the lantern. It was far too bright. But in its glare I caught a glimpse of everyone's faces—wide-eyed and afraid. They drew back from me, and flinched with every flicker.

For a while I was frozen. Then my hand began to shake, and I became aware of the heat generated by the light and a weird sensation that my body wasn't entirely mine. I dropped the lantern. It went out before it hit the ground.

When my eyes got used to the low light, I saw Tessa leaning against the wall. "All this time, I thought it was impossible that . . ." She didn't finish. She didn't need to.

How had I never realized what I could do?

I drew several quick breaths. "What am I?"

"An elemental. Same as everyone else."

"What kind of element is that?"

"You can channel energy."

I looked at my hands. They seemed the same as before. "How did you know? How do the Guardians know?"

"How do you think? You got your element the same way as everyone else."

"No. My mother was a seer."

"And your father?"

"He's Guardian of the Fire."

"Fire?" she sneered. "The man struggles to make a spark. That's what happens when you have more than one element—the second is weak."

Somehow I knew she was telling the truth. I knew it because I'd seen Alice facing the same struggle. Griffin too. They both had abilities that superseded the element we'd always thought they had.

I stole breaths, but couldn't get enough air. "Why did my father hide it from me? Why hide it from himself?"

"A good question. Or how about: Why did the Guardians keep Skeleton Town a secret? You must've realized that we all have reasons to keep secrets. All of us."

Was my *element* like Alice's? Was that what this was about? Was it something that couldn't serve the greater good? Even illuminating a lantern might have a purpose.

I felt the way I did when I ran after Alice, always a step or two behind, unable to catch up. I looked around for some sort of help, but no one except Griffin would even look at me.

"Why don't you say something?" I shouted. "After all these years, I have something. Why won't you look at me?"

Rose opened her mouth to speak, but stopped herself. When she cast her eyes down again, I felt the full force of their silence.

235

It wasn't shock; it was *shame*.

"Did you already know?"

"No," whispered Rose. "How could we?"

"Then why aren't you surprised?"

As she approached, she reached out like she was going to touch me. But she didn't. She turned her bangle around instead.

Suddenly it all made sense. The way Rose always pulled back. The way Alice had gritted her teeth the night we'd touched. The shock we'd felt as we touched the metal mast of the sailboat—it wasn't Alice who caused it, but me. And the pirate who attacked us near Bodie Lighthouse . . . had *I* done that to him? Had I killed a man?

My mind swam. My father was the only one who'd ever really held me. Alice had tried, but I'd known something wasn't right. But then, I was excited. Exhilarated. Where I'd felt heat and excitement, she must've felt only pain.

"What's wrong with me?" I shouted.

"Nothing's wrong with you," said Alice. "Your echo hurts us, that's all."

"When did it start?"

"It's always been there. But it's gotten worse each year."

"Why didn't you tell me?"

"The Guardians made us swear we wouldn't," said Rose plaintively. "They said it was a curse, and that we shouldn't make you feel bad about it."

I looked at Tessa. "Are they right? Am I cursed?"

She stared right back at me. "Is it a curse to create light in darkness?"

My head spun with the possible meanings of who I was. How could I help? Would the others even trust me, when none of them knew what I could do? From their expressions, I was sure I knew the answer.

I had to get away. I'd had years to get used to being an outsider, but this was different. I'd always known the Guardians didn't trust me, didn't value me. But I'd never thought I was a threat to them.

I leaped up, and was almost to the steps when I heard Tessa calling to me. "I don't blame you for feeling angry, Thomas," she said. "You *should* feel angry. But anger is a powerful force. Use it wisely."

I took the steps three at a time. On the grass outside I looked around and tried to decide where to run next. I had to get away from them, the ones who'd lied to me my entire life. They were my world, but my world meant nothing.

Behind me, the door clicked open, but I didn't look. I simply turned another corner and hid. I wouldn't speak to anyone anyway.

It only took Griffin a moment to find me. He pressed his hands against the ground, and then pointed at me. *I. You. Feel*, he explained. He looked around before continuing. *Feel. Everyone. But. You. Special.*

I guessed he meant that he could track me better than the others. Or maybe he was just warning me there was no use in running. One way or another, he'd find me.

He sat down like he was planning to stay.

Seeing the concerned look on his face, I calmed down a

little. The Guardians may have told everyone else to keep my element a secret, but not Griffin. They barely had the skill and the patience to communicate with him. All he'd kept from me was an echo he couldn't have understood. How could he when no one ever touched him either, for fear of triggering one of his seizures?

I raised my shaking hands to sign. *I. You. Hurt.*

He nodded.

You. Me. Not. Tell.

He shrugged. *Hurt. Only. Little.* He reached out and patted my hand, but he'd clamped his jaw shut so the discomfort wouldn't show.

I'd never felt as close to him as I did in that moment.

He lay down on the grass beside me and stared at the fast-moving gray clouds. I did too. Normally they'd have seemed threatening. Normally I'd have been worried. Now, as my pulse slowed down again, I felt almost nothing at all.

Finally I closed my eyes, just for a moment, to block out the thoughts crowding my mind. A few strikes passed before I opened them again.

CHAPTER 35

The others were on the grass beside the shelter. I heard them talking, smelled their dinner of fresh-cooked fish, but I didn't join them. I didn't want to see the way they looked at me.

I walked through Skeleton Town. The storm was growing stronger. Gusts of wind kicked up dust. Clouds whorled low in the sky.

Soon I reached the building with the storeroom where I'd found the cutlery. Alice had known the moment she saw the emblem on the handles that Skeleton Town hid secrets. But then, she'd known long before that. Perhaps that's why she found it impossible to respect the Guardians. Hard to see through lies and not hate the liar.

We were all liars, though. Alice had been right: We all had secrets—every one of us.

I entered the building and headed for the back. The storeroom looked the same as before. I wasn't sure why I was there until I reached for the top shelf and ran my hand along it.

The pendants were right where I'd left them.

I took one and put it in my pocket. I didn't look at the color, or the shape. It was a peace offering—nothing more. Rose would accept it or she wouldn't.

I stepped through the crushed glass and headed outside. Rose was on the street, peering through the broken windows of the clinic next door, long hair obscuring her face. When she turned her head toward me, she seemed surprised and then relieved.

"I heard you wake up," she said, walking toward me. "But you didn't join us. I've been waiting for you all afternoon." In her hands she held a cloth, filled with pieces of baked fish. "It's still warm."

I ate greedily.

"I think you should know: Alice has a plan. Once the pirates have imprisoned our families, we'll let them get halfway to Skeleton Town and then take the sailboats down the west side of Roanoke. We'll moor the boats near the ruins of Wanchese, and try to rescue everyone."

"Will it work?"

She shrugged. "Tessa says that if we can free the Guardians, the pirates won't want to fight us."

"Why? They didn't seem to worry about fighting the Guardians on Hatteras. Captured them pretty easily too."

"We don't know exactly what happened. Anyway, can you think of a better plan?"

"No."

Rose fingered her bangle. Her eyes remained fixed on the ground.

"How's Dennis?"

"Better. Whatever Tessa gave him was a miracle. He's eating now, trying to make up for lost time."

"Well, there's certainly enough fish to go around." I quickly realized how that must sound to her—all those dead fish strewn along the shore. "I didn't mean—"

"It's all right." Finally, she looked at me. "I'm sorry I snapped at you down by the water. I know you kept things from Dennis and me, but I think I understand why. He can't take much more. Neither can I, to be honest. To watch the sunrise this morning and realize how different today should've been . . ." She swallowed hard, fighting tears. "Anyway, I'm sorry. I just needed to vent. And who else could I vent to?"

I wasn't sure she expected an answer. Or that I could give her one. So I stuffed the remaining fish in my mouth and slid my empty right hand into my pocket. My fingers closed around the smooth, flat object inside. "This is for you."

For a moment, she just stared at the pendant dangling before her. Then she touched it with her fingertips and pressed it against her heart. "I knew it." She tied the cord around her neck as though she'd been practicing for years. "I just knew that no matter what else happened, you'd be the one to remember my birthday."

Her words lingered. It was my turn to speak now, but I said nothing, because the truth would only hurt her. In spite of everything, silence—another lie—was the kindest thing I could offer.

Rose reached out and took my sleeve. It was a careful, thoughtful move, and I didn't stop her. Holding just the cloth, she raised my arm and brought it toward her.

I touched her hair, ran my fingers through the strands draped over her shoulder. They were matted and coarse, coated in sand and blown dry with salt air, but it didn't matter. Her hair felt as wonderful as I'd always dreamed it would.

I raised a finger and eased the strands away from her face. She peered up at me with searching eyes, and I was sure I saw longing in her expression. Did she see the same thing in me?

"I can't braid my hair," she said. She held up her injured hands, no longer bandaged, but with angry scabs across both palms. "Would you do it for me?"

I moved behind her. She gave me instructions, and I followed them. I didn't touch her skin because I didn't need to. This was enough.

When I was done, she handed me a piece of twine so I could tie off the end. She shook her hair, and the braid flapped behind her. She faced the clinic again, and with me standing beside her, contemplated her reflection in a piece of broken glass.

"You make me feel pretty again," she said.

A shout from the water tower interrupted us: Alice announcing that the ship was getting closer. She didn't sound panicked, but there was no doubt that the time for resting was over.

We joined Dennis, who stood at the bottom of the tower, still eating. He looked well.

Tessa was beside him. "The tide has turned, so the ship was finally able to get through the inlet," she said. "I think we should prepare."

Rose collected the empty water canisters and placed them in a bag for me. I slung it over my shoulder and climbed the iron ladder running up the tower. It slid dangerously from side to side, the rungs so rusted that each one left a thick residue on my palms. The wind seemed to accelerate with each step. At the top, the whole tower shifted with each buffeting blast.

"They're moving fast," said Alice, pointing to the south. "Too fast."

Through the binoculars, I watched the ship's tiny flag dance along the treetops. Just ahead, there was a gap in the trees. I focused on it and waited for the ship to get there, so I could see the whole vessel.

It passed through quickly, and kept moving.

"The sails are full," I said.

Alice smacked the iron rail. "They're not stopping to the south at all. They're coming here, to Skeleton Town."

"But Tessa said—"

"I know what she said. And we believed her."

"You don't trust her?"

"I don't know. But that ship is heading this way. So we're going to need a new plan."

We filled the canisters and dropped them to Rose. By the time we were done, the ship was racing along the western shore of Roanoke Island. I'd never seen a vessel move so fast.

"What's happening?" Rose shouted. Her voice was whipped away by the wind, but I still heard her.

"We're not sure," I yelled back, stalling.

Alice curled her lip. "Not sure? I think it's a little late to protect her, don't you?" When she stared at the ship once again, she seemed to have made a decision. "Stay here and keep us posted. I'm going to get us ready to leave. There's no time to waste."

She climbed down the ladder with quick, confident steps. For half a strike I studied the ship barreling along the western shore. When at last they raised the sails and slowed down, I knew we had an even bigger problem.

"They're only four hundred yards south of the sailboats," I shouted.

I knew it would be difficult for us to sail away without being seen, but I hadn't considered that simply getting to the boats might be impossible.

"Come down," Alice yelled back. "We have to leave."

"What about our parents?" Rose added. "Can you see them?"

I focused on the ship, now anchored less than two miles away. The pirates had lowered a cutter—a rowboat—from the stern, and were climbing down a ladder to get in. Others slinked down a rope hanging beside it. Ten men squeezed inside the cutter and rowed to shore as a second boat was lowered.

"Come down, Thom," Alice yelled.

Another ten pirates shuttled to the shore as two men returned to the ship with the first cutter. This time their cargo was a long wooden box; it must have been heavy, because it required four men to get it on board.

"They're putting a giant wooden box into the cutter," I shouted.

Tessa was first to reply. "Describe it."

"Rectangular. About the length of . . ." A *body*, I was about to say. But I stopped myself. There was something weird about the box, and the way the four men carried it, faces a picture of concentration and solemnity. *Please*, I thought, *don't let any of our parents be dead.*

The second cutter returned to the ship and collected another group of pirates. I knew that the Guardians would disembark soon, but once again the boat set off without them.

"Have you seen our parents?" Rose called.

"They'll be next. I'm positive."

It took longer for the boats to return now. The water was choppy and they were fighting the wind, barely able to hold their course. By the time they made it to the ship, Dare was standing on deck. While more men boarded the cutters, he raised his telescope and surveyed Roanoke Island.

I was about to hide behind the tower when I realized he'd already seen me. With the binoculars pressed against my eyes, I watched Dare watching me.

Dare untied the rope ladder from the stern of his ship and let it fall into the cutter. Finally, he slithered down the remaining rope and onto the waiting boat. Then, in a gesture I remembered all too well, he raised his hands and clapped.

The Guardians were still on board.

CHAPTER 36

I gripped the ladder and hurried down. The others had gathered at the bottom of the steps, awaiting news. Griffin was at their center, his finger running through lines in the journals.

"They've left the Guardians on board," I announced.

"What?" Rose tugged my sleeve. "But if the ship capsizes, they'll drown. Anyway, you heard them talking. They said the Guardians would live until they had the solution."

"And they're coming here to get him right now," Alice reminded her.

Griffin watched us all. A moment before, he'd seemed energized by his journals. But panic had set in again now. He was aware of it, but not afflicted by it. And perhaps that was the key.

Dennis gulped deep breaths. "We're never going to see them again, are we?"

"Yes, we are," I replied firmly. I slowed down to make sure that I could sign to Griffin. He needed to understand. "This is what's going to happen: Alice is going to lead you to the sailboats. Take the route through the marsh and woods; Dare and his men won't cross a marsh with all their packs. When you reach the boathouse, wait for dark and sail out to the ship. Climb aboard and release the Guardians. Then take them ashore before the hurricane makes landfall."

"You make it sound easy," said Tessa. "There'll be pirates on board, remember?"

"Didn't look like it. Dare took the rope ladder with him when they left. Anyway, none of the pirates will stay aboard during a hurricane."

"You don't think they'll protect their vessel?"

"Why would they? They don't need it anymore. You said *this* is their new home now."

Rose looked at the sky. "Even if we get our parents ashore, then what?"

"They'll be alive. They can help us. Isn't that enough?"

"What makes you think the pirates won't come after us when they see what we're doing?" pressed Tessa. "They have boats too. Besides, we'll need several journeys to bring everyone ashore."

"Trust me—you'll have all the time you need."

"Why? Because it's getting dark?"

"No. Because they'll be too busy chasing the solution."

In the silence that followed, I turned to Griffin and signed that we'd be running from the pirates. Without hesitation, he nodded, just as I knew he would.

"What are you talking about?" cried Rose.

"Griffin and I will create a diversion. As long as Dare sees us on the island, he'll chase us. It's the solution he wants, not you."

"And he'll capture you both," shouted Alice. "Forget it."

"No." I tried to sound calm, although I was already panicking inside. "We'll have a head start. Plus, it'll be hard for him to see us in the dark."

"Not hard. Impossible."

"Not if I take the lantern. When we're a safe distance away, I'll illuminate it. Dare will see our faces. At the same time, Tessa can take one of the sailboats to the ship and start getting the Guardians ashore. Alice, you take the other boat, and head for the gap in the bridge. That's as far as Griffin and I will be able to go. When we get to the gap, we'll shout down to you. Then we'll jump."

"It's too high."

"Says the girl who did the exact same thing four strikes ago."

Tessa shook her head vehemently. "You can't possibly expect Alice to hold a sailboat steady in this weather."

"I expect more than that. I expect her to rescue us the moment we hit the water. Because if she can't do it, then no one can."

Alice huffed. "And if I rescue you, then what?"

"We head for the ship and shuttle the Guardians ashore."

She glanced at the sky and frowned. "I hope we get that chance."

Tessa led me into the shelter. "I don't like this."

"I know."

"It's too big a fall from the bridge. You could be killed."

"We'll be all right. And the water's choppy, which will help. Anyway, Alice jumped into much shallower water."

"That's not the point. You'll be jumping from twice as high as she did." She picked up the lantern. "You really believe Alice will find you at the gap?"

"I know she will."

"I hope you're right." Tessa rubbed her eyes. "I honestly didn't know they'd leave your parents on board." She emphasized the word *honestly* as though she expected me to doubt her. "The sacrifice of few for the good of many, I suppose."

"What?"

"It's just a saying I heard once."

Tessa placed a cloth over my hand and passed me the lantern. The material stopped it from illuminating so strongly, but the light was still there. I folded the cloth and experimented with different thicknesses. The lantern grew dimmer each time I doubled it up, but although there was less discomfort, I still felt fatigued. Finally, I placed it on the ground. I needed to save my energy.

"How did you power the lantern in the clinic?" I asked her. "For me to find, I mean."

"I was wondering when you'd ask that. There's a solar panel on the roof of the clinic—it's a device that takes energy from the sun and turns it into power. It barely works anymore, but it's strong enough for a lantern."

I thought about this. "Is that what I do? Transfer energy from the sun?"

"Who knows? Our elements have evolved over time, but yours is the newest. No one really understands it yet. That's why the Guardians tried to hide it from you. All of us fear things we don't understand, or can't explain."

"You could've told me, though. You've been living so close to the colony. You could've just stopped me one day when I was alone."

Tessa ran her fingers over my hair, the touch so light she was almost stroking air. "They exiled me for suggesting that you know the truth. Imagine what they'd have done if I told you myself." Her hand stopped moving. "Pirates aren't the only killers on this island, Thomas. Believe me, your Guardians have blood on their hands. I didn't want it to be mine."

I handed her the portrait I'd found of my mother. "It's time to go. Will you look after this for me?"

"Sure." She unfolded it gently and stared at the image. It seemed to stir something in her. She ran a finger over it as if she could somehow feel her daughter's skin. "She always told me he'd be the solution, you know."

"Who?"

"Griffin." She wiped a tear away. "Before he was born, that's what she called him."

"But . . . you said you didn't know who it was."

"I was lying. I just didn't want the others to know. You have support here—two girls who'll do anything to save you. I wasn't sure they'd do the same for Griffin."

I didn't know what to make of this news. But I was more

determined than ever that Dare wouldn't lay a finger on the solution.

"I never really understood what your mother meant about a solution, Thomas. Probably wouldn't have believed it anyhow. But now . . ." She shook her head. "Your mother was willing to die for him. You have to keep him alive."

"I will," I said. "No matter what."

We said our good-byes as the first drops of rain fell. Looking into Alice's eyes I knew that she was frightened—for herself, but even more for Griffin and me. I could see it in the way she glanced at his right leg, wondering if he'd be able to make it as far as the gap in the bridge, let alone get there before the pirates. The same thing had occurred to me. Choosing when to take the lantern from him and illuminate it would be critical.

Just before she left, Alice took Griffin's pack. "You don't need extra weight."

He closed his precious leather books and placed them gently inside.

"The sailboats have a small waterproof hold," she said. "The bags will stay dry."

"Thank you." I looked at the sky. "You sure you can handle this weather?"

Alice held up her hands, dotted with thick white calluses. "I'm looking forward to trying."

It was a typically defiant response. I might have found it amusing under other circumstances, but not now. "How come your hands look like that? You don't get much more time in canoes than me."

"I rub sand between my hands to toughen up the skin. My sister thinks it's disgusting."

"I can't imagine why," I said, which made her smile. "What about your parents?"

"My father thinks it's proof that I'm weird. But sometimes I catch my mom winking at me. I think she likes it that I'm not the same as Eleanor."

"You can say that again."

Alice looked over my shoulder at Tessa's retreating figure. Or maybe she was looking at Rose, lingering several yards away, waiting for the moment when we'd be alone.

"I'll be there, Thom. At the bridge. I promise I will."

As she turned from me, her fingers brushed against mine. Then she limped away.

Rose approached, biting her lip. "I need you to know, the reason I kept quiet about your echo wasn't because the Guardians told me to. It just never occurred to me that's what it was: an echo. I was afraid it was your *element*—that you had the ability to cause pain."

I flinched. "How could that be an element?"

"I don't know. But I think we're starting to realize there's a lot we don't understand. Anyway, that's why I never said anything. I didn't want to give you a reason to pull away from me."

"I know that now."

She glanced at our hands, so close but not touching. Perhaps we'd never touch. "Do you realize how exciting this is? Starting today, you get to discover what you can do."

"As long as we survive, you mean."

The wind snapped her vest, but her braid barely moved. "Yes. I guess that's true."

We stood in silence. The others were already a hundred yards away. "You should go."

Reluctantly, she nodded. "Hold out your hand first."

I did as she said, and she reached out so that our fingertips were only a hairsbreadth apart. I imagined I could feel her heartbeat pulsing through the air. I could feel mine too, getting steadily faster, and I knew I had to calm down. But I couldn't calm down.

Then we touched.

I felt the warmth, the energy, the power between us. It shifted like a living, breathing force. I let it fill my body until I wanted to explode in delight. And through it, Rose smiled. She *smiled*.

But the smile was all wrong—determined and fierce. And when she began to moan, I knew I was hurting her. There was no pleasure in this. The energy only seemed to go one way. And I'd seen firsthand where that exchange could lead.

I pulled back. "I'm sorry."

For a moment, I thought she was going to tell me that it was all right—there was no need to apologize. But then she seemed to think better of it. And when she stared at her feet, I knew there would be no more lies between us.

"Me too," she said. "More than you know."

CHAPTER 37

I watched them disappear among the trees. Tessa stood in the middle, the cat right beside her. Rose and Alice stood on either side, as separate from each other as they could be. Everything about them was opposite: their hair; their gait; Alice's fierce independence, and Rose's tight grip on her younger brother's hand.

Griffin began walking the other way. I followed.

Me. Afraid, I signed.

He shook his head and smiled. *Me. No.* He studied my expression. *I. See. Four. Death,* he signed, referring to Rose and Dennis's grandparents, whose boat capsized; and John, the boy who fell from the rope swing; and Lora, I hoped. *Four. Death,* he repeated. *Me. Never. Dead.*

Somehow I'd never considered *what* he felt when he foresaw someone's death. I'd just witnessed what those visions had done to him—how they'd left him broken and unable to communicate. What if he'd seen death itself, the actual moment when life ends? Was he destined to see his own end the same way?

We pressed on toward the mainland bridge. Weeds rose stubbornly from cracks in the road. Every hundred steps I glanced back to see if the pirates had entered Skeleton Town, but there was no sight of them. Darkness was falling fast, accelerated by angry clouds that seemed to suffocate the sky, and rain that grew heavier by the moment.

Another hundred strides. And another, but still no sign of the pirates. We were onto the mainland bridge now—so much longer than the one between Roanoke and Hatteras—and as I pictured the pirates landing their cutters close to Alice's boat-house, a terrible thought crossed my mind: What if they'd taken a shortcut to Skeleton Town through the woods and marsh, instead of the easier, longer route by road? It seemed impossible, given how much the pirates were carrying, but maybe Dare knew our plan. He was a seer, after all. Maybe he'd had a vision. What if he'd already intercepted Alice and Rose?

I stared at the coastline to the south. The pirate ship peeked out from the bay where Dare had lowered anchor, but I couldn't see around to the boathouse. There were no signs of our sailboats on the water either.

Stop, I signed. *None. Pirates.*

Griffin signaled that we keep moving.

Wait. I walked to the railing at the side of the bridge. I couldn't get a great view of Skeleton Town, so I leaned out farther. It was already dark enough that I could barely make out the sound frothing below us. The only light in the sky came from the dying embers of the sunset.

Griffin glared at me. *We. Move.*

But we couldn't move—not if we weren't being followed; and if the pirates weren't even entering Skeleton Town, they couldn't possibly follow us. If that happened, the others stood no chance of getting the Guardians ashore.

I glimpsed a dot of light emanating from Skeleton Town. It was so tiny that I thought I'd imagined it, but when I saw it again I guessed what it might be: a reflection of the purple-red sky on Dare's telescope lens.

Relief flooded over me. Our plan might still work. I pushed back from the railing and signaled for us to keep moving. A few strides later I looked back, and relief gave way to fear.

The pirates were lighting torches, one after another. When they had about ten lit, they began to walk briskly toward the bridge.

Griffin looked back too, and broke into a run.

We were supposed to be farther along than this. We probably had a thousand-yard head start, but I wasn't sure it would be enough. I hadn't realized how steeply the bridge sloped upward, or that the surface deteriorated the farther we went.

There was no point in hiding anymore—not if we risked losing our footing and injuring ourselves in a fall—so I took the lantern from Griffin and illuminated the ground before us. I lifted it high above me, hoping I'd be able to make out the gap in the distance, but the light only revealed an area ten yards in front of us. Stretching into the dusk, the bridge seemed endless.

Another hundred strides. I was about to look back, but

thought better of it. They would be gaining on us. I didn't need to see them to know that.

With every step, my pulse grew faster, and the lantern shone a little brighter. At the same time, I could feel my energy draining faster than before, as though I'd cut myself and was watching blood trickle out. The wind seemed to push us from everywhere at once; I couldn't imagine how hard it must be for Griffin. I doubled up the cloth in the palm of my hand and felt immediate relief as the lantern dimmed.

We were approaching the high point of the bridge when I heard it for the first time: the unmistakable sound of Griffin's foot dragging along the ground. His pace slowed. There was no use encouraging him either—the expression on his face told me it would be pointless.

I risked a backward glance and saw the pirates moving ever faster, encouraged by signs of our tiredness.

The lantern was no advantage anymore. It was giving us away—shining a light on our weakness—so I threw it onto the ground and let the darkness swallow us. The pirates would still know where we were, but at least now they'd have a harder job knowing exactly how far ahead we were.

Fierce gusts were more common than a lull now. The wind howled, but I could still hear Griffin breathing. He slowed down some more, and when I looked back I saw that the pirates had made tremendous gains. There was maybe four hundred yards between us.

Griffin grabbed my arm—to stop himself from falling, I figured—and let out a grunt. But his pace picked up again after that. He kept going for another twenty strides, and then grabbed my arm again, but this didn't feel accidental at all. And when he grunted and the pace accelerated again, I realized what he was doing: shocking himself to distract from the pain in his leg.

I counted every stride, not in groups of a hundred, but in tens. And each time I started the count over, I wondered if it would be Griffin's last. Another look back showed that the pirates were three hundred yards away at most. They were sprinting too. They clenched their fists and pumped their arms back and forth with every step.

The constantly shifting wind battered us all now. I wondered if we were even moving forward.

Another swipe from Griffin, but no grunt this time—just a pitiful cry, like a wounded animal. Tears filled my eyes, blurred my vision. Another grab and I cried out, from pain and the realization that we might not make it to the gap, let alone survive the fall.

Griffin forced himself to keep going, but his foot wasn't leaving the ground at all anymore. His cries were continuous and terrifying. I wished I could say something to him, but signs were empty now. I grabbed his sleeve and slung his arm over my shoulders. Grasping the material behind my neck, he kept moving. I focused on keeping a steady pace. Surely the gap couldn't be too much farther?

The wind changed direction again, and Griffin toppled over as though he'd been pushed. He hit the ground hard— didn't even have time to extend his arms and brace himself.

I knelt beside him and tried to help him up, but when I touched him, he screamed. I pulled back and sat on my haunches, just watching. When he turned his face toward me, I saw a gash running down the right side of his forehead. It bled into his eye and mouth. He spat the blood out angrily.

I wanted to scream too—for Griffin's pain, and for being unable to help him. I heard the pirates' voices carried toward us on westerly gusts. I couldn't make out words, but I could feel their excitement. They were gaining so quickly. They must have known we were spent.

Griffin bumped my arm. Somehow he was standing again. He wore a determined look that almost scared me. *Finish*, he signed, slicing the air with his flattened right hand. And again: *Finish*.

This time he led the way. He didn't make a sound either. The pain he was enduring had been locked inside of him.

"Close." I heard the word shouted from behind us. "Soon."

I was so busy tuning in to the pirates' exchanges that I didn't see it. Then again, there was nothing to see. One moment I was leaning into the wind, grinding out one and another step; the next, Griffin shoved me to the ground. I landed hard, but my head didn't make contact—it just hung in the air, in the space where the road used to be.

I couldn't see the water, but I imagined I could hear it far below me: violent and churning.

"Alice!" I shouted at the top of my lungs, but the wind took the word and smothered it.

I looked over my shoulder. The pirates were a hundred

yards away. I could see them smiling in the light from their torches: twenty men, maybe twenty-five.

So many men for just one boy. Could Griffin really be so important? Did Dare know more about him than I did?

"Alice!" I tried again, but there was no reply. We were up so high, I may as well have been staring into space.

Griffin pulled on my sleeve. I rolled over to face him. I was afraid that Alice wasn't down there; afraid that we would die. Beside me, Griffin looked stoic and fearless.

We. Jump, he signed, kneeling beside me.

I didn't want to jump.

"Almost there," came the pirates' shouts.

Jump, he repeated.

I looked down again, at the ragged edge of the bridge, and the endless blackness. As the pirates' footsteps pounded toward us, I took a deep breath and nodded once. Then I stood.

Side by side, we stepped into nothingness.

CHAPTER 38

My insides twisted. I couldn't inhale. I only had one thought: *This is the end.*

I was falling so fast that I didn't even feel the impact of the water. I just knew that one moment I was in air, the next I was fully submerged, breathless, with no idea which way was up. If I was hurt, I wasn't aware of it; all I could feel was the desperate need to breathe again.

I kicked to what I thought should be the surface, but I was still underwater. Somehow I thought of Rose in that moment—of how, years ago, she'd taught me to blow bubbles to find out which way was up. I tried it now, and although I couldn't see anything, I felt them running by my left cheek. So I turned to the side and swam. Moments later, I broke the surface.

I had just enough time to snatch a breath before the wave hit me. It pushed me straight under again, but I fought my way back up and looked for Alice's boat.

"Thomas!" I heard her voice, but she sounded miles away. "Thomas!"

I saw another wave coming and stole a deep breath before ducking under it. It rolled me over, but I surfaced easily.

"Thomas!"

I tried to shout back, but water sprayed against my face. I couldn't see the boat, or Griffin.

"Thomas!" She sounded desperate, but now I could tell exactly where her voice was coming from.

I turned and made out the silhouette of the mast. "Alice." Her name came out quiet. But the boat was being driven toward me by the waves. If I could just swim a few strokes, she might see me.

Another wave—this one big enough to lift the boat half a yard. I didn't even try to swim into that wave. I just took another deep breath and headed straight down. Then I swam underwater for several strokes. When I emerged again, Alice's boat was only five yards away, and I could see that Griffin was beside her.

Griffin was alive.

"Thomas!" Alice was turned away from me. She sounded desolate. "Thomas. Please, Thomas. *Please.*"

I was about to swim toward her again when I heard something crashing into the water. I didn't need to see to know it was one of the pirates. And he was close.

"Alice!" I summoned the word from a place deep inside me. Somehow she heard. She spun around, grabbed an oar, and held it out for me.

I heard a grunt to my left. I kicked hard to stay afloat while I stole a glance. It was a pirate, all right. He battered the water around him, trying to get to me, but he was no stronger a swimmer than I was.

Another splash. This one to my right.

I grasped the oar. The wood was wet and slick, and I struggled to hold tight as Alice dragged me to the side of the boat. I got hold of the edge and tried to pull myself up, but another wave tipped the boat toward me. It was all I could do not to let go.

Another splash, closer again. They must have spotted us from the bridge and were taking aim.

"We need to go!" Alice screamed. "They're on us."

Before I was even fully on board, she slipped to the opposite side of the boat and pulled the rope that drew in the sail.

I felt the tug of the water as we began to move. It forced my legs out to the side, but still I held tight to the boat. I'd survived chasing pirates and a massive fall. I wasn't going to let the undertow take me now.

Griffin grabbed the material of my sleeve to keep me locked in place, but as my legs dragged in the water, I could feel my grip loosening. His too.

"We're not moving fast enough. You've got to get in," Alice shouted over the wind and rain.

With a final effort I pulled myself onto the edge of the boat. Most of my body was out of the water now, and the undertow lost its hold on me. I swung my legs over the side. Before I crashed into the boat, Griffin grabbed the oar again and swung it toward my leg.

A cry split the air. When I tilted my head I saw one of the pirates drifting behind us, left in our wake.

"Behind me," shouted Alice.

I snatched the oar from Griffin and brought it down with a sickening crack. The pirate didn't make a sound as he fell away from us, but I'd splintered the wood.

More splashdowns now—not one or two, but several, getting faster and closer. It was madness: men leaping into stormy waters in a do-or-die effort to capture the solution.

"Two ahead," said Alice.

"Then turn," I shouted.

"Can't."

The boat drove toward the two figures bobbing in the water. I tried to knock one away with the oar, but he grasped it and almost pulled me in with him. By the time I let go, the pirate to our right had one hand on the side of the boat. His other hand swiped at Alice's tunic. When he got a fistful he whipped her backward.

I dove at him and gripped his arm. We were moving fast, but he was dragging us to the right. The sail protested by flapping awkwardly in the wind. We were slowing down. More pirates were landing nearby.

I tried to pull him away from Alice, but he wouldn't let go—not at first, anyway. But when our eyes met, I channeled all my anger and grasped his arm as though I intended to snap it in two. Immediately, his expression changed. He looked as if he was in agony. A moment later, he let go.

Another two ahead of us, but this time Alice didn't attempt to slide between them. She just tugged the rope, pulled the tiller toward her, and accelerated toward the one on the left. I heard his head collide with the hull.

"Watch the back," she instructed.

I did as she said, but there was no one there. Just as well, as I felt like I was watching in slow motion. Even the sound of their screaming was muffled.

Alice grunted. "Don't listen. They would've killed us, if they'd had the chance."

I turned to Griffin. He was slumped against the side of the boat, massaging his leg. We'd escaped the pirates, but neither of us was smiling.

"You survived," Alice shouted as we crashed into another giant wave. "You're alive."

I shivered. It wasn't cold, but the wind felt sharp against my saturated clothes. I was exhausted too, as if someone had sucked away my remaining energy. My body felt strange—not mine, somehow.

"You survived," she said again, looking straight at me. Her expression made it clear how afraid she had been for us.

"Yes."

Alice relaxed the sail. "You need to get down. We're going about."

Down, I told Griffin. I slithered beside him. Alice turned us around and the wind caught the sail once more, snapped it back and jolted us southward.

"It's only a couple miles," she said. "We're moving fast, but we can't risk capsizing. If we go over, we'll never get the sail out of the water."

I struggled to focus. "Should you loosen it?"

"No. As bad as it is, it's going to get worse."

She was right. As the waves picked up speed and size, they smacked the edge of the boat and spilled over the side. I cupped my hands and tried to bail, but my arms weren't responding. It was pointless anyway—the water was coming in too fast.

"Forget it," Alice yelled. "I need you to lie out over the water. I can't hold the boat down much longer. I'm not heavy enough."

I found the foot strap just inside the boat. So did Griffin. We eased ourselves over the edge, and the boat righted. Alice pulled the sail in tighter, and the boat rose up on our side again. With a deep breath I extended myself fully. The edge of the boat pressed into my calf muscles. When the boat righted once more, waves clipped the back of my head.

To either side of me, Alice and Griffin were lying out too: three horizontal bodies, fighting nature.

"Less than two miles," Alice shouted over the roar of the wind. "We'll be there soon. You have to hold your position."

I glanced to my left. "I can't see it," I mumbled.

"Trust me. Hold still."

I closed my eyes and let the wind and rain pummel me. I wanted to hold still for her, but I didn't have the strength to support myself anymore. My knees began to bend and my torso dipped lower.

"Hold steady. I need you full out."

"Can't," I said. It was just a fact: I had nothing left.

"Yes, you can! I need you to do this, Thom. Please."

Griffin was even worse off than me. He was supporting his weight on one leg. When he started to lose his form, he grabbed my arm. I felt the shock, the momentary pain, and Griffin screamed, but then his body stretched out again.

It had taken something from me as well, though, and left me breathless. It was terrifying to feel that way, so I tried to shut out everything but a single thought: Stay strong for Alice and Griffin.

I heard the words *one mile*, but they meant nothing to me. It seemed as though every time Alice screamed at us, Griffin touched me again, and a part of me disappeared.

I heard her say "almost there," but it sounded like she was talking to me from a mile away. She shouted "pull up," but I heard them as sounds, not words. I didn't know it was an instruction. I wouldn't have been able to act on it, even if I had.

The boat slowed. I was still stretched out.

"Up, Thom!"

My head glanced the surface of the water, and then dipped deep.

Griffin took my arm. I felt the familiar jolt, and the crushing emptiness that followed. Then the undertow torqued my body and ripped me from the boat.

CHAPTER 39

Underwater again. But this time was different. The current was even stronger than before, and I couldn't fight it; not just because I had nothing left, but because I was spinning endlessly, as helpless as a leaf in the wind. I didn't know how long my breath would last. I couldn't seem to care, either.

It was strangely peaceful in the water, away from the destructive groans of the hurricane and the shouts of the pirates. The water was powerful, but it cushioned and supported me. It seemed to be taking me somewhere.

Something brushed by me. I was vaguely aware of movement to my left. Then, from behind, two hands dug into my armpits. When I turned my head, I felt something slide across my cheek. A rope perhaps.

Suddenly I was moving again, propelled by someone a thousand times stronger than me. My pulse seemed to jolt to life. Energy coursed through me. I was conscious again. Alive again. And I needed air desperately.

Panic overtook me.

We broke the surface and carried on climbing until my entire body up to my knees was clear of the water. I gulped air before we splashed down. Still the hands remained clasped against me. I seemed to be skimming over the surface of the water, feet clipping the crest of every wave.

With no energy left, I drew what I could from the person behind me. My power surged in response.

When I finally stopped moving, I heard Alice's voice beside me.

"Stay awake." She tied a rope around my waist. "We can't lose you again."

I was next to the sailboat. Rose was beside me, bobbing up and down. She tried to pull herself onto the boat, but slid back into the water. Griffin held her fast and dragged her on board.

I knew Rose had saved me. I even tried to smile for her, but when she stared back at me I saw nothing but pain in her eyes.

Alice tied the rope around me in a tight knot. "You're not going anywhere now," she said. She turned to Rose. "Are you okay?"

Rose shook her head, no. She didn't speak.

Alice held Rose's hands, a gesture as touching as it was surprising. "You saved his life. What you're feeling now—the shock—it'll pass. Just try to relax. Conserve your strength."

Rose nodded, but her eyes never left me. She seemed transfixed. And somehow, in that moment, I deciphered her expression: not just pain, but fear too.

"We have to get inside the ship," shouted Alice.

"I'm passing down a second rope." Tessa's voice came from high above us.

I looked up and realized we'd made it to the stern of the pirate ship. Tessa had already climbed a rope and taken her position beside the ship's deck rail.

Alice called up to her. "Are there any pirates on board?"

"No. Not above deck anyway. They must've taken shelter on the island."

"Where are our families?" I asked. The words came out slurred. "We need to get them ashore."

Alice didn't reply; but then, she didn't need to. I felt the waves threatening to capsize our boat, and the rain driven horizontal by the wind. The time for rescuing was long gone.

She took the rope hanging down from the rail and handed it to Griffin. He gritted his teeth and began to shimmy up the rope, legs dangling below him.

"Where's Dennis?" I asked.

Alice pointed to the sailboat just beside us. The sail had been lowered, and Dennis was sheltering beneath it. The rain formed rivulets that ran through channels in the canvas and off the side of the boat.

"You next, Rose," said Alice.

Rose didn't move. She'd wrapped her arms around her body and was hugging herself. When I made eye contact with her, she burst into sobs that racked her body.

I'd done this to her. Hurt her. I wanted to apologize again, but what could I say to undo the damage I'd caused?

Alice turned to Dennis instead. "Go up," she told him. "Follow Tessa."

He did as he was told. His movements were slow and labored.

"Can you climb, Thom?"

I didn't think so, but there was no other way. "I'll try."

With a final glance at Rose, I grabbed the rope and coiled my legs around it to anchor myself. My wet clothes whipped against me. Twist by painful twist I forced my hands up the rope, feet locking me in place. The ship pitched from side to side, but I absorbed each shift by holding tight and waiting until I had regained my balance. Tessa shouted encouragement from above, Alice from below, but I could barely hear their words.

As soon as I reached the ship's rail, Griffin and Dennis joined Tessa and grabbed a part of my tunic. They were careful not to touch me, and I didn't blame them. As soon as I could, I swung a leg over the side and collapsed onto the deck. The rain lashed down so hard it stung my face.

"Come on, Thomas," said Dennis, grimacing. "We . . . we need to keep going."

At first, I thought he was suffering from seasickness, but that wasn't it, of course. It was his echo in the face of the hurricane. Whatever Tessa had given him was wearing off. We were losing him again.

I pulled myself onto all fours. Even that was difficult, given how much the ship was moving.

"Keep going straight," shouted Tessa, just in front of me.

"There's a hatch door about halfway along. I opened it already. Take the staircase below deck."

I thought of Alice, still waiting to join us aboard; and Rose, damaged by me. "What about the others?"

"Griffin and I will help them. You need to look for the Guardians."

I crawled along the deck, arm over arm, slipping on the wet planks. With the door open, the hatch was just a hole. A steep wooden ladder descended into pitch-blackness. I couldn't make out all the steps, so I faced the ladder and hugged it as I half climbed, half slipped down to the floor.

"Father," I shouted. I waited for a reply, but all I could hear was the wind and rain. I pulled to a stand, spread my legs wide for balance, and ran my hands across the wooden walls.

A sound from above pulled me around: footsteps— someone running across the deck. I recognized Alice's voice from the open hatch. She descended the ladder, and cursed as she slipped down the final few steps. I kept my distance so she wouldn't have to touch me.

"Thom?"

"Here. Is Rose on board?"

"Yes. But if we're all coming down here, we need a light. I can't even see the stairs."

"Where are we going to find a light?"

"Run your hands along the walls. There must be lamps."

I couldn't move. "I hurt her, Alice. Badly."

"Focus," she growled. "We're not out of this yet. Not by

273

a long shot. Rose saved you. If you can find us a light, you might just be able to save her right back."

I spread my arms again and shuffled to my left. I felt the rough finish of the wooden walls, and the seams between the planks. I must have gone a couple yards when my fingers brushed against something. It was high up, and I was sure it must be a lamp. I closed my eyes and clamped my fingers around it—quickly, before I could change my mind.

Weak yellow light illuminated a narrow corridor. The dark wood paneling stretched maybe ten yards until it was swallowed in darkness. There were several doors on either side, but they were closed. Keeping hold of the lamp, I turned around so that I could see in the other direction: another corridor, almost identical. If our families were still on board, there was no sign of them. Not a sound.

"Do you see—" I began, but stopped when I saw Alice's face, frozen in horror. "What is it?"

She pointed at the wall behind me, just below the lamp.

I twisted my body to see where she was pointing. Then I let go of the lamp, so I wouldn't have to look at all the blood.

CHAPTER 40

We need the light, Thomas," Alice yelled. "We're blind down here."

I didn't move. I imagined I could feel the blood splattered across the wall behind me. It had been deep red, still relatively fresh. Was it one person, or several? Was there anyone left to save?

"Thomas. The lamp!"

I swiped at the metal rod connecting the lamp to the wall. Through closed eyes I felt it flicker on. It was brighter than before too; my pulse was racing again.

When I opened my eyes, Alice was staring at me. "You have to hold on, Thom. Without you, we're . . ." She didn't finish the thought. "When I say so, let go of the lamp."

"What?" I figured I'd misheard her.

"Just do it." She leaped up and grabbed a wooden beam that ran across the ceiling. Her feet dangled beneath her. Then she brought her knees up to her chest and extended her left foot until it was almost touching the lamp. "Now!" she shouted.

I released the lamp, and she kicked it. There was a sound of splintering wood, and the lamp landed on the floor beside me. When I picked it up, the light returned. My hand shook from the pain.

Alice dropped to the floor. She spread her arms across the corridor to brace herself. "We've got to look for our parents."

There was a roar from the wind outside, and the ship tipped farther than before. I lost my balance and crashed against the bloody wall. I took a deep breath to try to calm myself, but the light shone brighter.

I heard cursing above us. The others were coming down the stairs, but rainwater cascaded over the steps, and no one seemed to be able to balance. Tessa had wrapped her arm around Rose, who was shaking. I had to look away.

"We're going to die tonight," said Dennis.

"No, we're not," Alice snapped. "There are no pirates here. We're in control now." Somehow she even sounded like she meant it.

As Tessa closed the hatch, Alice led us down one of the corridors, trying the handle of every door she came to. All were locked; I double-checked them myself. At the end of the corridor, another much shorter corridor ran at right angles in either direction. More doors at either end, but they were locked too.

Dennis began shouting his parents' names. I joined in. I glanced at Alice to see if she could hear anyone shouting back over the noise of the storm. Even if they were behind a door, she'd hear them as long as she was listening closely. Wouldn't she?

When we reached the final door, we retraced our steps. We moved faster now and wrestled with the handles on every door. As we passed the bloodied wall, I paused to block everyone's views. No need to think about that right now.

"They're all locked," shouted Dennis when we reached the last door.

"We have to take shelter," yelled Alice.

"What about my parents?"

"We'll find them once the storm has passed."

"How? They're not here."

The ship swung wildly. I hit the wall, collapsed onto the floor, and skidded a yard to the side, where I bumped into Alice.

She screamed.

I tried to get away, but I only had use of my left hand and couldn't balance. My wet shoes slid across the floor. Panic overtook me and her screams grew louder; after that, she swallowed them behind a choking sound that was somehow even more horrifying.

Finally I got some separation. It was small relief, because now I saw the looks of terror on everyone's faces. I was a danger in a storm like this. More than that, I was lethal. But no one could do without the light.

"Alice is right," I said, breaking the silence. "You must protect yourselves."

In response, Alice braced herself against the wall and kicked both legs against the nearest door. It shook, but didn't move. So she did it again. And again. Griffin joined in too. Two more kicks and the door flew open.

"Inside," she shouted.

It looked like a cabin for maybe five or six of the pirates. Bundles of blankets were littered across the floor, and a few chairs and tables had been thrown about by the storm.

"Get this stuff outside," said Tessa, grabbing a chair and shoving it out the door. "It could crush us."

One by one we pushed objects into the corridor. When we were done, Tessa pointed to the iron rings built into the walls. "Grab one of these, and hold tight. You cannot let go, no matter what happens. Do you understand?"

I looked around the room and saw everyone nodding. But they weren't looking at Tessa; they were looking at me. And I knew that every single one of them was wondering the same thing: What happens if Thomas lets go? What happens if Thomas slides into me in the night? What happens if I can't get away from him?

A length of rope lay on the floor. I kicked it to Alice. "Tie me up," I said.

"What?"

"You heard me."

She fed the rope through a ring in the wall and ran it around me like a harness, telling me where to lean so that she wouldn't have to touch me. When I was secure, she tied a knot and handed me one end of the rope. "If we need to abandon ship, pull this. The knot will untie."

I nodded once and tied the lamp to the end of the rope she'd given me so that I wouldn't lose it. The light was weaker now, and so was I.

"I-I'm going to have to let go," I told everyone. "I can't keep the lamp on all night."

No one said anything. Beside me, Rose closed her eyes tightly.

I let the lamp slide out of my fingers, and we were plunged into darkness. The relief was immediate.

I heard occasional gasps each time the boat lurched and we were pushed against the walls. Then a wave smacked the ship so hard I thought we'd capsize completely. I slid toward Rose. I couldn't stop myself.

The rope jarred me to a halt before I touched her. After an agonizingly long pause, the ship righted itself again, groaning like a tortured animal. I wasn't aware how close I was to Rose until I smelled the vomit on her breath.

"I'm sorry," I whispered.

Rose whimpered, and I knew it was because she was scared. Petrified, even, to find me so near again. When she inhaled, her breath shook. She was probably thinking up something reassuring to tell me—something typically Rose—but before she could speak, she began crying. The rest of the cabin grew quieter in response.

"I'm sorry," I said again, tearing up myself. "I'm so, so sorry."

"Don't be," she whispered. "It's not your fault. I just didn't realize . . ." She swallowed hard.

"What?"

"Nothing."

The ship rocked, and we all shifted again. The rope was tugging against my back. I could feel the skin beneath my shoulder blades being burned away by the friction. "What didn't you realize?"

I felt a movement as she raised a hand to her face, our tunics connecting momentarily. It reminded me of a time when we had touched. I was certain that could never happen again.

Then I heard another sound—the pendant being slid back and forth along the cord. She kept doing it, and my mind wandered to the moment that I had given it her, and the look on her face. It was the only time she'd appeared happy since all this had started.

The sound stopped, and Rose was still.

"What didn't you realize, Rose?"

She took a steadying breath. "How powerful your element is." She lowered her voice until it was almost inaudible. "I like you so much. You have no idea. But I thought I was dying. I-I think you almost killed me."

CHAPTER 41

homas."

I felt something tugging my armpits. The rope.

"Thomas!"

I opened an eye. The ship was barely moving. The howling winds had blown over. Through a porthole in the wall I saw the sky—dark gray, but with a hint of the approaching morning. I must have slept through most of the night.

I pulled the end of the rope toward me. The lamp was still there, and when I touched it, it shone.

All around me, the others were dragging themselves off the floor, trying to get their legs under them again.

"It's over," I said.

"No." Dennis sat upright, eyes closed, head lolling to the side. "It's just the eye of the storm."

"We have to look for our families," said Alice. "And we need to hurry. If we don't find them now, it could be a half day before we can try again."

I pulled at the end of the rope and the knot came undone,

281

as Alice had said it would. But my back was blistered from rope burns. Everyone waited for me before leaving the room. Without my lamp, they wouldn't be able to see anything.

We made our way along the corridor, trying every door. We shouted our parents' names, and listened in case they responded. Again, there was no sight or sound of them.

When we reached the stairs to the deck, Alice stopped. "I'm going up to check the damage," she said. "I hope the sailboats are all right. If you can release everyone quickly, there might be time to evacuate before the storm returns."

"No," mumbled Dennis. "The eye will pass soon."

Alice paused. "How soon?"

"Less than half a strike. Maybe only a quarter."

In response, Rose and Dennis continued along the corridor, screaming, "Mother. Father."

Griffin followed them. He ran his hands across the walls, trying to pick up a vibration, any clue at all about where everyone might be.

"What if they disembarked on Hatteras?" Rose called out. "Maybe they're not here."

"No," I said. "After the ship set sail, I scanned Hatteras with my binoculars. I couldn't see anyone."

It was looking more and more like something else had happened to our parents—something terrible. The others were thinking the same thing too. It was written all over their faces. When we reached the end of the corridor, we sat down, backs against the wall.

"Where's Tessa?" asked Rose.

It was a good question. The lamp illuminated the corridor, but I couldn't see her. I was about to check if she was on deck with Alice, when Griffin held up his right hand—a command for silence and stillness. Straightaway, he ran his left hand down the wall. He kept going until he touched the floor.

Rose pulled up her knees and hugged them. "What's he doing?"

Griffin placed both hands on the floor and began to retrace our steps down the corridor. We all followed him. Five yards later, he stopped and slapped the boards.

That's when I heard it: voices, faint and distant.

"Which room are they in?" Rose asked, breathless.

"They're not. He thinks . . . they're *under* us."

"How can they be under us?"

I knelt down and placed my ear against the boards. Sure enough, the sound was coming from underneath a floor so thick I couldn't even make out individual voices—just a kind of collective groaning. We never could have heard it above the noise of the storm.

I ran the lamp across the boards, looking for something—a mark, a scratch—and caught the shadow of a seam between the planks. There was a wooden ring, too, perfectly flush with the floor, and almost indistinguishable from it.

I jammed a fingernail into the seam and tried to pry the ring up, but it wouldn't move. Rose crouched beside me and followed my lead—Dennis too—and a tiny edge of the ring protruded above the surface of the floor. Quickly, Rose pressed her fingertips against it and lifted it up. When it stood out from the floor, I tried to pull it up, but the trapdoor it was attached to was either locked or extremely heavy. Either way, it wasn't going to budge.

Someone reached over me and took the ring. Tessa. I didn't have time to ask her where she'd gone before she twisted it a quarter turn and something clicked. This time it moved a little when she pulled, and with Rose and me joining her, we managed to raise the trapdoor a little. As soon as there was a space underneath, Griffin slid his fingers in and prized the door open farther. With all of us working together, the heavy door swung upward.

The noise rose to fever pitch. But that wasn't all. A foul stench filled the air, and when I retched, I wasn't alone. We all staggered back, gasping fresh air. Once I'd filled my lungs, I stepped forward and shone the lamp into the hole again.

I recognized the faces down there, but they were well out of reach, sprawled against the curved sides of the ship's hull. They closed their eyes and shrank back from the bright lamp. They had probably been in darkness ever since they were kidnapped.

"Are you all right?" shouted Rose.

"Rose?" I recognized Kyte's voice. "Rose, is that you?"

"Yes. Are you all right?"

"We're . . . alive." His hesitation worried me. So did the sudden silence of everyone around him. "You came for us." He practically choked on the words.

"How did you get down there?"

"They threw us down. Some of us have broken limbs. We'll need a rope to get out."

"Father," I called. "Where are you? Are you there, Ananias?"

"Yes." Ananias's voice came from the left side of the cavernous hold. Even when I lowered the lamp, I still couldn't make him out. "But Father isn't here," he added.

One or two of the Guardians tried to force their eyes open, but they just squinted until the discomfort became too much. Then they closed them again.

"Where is he?" I asked.

"I don't know."

Kyte stood directly under the trapdoor. "The pirates beat him, Thomas. Badly."

I thought of the bloodstained wall and began to wave the lamp around. I could see everyone in there, but not my father. "Where is he now?"

"We don't know. We're not sure he's still on board."

My mind flashed back to the previous evening, and the wooden box I'd seen the pirates lowering onto the cutter. It had been the right size for a body.

I tried to wipe the thought away, but couldn't. My breathing grew faster, and the lamp shone brighter. In its glow I saw the way the Guardians' faces had frozen in a grimace, as though the pain had gone on for so long that it couldn't be undone.

I stepped back. Tessa was behind me, but out of sight. I got the feeling she didn't want to be seen. Griffin was beside her.

Need. Rope, I signed. *Stern. Ship*, I added, hoping he'd realize I meant the ropes we'd climbed last night.

He nodded sharply and turned to leave. I held the lamp up for him so he could see the way to the staircase. Without the light shining on them, the Guardians groaned again.

"How do you know my father was beaten?" I shouted into the darkness.

Kyte quieted everyone. "We saw it happen. The pirates bound us, and then attacked him. They did it suddenly—sticks, ropes . . . whatever they could lay their hands on."

I was desperate to erase the image of that box leaving the ship, but now I could think of nothing else. I couldn't have lost both parents. I just couldn't.

"They made me watch, Thomas," said Ananias. His voice caught as he said my name, and I felt ashamed for not considering how awful the past few days must have been for him—knowing our father had been beaten; wondering if he would be next.

I tried to hold my voice steady. "We'll get you out. I promise." I turned to Dennis. "How long do we have?"

He stared into the hold and ran a hand through his hair. "Not long enough."

I raised the lantern to see if Griffin had reappeared, but I knew he'd need longer. With nothing else to look at, my eyes returned to the bloodied patch of wall again.

"Where was he when they attacked him?" I called into the hold.

It took Ananias a moment to answer. "On the deck. They

hit him . . ." His voice trailed off. "I'm sorry," he cried, like this was somehow his fault.

I could tell that he really was sorry. He sounded desolate, helpless, ashamed. But I felt only relief washing over me. The blood couldn't be my father's if he'd been beaten on deck. I wanted Ananias to know it too, but how could I explain about the bloody wall without worrying everyone even more?

Ananias continued to sob as the Guardians fell silent again. "For a quarter strike they hurt him," he continued. "Even when he couldn't stand. And then . . ." He choked on the words. "Then they pushed him through the hatch and down the staircase, and started beating him all over again."

CHAPTER 42

I couldn't wait any longer. If we were going to release the Guardians, we had to start now. I went in search of Griffin.

Looking up through the hatch, I saw the sky lightening little by little. Maybe it would be easier to face the hurricane if we could see what was happening.

I didn't mean to look at the wall behind me, but my eyes were drawn to it. All that blood, in long streaks that touched the floor—it was horrifying. It didn't end there, either. Drops of blood traced an uneven line under my feet. They continued all the way to the opposite wall, where they ended abruptly at a wooden panel beneath the stairs.

I ran my fingers across the panel. Then I knocked on it once, hard. For a moment there was silence, followed by moaning—quiet but insistent.

The lamp shone brighter, revealing the grain in the wood. I scrabbled about, searching for some kind of handle, like the ring I'd found embedded in the floor. Instead I found a tiny

gap running vertically from floor to ceiling. I dug my fingernails into it but couldn't lever it open.

I called out for Tessa to help me, but there was no answer.
When I scanned the corridor, she'd disappeared again.

Griffin pounded down the stairs. The rope was coiled over
his shoulder. He headed straight for my lamp.

"Is that Griffin?" shouted Rose from along the corridor.
"We need the rope. And the lamp. Dennis says the eye's about
to pass."

I heard every word, but I didn't reply. I needed the lamp
too. Just for a moment.

Griffin joined me. I didn't know if he'd guessed who might
be behind the wooden panel, or if he simply wanted to help.
Either way, I was so grateful to have him next to me.

"Now, Thomas!" yelled Rose.

There was desperation in her voice, but I couldn't stop.
Kyte was still alive. I had to know if my father was too.

Griffin pressed his nails into the gap and pulled, but the
panel still didn't move. The lamp dimmed as my energy
waned. Finally, I punched the wood in frustration.

It slid backward. Clicked once. And opened toward us.

Behind the wall was a tiny room, less than two yards deep,
high, and wide. A metal cage ran along the back wall, and
someone was trapped inside. He was sprawled awkwardly
across the floor, hands and feet bound behind him with
secure knots.

"Father!" I dropped to my knees and tried to reach him,

but I couldn't squeeze more than two fingers through the holes in the mesh. "It's me, Father. Thomas."

At the sound of my voice, he turned his face toward me. It was crusted with dried blood.

"Thomas," he rasped. "You came."

"I don't know how to get you out."

"Don't worry about me. Get the others."

I held the lamp closer and saw that his nose was bent to one side, lips and eyes swollen. When he opened his other eye, a wound on his forehead reopened. It oozed blood.

"I have to get you out."

"You can't," he said again. "Captain has the key."

"Maybe there's another key."

"No. He wouldn't take that chance . . . someone releasing me by accident."

"Why did they do this to you?"

He smiled, and one of the scabs on his cheek cracked. "Why, indeed."

He rolled over so I wouldn't have to see his injuries. Then he shuffled toward me and splayed his fingers against the side of the cage, so that our fingertips were touching.

I closed my eyes and savored the contact: skin on skin, without a hint of discomfort. As we touched, I realized this was his answer—that his touch was a threat to the pirates. Given everything I'd experienced in the past day, I could imagine why.

I slid my fingers onto the rope that bound his wrists. I picked at the knot, but it didn't give.

"Don't bother," he said. "They spend their lives making knots. They won't have made a mistake with me."

I remembered Griffin then, and felt ashamed that he remained in the background, excluded. I moved aside so he could join us. I pointed to Father's hand against the mesh, meaning for them to touch.

Griffin shook his head. He no doubt remembered the last time they'd touched. Or maybe it was the sight of our father's blood-soaked face. If he was going to die soon, Griffin didn't want to know.

Rose screamed my name again, but I couldn't leave until I knew the truth. "What are we, Father?" I whispered.

Though he barely moved, I could feel his surprise in the way his fingers stiffened. "You found out." I detected a note of pride in his voice.

"Tell me about our element. I have to know who I am."

"Element?" He snorted. "Dare can handle an *element*. But he's plenty afraid of what you and I can do. I hadn't seen that man in thirteen years, but the look on his face when he saw me . . . he's as scared of me now as he was then."

"Because our touch hurts people?"

"That's a part of it, but there's so much more." He seemed energized by our conversation, as if he'd waited all his life for this moment. "I'm older now—much older—but you can see, Dare wasn't taking any chances. And if he knew you had it too—"

A scream from above deck spun me around. "What was that?"

Another scream.

Alice.

I rounded the stairs to the deck and sprinted up. Alice was at the stern, pointing into the swirling mist.

As I joined her, I couldn't see anything at all.

"Put the lamp out," she snapped. "It interferes with my vision."

I dropped it at once. "What's out there?"

"Six," she whispered. "Six separate paddle strokes. So at least six men."

When I squinted, I could make out a tiny dot of light searing through the mist. It bobbed up and down. "Who is it?"

"Pirates. I can hear their voices."

Footsteps drummed against the deck planks as Griffin, Rose, and Dennis joined us.

"Oh, no," murmured Alice.

"What?"

She didn't answer. The light was near enough now that it illuminated the space immediately around it—including a man's face and his colorful arms.

CHAPTER 43

They're less than a hundred yards away," said Alice.

Dennis pressed himself against the rail. "They're crazy. The eye of the storm . . . it's almost passed."

As if it were under his command, the wind picked up.

"Do we have time to release the Guardians?" I asked.

He shook his head.

"Why is Dare doing this? Why not wait for us at the shore?"

"Because he doesn't think you'll come ashore," Tessa explained with eerie calm. Once again, I hadn't seen or heard her arrive. "He thinks you intend to escape in his ship."

I glanced around me at the vessel, larger than all the colony's cabins put together. It seemed ridiculous that we would attempt to sail the ship—although with the Guardians' help, perhaps not impossible. Maybe Dare thought his only hope was to recapture the ship before the storm passed and we released our parents.

But how could he be sure we hadn't released them already?

The light in the cutter was growing brighter with every

293

stroke. Dare stood in the middle, lantern raised, smile fixed. It occurred to me that with the light so close to his face, he wouldn't be able to see us. But then, that wasn't the point. He just wanted us to see *him*.

"How far away are they?" I asked.

Alice stared at the light. "Seventy yards. They're moving fast."

"The tide is with them," said Rose. She stared intently at the expanse of black water as though she were uncovering its secrets. "It'll push them south."

To my left, something creaked loudly. Griffin was pulling the winch that raised the anchor, his face a picture of determination.

"What's he doing?" shouted Rose.

I ran to help him. "Weighing anchor. If we can get the ship moving, we might be able to avoid them."

"But there are two anchors," yelled Alice. She sprinted to the bow and began heaving the winch there as well.

"Rose, stay there and tell us how close they're getting," I said. "Dennis, we need to know when the eye's about to pass."

They nodded at the same moment that Griffin's winch jammed. I grabbed a part of the wooden handle and we both tugged it. Little by little it began to move again. I was surprised at how easily the chain links slid up, clicking against the pulley aside the ship. This was no ordinary vessel.

"How far, Rose?"

"Maybe fifty yards."

Another turn of the winch. Our hands slipped on the

wet handle, but we kept turning it around and around. The anchor chain slithered upward.

"Forty-five."

I heard the anchor splash out of the water. We all looked to the stern, and the light that wasn't so little anymore.

"Forty."

"It's done," said Alice, rejoining us.

"It won't be enough," cried Rose. "A ship this size needs time to move."

"Then we'll use the sails."

Dennis glanced up. "You can't. When the hurricane returns, it'll destroy a sail."

"Thirty-five yards."

Alice looked straight at me, and an understanding passed between us: If Dare stepped foot on the ship, the sails were the least of our concerns. "Let's raise the jib," she said.

Griffin and I ran after her, past the mainmast to the bow. Dennis followed up the rear.

"Thirty." Rose's voice carried on the wind.

Alice and Griffin crouched beside a winch and began turning the handle. Like the anchors, the jib hauled upward with surprising ease. I tried to keep the sail from catching on any obstacles.

"Read the wind, Dennis," I called out. "Tell us everything."

"It's building," he said. "Eighteen knots—no, nineteen. It's about to rain. It'll be heavy right away."

The sail was unfurling, but not quickly enough.

"Twenty yards." Rose sounded frantic.

At last the jib billowed as the wind filled it. Alice locked the winch in place and looked at the sound to see if we were moving.

"Fifteen yards!"

"Twenty-two knots," muttered Dennis. "It's not enough." He stared at the sail, which snapped taut as a gust swept across the deck. "Twenty-eight." The ship groaned. "Thirty-one."

"Ten yards," Rose screamed. "They're about to reach the sailboats."

The sailboats. I'd forgotten they were tethered to the stern.

A ferocious gust knocked me right over. From above us came the sound of tearing fabric.

"Sorry," muttered Dennis. He seemed shocked, as though he'd just awoken from a trance. "I didn't mean—"

None of us waited to hear what came next. We ran to the stern, flat footsteps to keep from slipping on the damp planking.

"Get back from the railing," I yelled, but Rose didn't move. Instead, she was leaning over it, dragging up the rope that still dangled over the side.

"They'll use it to climb," she shouted back.

As soon as I reached her, I grabbed the rope too, but it wasn't budging. I drove my foot against the rail and used my full body weight to pull, but it stayed fast.

"Help us, Alice. We can't—"

A sound split the air, short and sharp like lightning splitting a tree.

"Get back!" screamed Tessa.

Rose slipped on the deck and almost fell down.

"Where have you been?" I yelled. But Tessa didn't reply. Instead she pulled Rose around and looked over her whole body.

"What was that sound?" asked Rose.

Tessa huffed. "Something else your Guardians didn't tell you about."

The rope shifted from side to side, and I knew that someone was climbing—someone much heavier than me.

Alice picked up the rope coil that Griffin had been carrying. She ran her free hand back and forth across it, faster and faster. I smelled burning. A spark became a flame, and soon the rope was consumed by fire. She threw it overboard.

Cries erupted from the boat below. But the rope attached to the rail didn't loosen.

"Stay back," said Tessa. She pulled a knife from the folds of her tunic, unsheathed it, and drove it into the rope. She began to saw back and forth.

The sound split the air again.

Tessa wasn't sawing anymore. In fact, she wasn't moving at all. Finally she staggered back and collapsed onto the deck, her right hand clasped against her left shoulder.

I knelt beside her. "What's the matter?"

She wouldn't let go of her shoulder. I grabbed a fold of cloth and eased her arm away, careful not to touch her. There was something damp and sticky on her sleeve.

"What happened?" asked Alice.

"I don't know. She's bleeding. A lot."

Tessa clenched her teeth. "Don't fight him, Thomas. His weapon will kill you." She stole a breath, but it seemed to hurt her. "Get below deck. Lock the hatch."

"What about you?"

"I'm not afraid of pirates. Now go!"

"Too late," shouted Dennis.

A hand appeared on the rail.

CHAPTER 44

I snatched the knife that lay on the deck beside Tessa, leaped toward the rail, and brought the blade down into the center of the pirate's hand.

His scream was excruciating. When he slipped away, the knife was embedded so firmly that he took it overboard with him. There was a splash as he hit the water.

Alice tugged on my tunic. "Get back, Thom."

I shrugged her off and peered over the rail. We had to know what we were up against.

The cutter was almost touching the ship, tethered to the rope hanging from the rail. Our capsized sailboats looked small beside it. Five men were lined up at the bow, ready to board. Alice's burning rope had been tossed aside.

The mysterious sound rang out again. A piece of the rail splintered off beside me and snapped against my cheek. I touched the spot and felt blood trickling from the cut.

Each of the pirates held something—a dark cylinder aimed right at me. Whatever those things were, they had the power to break wood, and had hurt Tessa in a way I'd never seen before.

"Raise your hands and stay where you are," shouted Dare. "We don't want to hurt you."

I stared at the cylinders aimed at me. I couldn't surrender—we'd worked too hard to escape—but Tessa was right: I couldn't fight those weapons. I pushed off the rail and dove to the deck.

"Wind at thirty-five knots," said Dennis. "We need to shelter."

Again, as if it took orders from him, the wind kicked, and this time brought rain in a thick sheet.

"Let's go," Alice shouted. "We'll barricade the hatch at the top of the stairs. If the pirates are stuck above deck, the wind and rain will take care of them for us."

I pointed at Tessa. "What about her?"

Alice rubbed her hands together again and conjured a flame. She brought it close to Tessa's shoulder so that we could see the wound. Then she extinguished the flame just as suddenly. It was too late, though—we'd all seen it.

So much blood. It seemed impossible.

"We'll drag you," I told her.

"No," spat Tessa. "Just go."

"Not without you."

"Then I walk."

With difficulty, she stood. Rose stepped forward and eased Tessa's good arm across her shoulder. They staggered toward the hatch, pausing after every step.

A new sound pulled me around—Griffin pushing a large

wooden chest across the deck. It slid easily on the slick planks. I didn't realize what he was doing at first, but then I understood. "Here, Alice. Help Griffin."

Together, we pushed the chest toward the stern. It was heavy, but when Dennis joined us we took a corner each and managed to lift it so that it balanced on the rail. As soon as it was stable, something hit it, and a piece of wood splintered off again.

"Push," I said.

Perched precariously on the rail, the chest tipped over the side and crashed against the cutter. I leaned over and saw that it had sliced off one side. The boat was taking on water. The pirates still aboard had lost their footing and were floundering about in the swell. One of them clung to his seat and bailed water in a hopeless attempt to keep the cutter afloat.

But there was still another pirate. He hung on to the rope half a yard below me, his weapon inches from my face.

Dare's stare was icy. "Get back or I'll kill you."

I stepped away. The others did too.

He kept me in his sights as he swung his leg over the railing. When he had both feet on the deck, he smiled. "Hello, Griffin."

I didn't understand. Why would he think I was Griffin? Or didn't he know? I narrowed my eyes and remained silent.

He shrugged and turned to my brother. I expected him to repeat himself, but he didn't. In fact, it was clear from his expression that he'd already worked out that Griffin was his *solution*—his prize. But how?

You'll know him too, just as soon as I call his name.

The words played in my mind. Dare knew that Griffin was *deaf*. The moment I reacted at all, it was clear I'd heard him. But the weapon remained pointed at me, not at Griffin.

Another fierce gust seemed to knock him off balance. In a flash, Alice launched herself at him. She was as quick as lightning, but she didn't even lay a finger on him before he swung his arm around and the weapon cracked against her face. She landed on the deck with a sickening thud.

"Stupid girl." He pointed his weapon at me again. "Am I going to have to do that to you too?"

I shook my head.

"Good. Then start walking toward the stairs. Now!"

Alice didn't get up. She wasn't even moving.

"I'm not leaving her."

"No one said anything about leaving her. Now get back." Over the roar of the wind and rain, I heard his weapon click. "I can live without you, Thomas. Your brother is the only one I care about. So if you want to live, walk." He waited for a moment, then smiled his cold empty smile. "Bad choice."

I didn't even see his hand move, but the weapon caught me square across the jaw. My feet flew out from under me and suddenly I was on the deck beside Alice. Her eyes were closed. I couldn't tell whether she was alive or dead.

I tasted blood in my mouth and spit it out. When I looked up, Dare towered over me, an expression of surprise on his face. As our eyes met, he turned away. He grabbed Griffin and tried to push him toward the stairs, but Griffin fought back.

"Stop it, Dare! They're children." Tessa's voice was weak, barely audible above the wind and rain, but the words stopped him in his tracks. "Isn't it enough that you shot me?" I could hear the pain in her voice—she almost choked out the words.

Dare stared at her, and at Alice and me. Everyone who had crossed him was injured.

"Look around you," she continued. "There are no Guardians here to stop you. You've won. Now put your gun away."

As he studied the mess of bodies on the deck, Dare seemed confused, almost hypnotized.

It was all Griffin needed. He spun around and kicked at the back of Dare's legs. The pirate dropped hard.

I clambered up and dove for the weapon in his hand. The thin cylinder was cold and smooth in my palm. In the back of my mind, I willed Griffin to escape. If there was one thing I knew for certain now, it was that nothing was more important than him. I didn't need to believe in a solution to know that if Griffin could get away, we'd still have everything that Dare wanted. We'd have the upper hand.

But Griffin wasn't moving. And neither was Dare.

That's when I felt it—an ache that grew from my hand and spread along my arm and up my neck. My chest tightened too. Dare pulled the handle of the gun so hard that I could hear his teeth grinding.

The pain was inside my head now, and spread across my body like heat emanating from a fire. I felt the gnawing pressure, the sensation that my life was ebbing away. I wanted it to stop. I needed it to stop. Dare's mouth twisted into a smile.

I closed my eyes and tried to harness my fear and uncertainty and anger. So much pain, but when I concentrated, everything converged. It was like a wildfire confined to a small space in my brain. And still it grew.

My breaths were short and fast. The fire became an inferno that left me blind and disoriented. I saw nothing, heard nothing, smelled nothing. I was just a vessel for the force consuming me. It was ready to be unleashed.

In an instant, the inferno shot through me and into him.

The look in Dare's eyes shifted from triumph to horror. He began to shake—not just his hand, but also his arm. It spread to his head, and then his entire body was contorting. He couldn't seem to pull away anymore. The realization produced another jolt of energy that surged through me and into him. Now his eyes expressed nothing at all—simply flicked up and back until there was only white. His body relaxed so suddenly, it was as if I'd liquefied his bones.

"Enough, Thomas. Stop!" cried Tessa. "Don't become him."

Her words snapped me back to consciousness. I gulped deep breaths and rolled away.

"You were close. Too close."

I knew what she meant. I'd felt it the moment I saw Dare panic, and again as his eyes had rolled back. It was an awesome feeling—power like I'd never known. I could've killed him, I realized. But who would I be then?

The weapon lay on the deck between us. I kicked it away. There would be time to ask the Guardians about that when the hurricane had passed. For now we had to get below deck.

"Tie him up," said Tessa. "Let the Guardians decide his fate in the morning."

Griffin took a fistful of Dare's tunic and pulled him upright. Dennis joined him. They seemed to have him in a seating position when Dare's eyes slipped down again.

He pushed Dennis to the deck and grabbed Griffin by the throat. He staggered toward his weapon. His expression had changed now—wild, as though his animal instincts had taken over. He was choking my brother to death.

I crawled across the deck and lunged for the weapon at the same moment as Dare. This time I didn't wait for the power to surge through me—I just poured everything into him. He fought again, but he was stumbling backward toward the rail. It didn't take much to press him against it.

Griffin wriggled free, and a moment later he had Dare's torso hanging over the rail.

Tessa shouted "No," but Griffin couldn't hear her. He just pushed harder still, and didn't stop until Dare's body slipped overboard.

I barely heard the splash.

I looked down, waiting for him to reappear. But the surface of the water was covered with silver scales—not one fish, but several. Maybe hundreds. Thousands.

Just behind me, Rose stood still, eyes closed. The look on her face was pure concentration.

Griffin and Dennis helped Alice get below deck, their arms around her waist, her legs dragging behind. Tessa crawled

305

after them. Finally, Rose opened her eyes and the fish dispersed. But the sound was no calmer. Storm gusts whipped salt spray against my face. The ship lurched beneath me.

We were battered, but alive. Relief washed over me, and my pulse slowed down. The fire that had consumed me was gradually extinguished, and my body shifted through several states, like colors bleeding into one another in a rainbow: invincible, powerful, relieved, vulnerable, weak, exhausted, empty—

I fell to the deck face-first. I didn't even brace myself with my arms.

I couldn't.

CHAPTER 45

As I lay there, I thought of Dare, presumably drowned, and felt no remorse. I thought of Griffin, and was relieved to know he'd escaped. I thought of my father, and how much I still had to learn about myself. I thought of Alice, and hoped she was still alive.

Griffin and Rose appeared above me. They hadn't been gone long, but the hurricane was in full force once again. Rainwater ran off their hair in torrents. They fought to hold steady against the wind.

Dennis was beside them. He raised his face to the sky, and the wind calmed a little. I tried to make out what he was doing, but everything looked blurry.

Relax, Griffin signed.

I understood that he needed my pulse to be slow so that I wouldn't hurt them. It wasn't hard—I was barely conscious. I couldn't even raise my head.

He and Rose gripped the material under my armpits and dragged me on my back across the deck. They struggled to keep their footing, but Dennis fell in step beside us, and if I doubted it before, now I was certain: He was keeping the wind at bay.

When we reached the hatch, they eased me down the stairs. As soon as I was on the floor, Griffin hobbled back up and locked the hatch door. The ship was rolling about again, walls creaking. The hurricane sounded almost as loud below deck as above.

Rose leaned over me. It was dark, and I couldn't see her. But I felt every snatch of breath, every tear that fell on me, the end of her braid tickling my face. She wasn't even pulling away.

"Alice," I croaked. "Tessa."

"Tessa's back in the cabin," said Rose. "Alice too. She's unconscious, but Tessa says she'll be all right."

"Anchors."

"We lowered them." Her hair ran across my face again. I wanted to touch it, but I couldn't raise my arms. "Relax now, Thomas. We need to get you to the cabin."

"No. Father."

It was obvious that she didn't want to put me with my father, crushed between a cage and the wall. But in the silence that followed I knew she'd thought of something else too: that it was the best way to make sure I couldn't harm anyone.

Rose and Griffin grabbed fistfuls of my tunic and pulled me into the tiny room. My legs tangled beneath me. My head collided with the door frame. I clamped my mouth shut so I wouldn't cry out.

"I'll be back as soon as the storm passes," Rose said. "I promise."

Without another word, she and Griffin climbed around me. They were being tossed about like driftwood now, and just getting through the doorway was difficult. As their footsteps receded, I imagined I could still hear Dennis's voice keeping track of the wind's incessant acceleration: forty knots, fifty, sixty.

I felt empty. It was a painful emptiness too, like every muscle in my body had been strained, torn, obliterated.

"Thomas?" My father's voice cut through the emptiness. "Are you all right, son?"

Even breathing was hard. "My body . . . doesn't work."

Another gust or wave pushed me against the cage. The metal mesh dug sharply into my side. I couldn't roll away. A groan escaped me, but I wasn't aware of making it.

My father pressed his fingers through the mesh and touched my hand. Warmth radiated through his fingertips. "Stay calm," he murmured. "Breathe deeply and concentrate on your heartbeat—keep it slow and steady. You need to find equilibrium if you want to overcome the echo."

"Echo?"

"Shh! No talking now. Only deep breaths."

I did as he said, and little by little my pulse slowed. I might have been imagining it, but it felt like something was returning to me, like an empty canister being filled with water.

Another violent gust, and our hands separated. I heard him

curse, but a moment later he'd found my fingers again. We held each other tightly.

I couldn't remember a time I'd felt so connected to my father.

I came to as footsteps drummed on the stairs just outside the door. At least, that's what I thought I heard, but a moment later they were gone. After that, there was nothing but the sound of the weakening storm.

I stretched. Though I ached all over, I was in much less pain than I would have imagined. My father still held my fingers.

"Feel better?" he asked.

With my free hand, I raised a finger to my mouth. Dare's weapon had split my lip, but nothing more. "Yes. But . . . how?"

He ignored my question. "What happened up there?"

"Dare tried to take back the ship. He had a weapon. When I grabbed it, he started to shake. Griffin pushed him overboard and now I think he's dr—"

"Shh. It's all right now." His fingertips brushed against me. "How is Griffin?"

"He's safe."

"Good. And the others?"

"Dare hurt Alice badly. Tessa too—"

A wave of energy pulsed through his fingers, sudden and sharp. I yanked my hand away.

He muttered a curse, but calmed himself with a deep

breath. When our fingers touched again, his energy level was normal, just as suddenly as if he'd blown out a candle.

"Tessa." The way he said her name sounded odd, like a question—as if he was trying to remember where he'd heard it before. "She came back."

"She helped us. But she's hurt now."

"What happened?"

"I don't know. Dare wasn't even beside her when he did it."

Father didn't say anything for a moment. "You're sure it was Dare?"

"I think so. Why?"

"Just . . . be careful around her. Remember, she chose exile over staying with you."

I shifted my weight, but nothing felt comfortable. "Why did you tell me she was dead?"

"Because that's how she wanted it. We make decisions, and we live with them. No matter how much we regret them."

I needed to know about those decisions. "I found a picture in Bodie Lighthouse. Our family. Before Griffin was born."

"Your mother . . ." He spoke quietly, and though he tried to hide it, I knew he was fighting tears. "I wish I could go back. Change everything."

"In the picture she's holding Ananias. Did she ever hold me? Or were you the only one who could stand it?"

Another pulse, but this one was different: a wave of soothing energy. Maybe I was imagining it, but it felt like a gesture of love.

"Oh, Thomas. Of course she held you. She adored you.

Nursed you for over a year when you were a baby, but only when you were almost asleep. Your pulse would slow down then—gentle enough for her to cope."

"Will anyone else ever touch me?"

"Yes. You'll learn to listen to your heartbeat—control it too. You just need time."

That was what I wanted to hear, but it still didn't answer the biggest question of all. "Why have we been hiding our element?"

Yet another jolt—small, but this one scared me. It was the quality, as if he were channeling raw power. Anger, maybe. I wondered if it was the kind of energy I'd seared into Dare.

"We hid ourselves because of a promise," he growled. "A stupid promise I should never have made. One I've regretted every day since."

His breathing accelerated. It seemed to trigger a reaction in me, and my pulse quickened. He pulled away to prevent me from having to do it first.

"Sorry," I said.

"No, it's my fault. Our element is symbiotic. In the old times, a parent would teach it through touch—I would've adjusted your heartbeat and energy levels myself to show you the effect. But the Guardians stopped all that."

"So why did you make the promise?"

"It seemed like the best choice."

"But it was a lie. How can that be best?"

"Because the alternative was exile."

"Like Tessa?" I tried to make sense of it. "Why would they exile you?"

"Not me. *Us*." His voice sounded low and distant. "They fear us, Thomas. Their elements take one energy source and transfer it into another. But no one knows the limits of what we can do. Even me. I've wanted to tell you so many times, but how could I do that and make you promise not to think about it ever again?"

I couldn't answer. It was a decision I'd never had the chance to make.

"On your sixteenth birthday, they wanted to make you an Apprentice. But I wouldn't let them."

"*You?*"

"Of course me. I wouldn't let them fob you off with some pretend skill that had no real connection to you. Not while you had no idea who you really were." He kicked out against the end of his cage. "I've lived the last sixteen years struggling to make a simple fire, while Ananias watches me pityingly. And all along, I've been hiding miracles the other Guardians can't even comprehend."

"I can make a lantern shine."

"A lantern?" He snorted. "The energy you transferred to Dare wouldn't illuminate a lantern, it would illuminate a hundred lanterns. Anger is the strongest force of all. But it's unpredictable and exhausting—as dangerous for you as the person you touch."

I thought of Dare, and the pirate who'd tried to capsize our sailboat under the bridge, and the one who had tried to stop us in the creek near Bodie Lighthouse. My element had served us well then, but at what cost? I'd been unable to stay conscious afterward. Father was right—I couldn't lose control. I may not always have friends to save me.

"My energy travels through metal too."

"Yes. That's why the Guardians have tried to keep metal objects out of the colony as much as possible. They knew they'd never be able to explain your element, or the things you might do with it."

"Like what?"

"On Roanoke you powered a lantern. But on this ship . . ." His tongue clicked. "When the hurricane passes, you need to look around. Dare will have instruments, machines, I'm sure of it. Only you and I can make them work—especially you. Your power is unthinkable, you hear me? *Unthinkable*."

"Then so is yours."

"No. We're not the same."

"You can't know what I'll be able to do. Even I don't know."

"Believe me, I know." He found my fingers again, and his breathing grew slower. As quickly as he'd grown animated, he now seemed to be drifting toward sleep. With energy flowing freely between us, it was as though he was sending me to sleep too. "I just know."

CHAPTER 46

hen I woke again, I felt surprisingly fresh. I'd ache all over when I tried to stand, but at least the crushing emptiness had passed.

Rose stood in the doorway, silhouetted by a dull light. Somehow, her face was unblemished. The rain had even cleaned off the grime.

"Dennis says the hurricane has almost passed," she explained. "It's barely a storm now."

It took a moment for the words to seep in. We'd survived. It seemed impossible. How could we have overcome Dare and his men?

"How's Alice?"

Rose moved aside and Alice stepped forward. The left side of her face was hideously bruised. Her eye was partially closed.

"Oh, no."

"It's fine," snapped Alice. "Tessa says it'll heal eventually. Anyway, you don't exactly look great yourself."

"How is Tessa?"

"Not well. She won't let us touch her shoulder."

"And Griffin? And Dennis?"

"They're all right. Dennis found a rope in one of the drawers from the cabin. He's lowering it to the Guardians right now. But we need your help."

My father seemed to be sleeping peacefully as I left the claustrophobic room. It was a relief to see him relaxed; he was worse off than any of us. In the weak light, I could make out the trail of blood leading from the floor of his cage, out the door, and across the corridor to the opposite wall. It looked as terrifying now as before, but he'd survived. That was all that mattered.

Toward the end of the corridor, Dennis stood beside the trapdoor, the rope dangling from his hands. He looked fully recovered, as though the headaches that had plagued him for days were finally over.

In the hull below, the Guardians moaned, desperate to leave their prison. When Kyte announced that he'd be going up first, no one argued.

Once Kyte had a good grip on the rope, we all began to pull. He was heavy, and the rope scraped against the edge of the floor, which slowed us down. Finally his hand emerged, and he grabbed the floor and took some of his weight. Even then we kept pulling, until he was able to swing a leg up. When he was out, he rolled toward us.

Dennis fell down beside his father and wrapped his arms around him. I expected Rose to do the same, but she hesitated. I was proud of her for that. It meant she'd accepted that the world could never be the same. Kyte would still be at the center of it, but that was the problem. The strong, steady influence he'd brought to bear for years had been built on lies as poorly constructed as the colony on Hatteras. The flames that devoured our cabins had destroyed his imaginary world almost as quickly. She wouldn't let him forget it.

As Kyte saw his daughter staring down at him, a flicker of understanding passed between them. "Aren't you going to help me up, Rose?" he asked with typical bluster.

Rose brushed my sleeve—a fleeting gesture to let her father know whose side she was on. She crouched beside him, but she didn't kneel. "Do you need help, Father?"

Kyte sat upright. Gritting his teeth to mask the pain, he pulled himself to a stand. Even with their positions reversed, Rose didn't look intimidated.

"It would be a nice gesture for you to help the other Guardians," he said.

Rose returned a straight-lipped smile. "Of course I'll rescue the others as well. It's why we came."

Kyte gave her a piece of the rope and took a handful himself.

"Looks like this is under control," I whispered to Alice. "I'm going to check on Griffin. Is he in Tessa's cabin?"

"I guess so." She picked up a loose coil of rope and prepared to pull too. Then she smiled. "Hey, can you do me a favor?"

"Sure."

"Can you think of a way to get my mother out of the hold

but not my father? The past four days are the best we've ever gotten along."

She laughed then, and so did I. It felt strange, but good. Like I'd been holding my breath for days, and could finally exhale again.

I made my way to the stern. Even though the ship was steady, I imagined I could still feel it rocking from side to side. The hurricane had branded itself on my memory.

Tessa's door was ajar. Pieces of wood had splintered from the door frame where Alice had kicked it open the night before. Tessa lay on her back on the floor, head tilted to the side. But Griffin wasn't there.

"Good. You're alive," she said, opening one eye. "Won't even look too bad once we clean up the blood."

"Wish I could say the same for you."

She chuckled, and grimaced. "So, I saw what Dare did to you. But I also saw what you did to him. I tried to tell you to stop—to save your energy—but . . ." She took a deep breath. "What happened to him when Griffin pushed him overboard?"

"I don't know. He didn't resurface."

Tessa closed her eyes. "Good."

I knelt down and eased back the shreds of material covering her left shoulder. The caked-on blood seemed to emanate from a single tiny spot. It seemed impossible that such a small wound could cause so much bleeding.

"Are you going to be all right?" I asked.

Tessa swallowed hard. "You mean: Am I going to live?" She pursed her lips. "It's not so bad. I'll be fine in a while."

She shifted on the blankets. The underside of her shoulder was caked in blood too. Without material to cover it, I could see that the wound was another tiny hole, the same as on the front of her shoulder.

"There are holes both sides."

"Yes. I was lucky. Dare's weapon is called a gun. It sends a tiny piece of metal—a bullet—at very high speed. The bullet bursts through skin and muscle and flesh . . . does a lot of damage. I won't be able to use my shoulder until the wound is fully healed. Even then, it might not be the same."

"What can I do?"

"Get my medicine bag from the hold in the sailboat, for a start."

"What if the boats aren't there?"

"Then we're all in trouble. Some of the Guardians may need treating if they've been stuck in the hold for days." She licked her lips. "I'd really like some water as well, please. Then I just need to rest."

Looking around the room, it occurred to me that something else was missing too. "Where's your cat?"

Her expression shifted. "Cats aren't water creatures. And in a storm . . . well, let's just say he chose to stay home."

"I'm sorry."

"So am I. Now let me rest."

I was about to leave, but there was another question I had

to ask: "Where did you go last night? A few times I looked around and couldn't see you."

"I don't know what you mean. I was there with you. Where else would I be?"

She was keeping something from me, but there would be time to press her on that. As she closed her eyes, I stepped quietly out of the room and pulled the door closed behind me.

Toward the end of the corridor, the trapdoor appeared to be open, but everyone had gone. They'd worked even quicker than I'd dared to imagine. Snatches of voices came from the deck above—the sound of families reuniting, or perhaps Alice and Rose demanding answers. The truth would come out now, whether the Guardians liked it or not.

We were safe again. Whole again.

It was time for healing.

EPILOGUE

I closed my eyes and savored the peacefulness. I was so distracted I didn't realize Griffin was standing behind me until he grabbed my sleeve and twisted me around.

Come. Look, he signed.

He turned and headed through an open door behind him. I didn't follow, though. I just peered into the room and wondered how he'd managed to get in, when it had been so securely locked only a few strikes before.

I waited for Griffin to face me again. *How. You. Here?* I signed.

He understood me well enough. *Door. Open.*

Who. Open?

He had no answer.

I inspected the lock. There was no key, but the door handle turned freely. Had it just been stuck? Or had someone found a way to break in?

The room was remarkable: full of books on shelves, and

maps on walls. Mechanical instruments had been tied down onto tables with elaborate knots. There wasn't any wasted space. Even the low bed in the corner was stuffed behind a desk. The blankets that lay neatly across it seemed undisturbed despite the ship having seesawed through the night.

Griffin stood at a desk to the left, poring over an open book. A small porthole near the ceiling cast a sliver of golden light across it, but most of the room's light came from the row of windows in the far wall.

Read, he signed. He was breathing fast and shallow. The look on his face told me he'd already read it, and didn't like what he'd seen.

I took in line after line of handwritten words—neat and clear, not a single mistake or crossing-out. The first line was a series of numbers and letters I couldn't decipher: 35°52°N 75°40°W Y:18 D:38. Then, underneath, it said: *Barometer readings suggest hurricane. Shelter W of Roanoke I. Children hiding in remains of Manteo. Solution within reach.*

I pointed to the word *Manteo*.

Griffin nodded briskly. *Skeleton. Town*, he explained.

I knew he must be right. But in that case, the words must have been written the previous day. And if this was Dare's log, presumably the cabin was his too. Judging from the number of similar-sized books on the shelves, Griffin would have days of reading ahead of him.

Where. Find. Book? I asked.

Griffin shook his head. Then he pointed at the desk,

showed open hands with palms up, and finally stabbed the page with his finger. He'd found it right there, just waiting for him.

How convenient.

I imagined Dare working on it just before he left the ship. But how could a book stay in the middle of a desk during a hurricane? And how could he be sure we'd find it?

As soon as the thought entered my mind, I knew the answer: He was a seer. He may have seen it all already.

But then, why had he attacked during the night? If he'd already envisaged the outcome, surely he wouldn't have willingly gone to his death.

Griffin flicked back through the book and pointed to a new page:

35°54'N 75°35'W Y:18 D:36. Fortuitous timing. Tropical storm provided perfect cover. Islanders offered no resistance. Call themselves "Guardians" now. Such beautiful fiction! Refuse to surrender solution, of course—always did value their own lives above the multitude. Doesn't matter—he'll have to come out of hiding soon. Nowhere else to run.

On the previous page, there was another passage:

Visions kicking in again—first time in years. Fuzzier than before, but promising. I see them both—indistinct, but so near. Eighteen years and thirty-five days, but the endgame is in sight now. I thank the Gods for this opportunity. I know They will not let us fail.

Again, there was so much I didn't understand, but Griffin

was pointing at the final figures on the top line: *Y:18 D:35.*
Then he pointed to the words a few lines down: *"Eighteen years and thirty-five days,"* I read out loud.

Numbers. Time, he signed.

I read the passage over and over. Eighteen years ago would have been around the time of the exodus and the Plague. How had Dare and his men escaped it?

Griffin ran a finger along the spines of the other books. Dust spilled from each one and swirled in the sunlight filtering through the window. When he reached the leftmost book, he pulled it from the shelf and placed it on the table beside the other. He opened it and flicked back through the pages until the top line read *D:2.*

He turned the final page.

35°54'N 75°40'W D:1. The day has come, as we predicted. They're calling it the end of the world, but they are wrong. It is the end of the human race, not the world. Now it is time for another new world to emerge, and we will build it, just as we built the first. The Gods have made us thus, and the Gods will ensure that we succeed. We are unique, we are perfect, and we will no longer hide. Today is Day One. Long live the elementals!

I was breathing faster than before. Something felt wrong—off kilter—and I didn't understand why. We already knew we were what remained of the world. We'd worked out what had caused the devastation, and when it had occurred. The only new information here was a precise date for those events.

Griffin moved his finger across the page and settled on three words: *We are unique*. He furrowed his brow. *We. Unique?* he signed.

Suddenly that word felt bigger than the others, loaded with meaning. And I knew exactly why. My mind flashed back to the night we'd spied on the pirates—how not one of them had realized we were so close. I recalled the pirates chasing Griffin and me; how they'd jumped off the bridge and thrashed about in the water, desperate to catch the solution, but unable to save themselves. I pictured the clan ships that never ventured into Hatteras waters, in spite of the fact that they were friends, fellow traders, possibly allies. But most of all, I thought of the pirates who had attacked the ship last night, and the way we'd repelled them with our elements.

Why hadn't *they* molded the wind, controlled the fish, threatened *us* with fire?

Pirates. No. Elements, I signed. My hands shook. The gestures felt too large, but I couldn't help it. The world had changed again, and I was struggling to keep up. All this time, I'd thought the Guardians had been keeping people away because of the Plague. But that wasn't it at all.

They'd been *hiding* us, so that no one would find out what we could do. That we had powers other humans didn't possess.

Still Griffin rested his finger beside the words in Dare's log, as though waiting for me to make sense of them. Finally, he tapped the page in frustration. But now he wasn't pointing at the phrase at all, only one word: *We*.

That's when I understood his true meaning. Griffin wasn't worried about being an elemental, or being unique. He was worried because Dare was an elemental too.

Dare was one of us. And only one family bloodline produced seers.

Ours.

ACKNOWLEDGMENTS:

In roughly chronological order, I'd like to thank:

Ted Malawer—agent, sounding board, advisor, and friend—who got behind this novel the day it was conceived, and offered encouragement every day after.

Liz Waniewski, my inspiring editor, who believed that my seeds for a book might blossom into something special, and worked tirelessly to ensure that they did. Her influence is felt in every page of this novel, and each one is significantly better for it.

The many people on Roanoke and Hatteras Islands: Chris Wonderly, Park Ranger at Bodie Lighthouse, who answered questions, shared technical information, and even emailed photographs of the (closed) lighthouse, so that I could accurately portray it; the staff at the Outer Banks Visitors Bureau and the Whalebone Junction Information Station, who offered the kind of insights into tides, weather, and insect life that only locals can offer (oh, and maps; lots of maps); John and Connie Booth, who provided delightful accommodations on Roanoke Island; and Sue and Sadie Daniels, who ensured that I left Wanchese exceptionally well fed.

The indefatigable librarians of the Schlafly Branch of St. Louis Public Library.

Rick and the folks at Northwest Coffee, for caffeinating me and providing the ideal place to write.

Audrey and Clare — *again* — for reading every page, frequently many times. It's a true gift to have readers who really get what I'm trying to do, and are so willing to help me achieve it.

Tony Sahara, whose terrific cover expertly captures the world of *Elemental*. And Steve Stankiewicz, for the beautiful and informative map.

The entire Dial team: Regina Castillo, my amazing copyeditor who continues to educate me on the finer points of the English language; Heather Alexander, who reads everything and never fails to offer great advice; Jasmin Rubero, who brings true artistry to every page; and Lauri Hornik, Kathy Dawson, and Scottie Bowditch, for whose behind-the-scenes efforts I remain extremely grateful.

TURN THE PAGE FOR A SAMPLE OF
THE NEXT BOOK IN THE TRILOGY. . . .

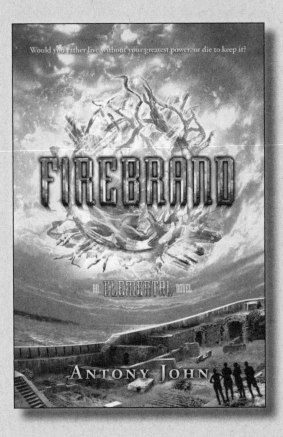

CHAPTER 1

It was hard not to feel as though the world was ending. I stared at my tattered clothes, touched my bloodied lip, and winced from the pain of opening my mouth. I'd been able to block everything out as long as we were fighting for survival. I'd even relaxed for a moment at the thought that we had won. Now I wasn't sure what winning meant.

Below me, the ship, still at anchor, tilted gently from side to side. Light filtered through the bank of windows that ran along one side of the cabin. After the night's hurricane, everything seemed still. But the sense of foreboding that had consumed us for three long days was very much alive.

We. Go, signed my deaf younger brother, Griffin. He looked as ragged as I felt, with disheveled hair and cuts across his face and arms. Beneath the grime, though, he seemed more alive than ever. *They. Find. Us*, he added.

I understood him well enough. This was no ordinary cabin. It belonged to Dare, the pirate captain who'd kidnapped our families and destroyed our remote Hatteras Island colony a few days earlier. And we'd just discovered that he was our uncle. His cabin had been locked all night, but now it was mysteriously open. Until we could explain everything, Griffin was right: We couldn't afford for our colony's Guardians to find us here.

But what about the logbooks arranged in chronological order above the desk, and the machinery bolted onto the shelves? There were answers in this cabin, explanations about who we were and where we came from.

Just. Little. Time, I signed.

Griffin's eyes shifted to the door and back to me again, reminding me of the stakes if we got caught. But what he signed was, *All. Right.*

As always, we were a team. And neither Dare and his pirates nor the Guardians' lies about our past had done anything to break that bond. If anything, we were stronger than before.

I ran my hands across the machines and watched them spark to life at my touch. My element, whatever it was, still felt new. Power pulsed from me instead of flowing. I picked up a thin metal cylinder and focused my energy on controlling the light that instantly shone from one end. The beam seared through the dusty air and cast a yellow circle on the ceiling. It grew dimmer as my concentration waned.

I put it back carefully on the shelf.

Griffin turned his attention to a large map hanging beside a desk. Meanwhile, I touched each machine in turn, watching in wonder as they responded with lights and sounds and dials swinging wildly. Dare wouldn't have kept them all these years unless they were important, but I had no idea what they were for. It was exhilarating and frustrating. I was glimpsing something extraordinary here, but the picture made no sense.

I moved along to the final machine: a black metal box with two protruding knobs. I placed my fingers on it and channeled energy as before, wondering whether I'd be rewarded with lights or something else.

I leaped back as a man's voice filled the room. Heart pounding, I looked around for whoever had spoken, but the room was empty. Silent too. I studied the machine more closely. It couldn't have come from there. What machine could possibly trap a human voice?

Griffin had turned to face me. He must have felt the floor move as I jumped. Now he waited for an explanation.

He wasn't the only one.

With a deep breath I placed my fingers on the machine again. The voice returned instantly: "Fort Sumter, Charleston, South Carolina. This is a recorded message. All Plague refugees are advised to join the self-sufficient colony at Fort Sumter, Charleston, South Carolina. This is a recorded message. All Plague refugees are advised—"

I pulled away. I recognized the name *Carolina*—I'd seen it on a map of the mainland—but I had no idea what the other words meant. I knew what Plague refugees meant, though. Unless we could recapture Roanoke Island from the pirates, that's exactly what we were.

I wanted to tell Griffin what I'd heard, but we didn't have

signs for the new words. I still couldn't believe I'd made the machine work at all.

Griffin was back to studying the map again. He swept his fingers across it, committing the details to memory in case he never saw it again. It wasn't an ordinary map, either. Hatteras and Roanoke Islands were just ghostly outlines, whereas the areas of water that surrounded them were filled with indecipherable details. At the top was a large inland waterway marked *Chesapeake Bay*. Farther down was the sliver of Hatteras Island, our former home. Toward the bottom was a place called Charleston. And at the mouth of Charleston harbor, someone—presumably Dare—had added four words: *Fort Sumter refugee colony*.

Griffin raised a hand. I assumed he was going to sign again, but instead he was completely still. As a panicked expression darkened his face, he pressed his other hand flat against the wall, closed his eyes, and felt for vibrations.

I didn't ask him if he'd picked up on something. I could hear the footsteps.

Go, he signed. But he must have known it was too late for that. We'd be seen leaving, and forced to answer questions about things we barely understood.

"Thomas!" Kyte's voice rattled along the corridor. He was self-appointed chief of the Guardians and my greatest critic.

Who? demanded Griffin, unable to recognize anything but the vibrations of the footsteps against the ship's worn planks.

Kyte, I returned.

For a moment, I considered calling Kyte to join us. I imagined his surprise as he realized what I'd been able to accomplish with my element—the one he'd kept secret from me my entire life. But then reality kicked in. It was more likely that he'd turn against us. He'd link us to Dare, our uncle, and hold us responsible for what had happened to the colony. He'd always hated me, after all.

I closed the cabin door noiselessly and leaned my weight against it.

Kyte was trying each door, so I grasped the handle as he reached ours. He twisted it sharply, but I held it fast. His breathing was heavy on the other side of the wooden door.

"Thomas?" he said quietly.

I held my breath and waited.

"Thomas?"

I closed my eyes.

A few moments later, he turned on his heel and walked away. His footsteps grew quieter. I breathed again.

Griffin leaned against the wall as though he were tired—of running, and fighting, and hiding. And lying. I knew how he felt. Over the past few days, we'd dragged the truth from a lifetime of lies. But already the deception was starting up again.

The difference was that this time, we were the ones with the secrets. And I didn't feel bad about that at all.

CHAPTER 2

We had to leave immediately. Kyte would have suspected that something was wrong when he couldn't find us. Other Guardians would be joining the search soon.

Griffin's eyes were fixed on the door handle that had mysteriously come unlocked during the night. I knew without asking that he was thinking the same thing as me—that someone had wanted us to see this cabin, with its mysterious machines and logbooks that chronicled the history of our world. Had that same person wanted us to learn the truth about Dare being our uncle? And that our Guardians, every last one of them, had always known it?

We left together and latched the door behind us. Toward the end of the corridor, the trapdoor to the ship's hold was closed. The stench from below still lingered, though, a reminder of the days our families had spent locked up in the belly of the ship.

Unfortunately, there was still one prisoner on board.

I covered my mouth with my tunic and checked on our

father. He was imprisoned in a metal mesh cage in a room beneath the stairs. We wouldn't have discovered him at all except for the trail of blood that led to a hidden door. The lock on his cage was too strong to break.

Father hadn't moved. Aside from the shallow rise and fall of his chest, he looked like a corpse, battered and bruised.

Griffin touched my sleeve lightly. Until we could find a way to get Father out, it was best to let him rest.

Up on the deck, we filled our lungs with the fresh salt breeze. The last of the heavy dark clouds had flown away to the north, and the late-summer sun was searing through the wisps that remained. In the bright light, the events of the past three days seemed like a nightmare from which we'd finally awoken. But it had been real, all right.

Four days before, a storm had caught the Guardians by surprise. They'd sent us to the hurricane shelter on Roanoke Island. When we'd emerged the following day, we'd discovered that our colony was on fire. Pirates had kidnapped our families too. Only five of us were left: me and Griffin, my friends Alice and Rose, and Rose's younger brother, Dennis. Finally, the pirates had come after us, which enabled us to slip aboard their abandoned ship.

Somehow we'd survived. It should've been something to celebrate. But as I looked around me now, I felt nothing but panic.

The four Guardians were sprawled across the deck like a school of dead fish washed ashore at high tide. Having been cooped up for days, I'd expected to see them stretching. But

7

only Kyte was well enough to move. The others lay still, heads turned toward the sun. Their faces were gaunt, lips chapped.

Rose bustled around the deck, handing out water canisters. She pointed to the stern, where we'd tethered our sailboats the night before. "I got the bags from the sailboat holds," she said breathlessly. "The boats were ruined, so I cut them free. But the bags are fine."

Her clothes hung slick against her. Her long blond braid flopped against her back. Of all of us, she'd been most desperate to rescue her parents—not just for herself, but also for Dennis. Now that they were reunited, she looked tired and relieved. Watching them, I wondered how things would change from now on. Rose and I had felt closer than ever on Roanoke, but it was no secret that her parents disliked me.

I rummaged through the bags and removed the remaining water canisters. Along with a little medicine, it was all we'd been able to bring with us from Roanoke Island. There'd been clothes and fruit and metal implements too, but we hadn't been able to carry it all. That would have to wait until the Guardians were strong enough to return. *If* they got strong enough.

Alice sidled up. She was the same age as Rose, but taller, with unkempt black hair and a perpetually suspicious expression. "It could be worse," she muttered, looking around the deck at the motionless Guardians.

"How?" I asked.

"Well, we didn't find any dead bodies," she said with typical directness. "Your father, my parents, Rose's parents . . . they're all here. Ananias and Eleanor too."

As if he'd heard his name, my older brother staggered toward us. Ananias rubbed his legs, trying to get the muscles moving again. Apart from his soiled clothes and bruises on his arms, he looked mostly unharmed. The look on his face showed that he was as relieved to see us as we were to see him.

"What's wrong with everyone?" I asked him quietly.

He looked around as if he wasn't entirely sure. "They're dehydrated. The pirates wouldn't give them food or water."

"*Them?*"

He lowered his voice to a whisper. "They kept us separate from the Guardians at first—me and Eleanor. Locked us in one of the cabins with blankets and water and food."

He tilted his head to the left, where Alice's sister, Eleanor, sat alone a few yards away. Ananias and Eleanor were usually inseparable, so it was alarming to see them apart. Not as alarming as the bruises that ran along both her arms, though. They were yellow-brown, not purple or red, which meant that she'd been beaten a few days before, when everything started.

"What happened, Ananias?" I asked gently.

"The pirates kept asking us questions," he said, voice barely a whisper. "Stuff about a seer and a solution. Maybe they figured we'd give in quicker than the Guardians, but we didn't know what they were talking about. So they hurt her. In the end, they threw us in the hold as well."

It was killing him that they'd hurt Eleanor instead of him, and that he'd been unable to stop it. He'd feel even worse

9

once he discovered that it was Dare who had made sure he wasn't harmed. An unwanted gift from the uncle he didn't even know he had.

Ananias stared at his hands. "I wanted to use my element to escape. I thought . . . maybe if I created fire, I could burn a hole through the side of the ship, and escape through it. But we were below the waterline. I'd have flooded the hold and drowned us. Either that, or suffocated everyone with smoke." The words came out fast, as if he was protesting his innocence.

"What exactly did they say about a solution?" I asked.

Nearby, Kyte coughed loudly. "What does it matter? The *solution* is make-believe."

"You've heard of it?" murmured Ananias, incredulous.

"People have talked about a cure for the Plague ever since it started. Doesn't mean there is one."

"Dare believed it," I reminded him.

"Dare was a delusional tyrant. Anyway, Rose tells me he's dead. Drowned, she says." Kyte pointed to Roanoke Island, only two hundred yards to the east, and choked out a single laugh. "With him gone, none of the pirates will be stupid enough to believe in this folly anymore."

Alice, who was inspecting the massive sails for damage, spoke up: "We can't take that chance." She waved her arm across the deck. "You all need time to recover. And while you do, we need to stay away from this place. They still have guns. Remember?"

"No! If we leave this place, our elements will fade."

Everyone fell silent. Even Kyte must have realized the

10

enormity of what he was saying, because his hands shook as he swigged from his canister.

"What do you mean, *fade?*" I asked.

"Don't pretend you didn't notice what happened to you on Roanoke. How everyone's elements are more powerful there." He wiped his mouth with a filthy sleeve. "You leave this place, you risk losing your element completely."

"What element would that be? The one you've kept from me my whole life?"

Rose raised her hand. "Please! Can we all calm down?"

"Calm down?" repeated Alice. "We're next to an island that's crawling with pirates. The same pirates who kidnapped our families and tried to kill us. How can we be calm?"

"I'm just saying . . . let's talk it through. Be reasonable."

"Reasonable like your father, you mean?" Alice sneered. "What do you think of that, Thomas? Your dear Rose thinks her father is reasonable."

I wished she hadn't said that. She was just trying to get a rise out of Kyte, but at our expense, not hers. Sure enough, Kyte's eyes flashed from Rose to me, simmering with anger.

Alice flashed a triumphant smile. "You should be happy, Kyte. You've done everything in your power to get Thomas and Rose together."

His eyes came to rest on me. "I've done nothing of the sort," he growled.

"Please, Father," began Rose, "try to understand—"

"Stay out of this! You have nothing to say."

"Leave her alone!" I shouted. "Without her, you'd be dead.

You call yourself a Guardian, but what have you been *guarding* the past two days? Apart from the locked hold of a pirate ship."

"We tried to resist the pirates, but we were outnumbered."

"We still are now. And nothing we have is a match for those weapons. But then, you know that already, don't you? Just as you know that Roanoke Island is perfectly safe for us. All those years you told us to stay away from it, and it turns out you used to live there."

I threw a quick glance at Ananias and Eleanor to make sure they were listening. They'd been lied to as well. Now they deserved to know the truth.

Kyte gritted his teeth. "Yes, there was a time we lived on Roanoke Island. Most of us were born there. Eighteen years ago, when everyone else evacuated during the Exodus, we decided to stay. When we heard about the Plague decimating the country, we knew we'd done the right thing. But sixteen years ago, the pirates paid us a visit and destroyed everything. After that, the colony was unsustainable, so we moved to Hatteras."

"Why not rebuild?" I asked.

"We had neither the materials nor the means to repair anything—buildings, windows, roads, bridges. A town that can't be kept alive is dead—a Skeleton Town, nothing more."

"What about the water tower? The boats? The clothes?"

"What about them?" Kyte sounded bored, as though my questions were irrelevant, instead of getting to the very heart of who we were. "They were just reminders of what used to be. Historical artifacts. Why would we show you things you couldn't build or repair? It would've been cruelty to tease you with seemingly magical objects that would never work again."

"So hiding everything . . . spreading lies . . . it was all for us, then?"

"Open your eyes, Thomas. The only people you've ever seen are clan folk trapped on floating cities, or pirates who pillage other colonies to survive. We alone built a sustainable colony."

"It was built on a lie," I shouted.

Alice's mother, Tarn, raised a hand. She was tall like her daughter, and normally as defiant. Now she stooped forward, hugging her knees. "Come on, Kyte," she said. "After everything they've been through, they deserve to know the truth."

Kyte turned on her. "The *truth*? The whole truth, Tarn? Every little detail?"

Tarn reddened. As Kyte stared her down, she lowered her hand, bullied into submission.

Kyte grasped the ship's wheel and pulled himself upright. He wanted to be eye-to-eye with me, never mind the pain. "Our colony was a place to live and grow. A place where we could nurture and protect you."

"*Protect?*" I wanted to laugh, but I was too angry. "The pirates burned it to the ground. Look around you, Kyte. Is this your idea of protection?"

"We did our best. We counted on our elements to help us survive."

I let him recognize the hypocrisy for himself before spelling it out. "Except mine, you mean."

Kyte flinched, but recovered with a deep breath. He took a faltering step toward me, fists clenched at his sides. "Your element is a mistake. An anomaly. So is Griffin's ability to see the future. A generation ago you'd have been banished, sent far away where you'd be spared from knowing your true nature."

I stepped forward to meet him. "How do you get to decide what's an element and what's not?"

"It's been that way ever since the beginning of the New World." His voice was fading, but the hollow words still erupted from him. Spittle flew out of his mouth. "Earth, water, wind, and fire. Four boys. Four elements. One lost—"

He stopped speaking at the same moment that I heard a faint popping sound. Immediately, his fierce expression turned to one of surprise. His eyes grew wide. And then, quite suddenly, he dropped to his knees.

Rose jumped forward, but she couldn't catch him before his legs buckled and he hit the deck. Eyes blank, he clasped his hand against his chest.

Blood glistened vivid red against his filthy tunic.